EYES
ONLY

Books by Fern Michaels

A Family Affair
Forget Me Not
The Blossom Sisters
Balancing Act
Tuesday's Child
Betrayal
Southern Comfort
To Taste the Wine
Sins of the Flesh
Sins of Omission
Return to Sender
Mr. and Miss Anonymous
Up Close and Personal
Fool Me Once
Picture Perfect
About Face
The Future Scrolls
Kentucky Sunrise
Kentucky Heat
Kentucky Rich
Plain Jane
Charming Lily
What You Wish For
The Guest List
Listen to Your Heart
Celebration
Yesterday
Finders Keepers
Annie's Rainbow
Sara's Song
Vegas Sunrise
Vegas Heat
Vegas Rich

Whitefire
Wish List
Dear Emily
Christmas at Timberwoods

The Sisterhood Novels
Eyes Only
Kiss and Tell
Blindsided
Gotcha!
Home Free
Déjà Vu
Cross Roads
Game Over
Deadly Deals
Vanishing Act
Razor Sharp
Under the Radar
Final Justice
Collateral Damage
Fast Track
Hokus Pokus
Hide and Seek
Free Fall
Lethal Justice
Sweet Revenge
The Jury
Vendetta
Payback
Weekend Warriors

The Godmothers Series
Classified

FERN MICHAELS

EYES ONLY

**Doubleday Large Print
Home Library Edition**

ZEBRA BOOKS
KENSINGTON PUBLISHING CORP.

ISBN 978-1-62953-292-9

Zebra and the Z logo Reg. U.S. Pat. & TM Off.

Printed in the United States of America

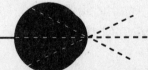

Prologue

Jack pulled his car into the driveway of Harry Wong's dojo and carefully maneuvered around to the back of the building. He sat for a moment, shivering, even though he had the heater going full blast. He looked at the clock on the dashboard—6:20 A.M., an ungodly hour to be making a visit to anyone. But he couldn't leave without saying good-bye to his best friend in the whole world. He and Nikki were heading to the islands for a whole year of sun and fun, and not necessarily in that order. Dennis West had been magnanimous in offering the use of his private plane, an offer Jack snapped up in a New York minute. Wheels up was scheduled for ten o'clock that morning out of Dulles.

A whole year's vacation. Nikki had gone over the moon when he showed her the rental villa, which came with a staff of three to see to their needs. The best part was that they were allowed to take their dog, Cyrus, with them. Jack could hardly wait to feel sand between his toes and the warm sun beating down on his shoulders. He grinned when he remembered Nikki showing him her new bikini, which would fit in his ear. Oh, yeahhh.

It was almost full light by then. Jack turned off the car lights, then fished around in his pocket for the key to the dojo. How well he remembered the day that Harry had handed him the key like it was the Holy Grail. And in Harry's mind, it was. That day, he and Harry crossed the Rubicon together. He knew in his gut he would lay down his life for Harry Wong, and he knew in his gut that Harry would do the same for him. Harry was the brother he'd never had, and he loved him as such.

Key in hand, Jack sprinted from the car. The arctic air body-slammed him. He slipped on a patch of ice, managed to right himself, and then he was at the door. He ripped off his glove, placed his hand on the palm reader, waited for the light to turn green, removed his hand, pressed in the digits of Lily's birthday, and inserted the key. The massive door opened slowly on its well-oiled hinges. Jack waited for the door to close behind him.

He knew the dojo like he knew his own house. He recognized the smells, the disinfectant, the sweat, the eucalyptus, the lingering odor of the shitty tea Harry brewed daily. He knew every squeaky board, every cracked tile in the building, the sound of the wheezing air conditioner in the summer, the grumble of the furnace in the winter.

Silence.

The fine hairs on the back of Jack's neck moved. The heat hadn't come on. Spook that he was, Harry should have called out his name by now, demanding to know why he was here at such an early hour. Because . . . Harry had security upstairs that showed both the front and back doors of the dojo and anyone even approaching the alley and the special security door he'd just entered. Plus . . . Cooper hadn't barked.

Cooper always barked. A friendly bark, but still a bark. Jack had always taken the bark to be a greeting, the same way Cyrus barked when someone came to the house.

Total silence.

Something's wrong.

Jack debated a moment as to whether he should go back out to the car for his gun. He nixed that idea immediately. As Harry always pointed out, he was his own weapon. A third-degree black belt meant he could, if necessary, kill with his bare hands.

Jack looked around the dimness of the dojo. The only light coming through was from the shuttered windows in the front of the building. And it was just slivers of light. Harry locked things up tight at night.

He moved then through the locker room to the main training room of the dojo, out to the hall, down another hall, which led to a staircase that would take him to Yoko and Harry's living quarters. No one ever dared approach the stairs unless invited by Harry or Yoko. No one. Except for him. He approached the stairs now, cautiously, his heart pounding in his chest. By now, Harry should have swooped down somehow, someway, and had Jack's head in a vise.

And Cooper wasn't offering up a greeting. **Something's wrong.**

Jack moved then, quicker than he'd ever moved in his life. He took the steps three at a time and banged on the door with both fists, shouting Harry's name at the top of his lungs. When the door opened immediately, he lost his balance and fell right into Harry's arms.

"What the hell! Jesus, Harry, I thought you were dead or something! What the hell is going on? Why didn't Cooper bark? Where's Yoko? Are you guys being held hostage? Talk to me before I beat the living shit out of you, Harry. I mean it. Why are you looking at me like that? Your eyes are round. You need to talk to me like **now!**"

"You want some tea, Jack?" Harry asked in the strangest voice Jack had ever heard.

"No, I don't want any damn tea, Harry. What I want is to know what's going on. Where's Yoko?"

"I'm here, Jack," Yoko said, appearing out of nowhere. "Are you sure you wouldn't like some tea?"

"I don't want any tea. Maybe you can tell me what's going on here. Your husband, my best friend in the whole world, is acting like . . . Hell, I don't know what he's acting like. And you, Yoko, are starting to scare me. Where's Lily? Where's Cooper? If one of you doesn't talk to me right now, I'm going to bust this place up on the count of three."

Lily took that moment to bound into the room, followed by Cooper. Jack knew his sigh could be heard all the way downstairs. The little family was okay physically.

"Did you come to tell me good-bye, Uncle Jack? Are you going to miss me?"

Thinking the little girl was talking about his own trip, he missed the eye exchange between Yoko and Harry. "I won't be gone long. I'll be back before you know it, and when I do get back, I'll have lots and lots of presents for you and Cooper."

"You're silly, Uncle Jack. That's not right, what you said. When I come back, I will bring presents for you and Aunt Nikki. Cooper is going away, back home, because he has a new job. Daddy, tell Uncle Jack about Cooper's new job. See all his stuff by the door. Cooper's ready to go after I go. He did his job. See how silly that is, Uncle Jack."

"Harryyy."

As Harry led Jack into the kitchen, he

could hear Yoko speaking softly to Lily, asking her if she was sure she had everything she wanted to take with her.

Harry pushed Jack down onto one of the kitchen chairs, his hands on the arms, pinning Jack in place. "Yoko and I should have told you. We didn't, because we knew this would be your reaction. I'm sorry for that, Jack. I know you aren't going to understand what I'm about to tell you, but Yoko and I both ask that you at least try to understand and to take our feelings into consideration. Right now Yoko and I are both . . . saddened beyond belief that we are sending our little girl away. We knew this day would come the day she was born. We've talked about it with Lily from day one so she would understand when the day arrived. Believe it or not, she understands. She's handling it better than Yoko and I. Even Cooper understands.

"Speaking of Cooper, you have to remember the strange encounter we had with him when we went to Julie Wyatt's in Rosemont, Alabama, when Julie's granddaughter Olivia said her spirit daddy had told her that Cooper was to go with me because he had a job to do. His job was to look after

Lily until it was time for her to . . . to leave. You remember that, don't you, Jack?"

All Jack could do was shake his head yes.

"Two days ago, Cooper started piling his stuff up by the front door. He knew it was time to go before we knew it. But Lily knew. She started packing up all her junk. Or her treasures, as she calls them. Then Julie Wyatt called and said she had a dream that it was time to pick up Cooper. I don't know how all that happened, Jack. I'm driving to Atlanta with Cooper after Lily leaves. Julie will meet me there. Halfway for each of us.

"Lily is going to Shaolin Monastery, or, as it is sometimes called, Shaolin Temple. It's a Chan Buddhist temple on Mount Song, near Dengfeng, Zhengzhou, Henan Province, China. It is led by Abbot Shi Yongxin. It was founded in the fifth century. It has been long known for its association with Chinese martial arts and particularly Shaolin Kung Fu. It is also the best-known of the Mahayana Buddhist monasteries around the Western world. I lived there, Jack. I promised in an oath of blood that all my children would be given up to them to train, as I was. Boys or girls, it doesn't matter. I am who I am today because of the monks who loved and taught me. I know you don't believe me, but Lily will love it there, as I did.

"And before you can ask, yes, it is killing me and Yoko that we are sending our baby girl away, but it is our way, Jack. I would kill myself before I would break the promise I made to the monks. Just so you know."

Jack struggled to find his voice. "But, Harry, she's so little. She needs you and her mother. You're right. I don't understand."

"I was the same age Lily is when I was sent there. My parents were so proud of me. I missed them, of course, but that life was a life I was destined for. Even as a child, I knew that, as did my parents.

"Cooper . . . Cooper was sent, we believe, to remind us of this day. Jack, I can't explain it any better than I have. It will be okay. Today things are more modern. Lily will be able to Skype us once a month. We can visit once a year, but we have to go there. She cannot leave until it is time for her to leave."

"Promise me something, Harry," Jack said, his head reeling with all that Harry had told him.

"What?"

"That I can go with you when you go to see her and that you'll let me know the day you plan to Skype."

"Deal!" Harry said, his hand outstretched. His face contorted into something that was supposed to be a smile. Jack's own smile was sickly.

The front doorbell of the dojo rang. Yoko came on the run, Lily right behind her, with Cooper bringing up the rear.

It was time.

Jack felt sick to his stomach as he stood on the side and watched what he later described as the **send-off.**

Lily, dressed in a cherry-red coat with a white faux-fur collar, kissed her mother and father, her eyes bright and sparkly. She didn't dwell on her good-byes. She hugged Jack and made him promise not to forget her. Jack, his eyes wet, nodded. But it was with Cooper that the little girl spent the most time. She hugged him, rubbed his belly, then whispered something in his ear that took a good two minutes. When she was finished, Cooper backed up a few steps and barked three times. Lily smiled and gave the dog another hug before she headed for the door and the people who would take her to China and her new life.

They looked like gentle, caring people, with kind eyes and happy smiles. Lily reached up for the leader's hand and said, "I'm ready. Bye, Mummy and Daddy. I will always love you, Cooper."

The door closed. Cooper lay down across the length of the door and put his big head on his paws.

Yoko shrieked her misery. Harry ran after her.

Left alone, Jack dropped to his haunches and stared at Cooper. "Listen, big guy, I'm not into dog speak, but I need to know how, what, and when. And add why to my list."

Cooper opened one eye and looked at Jack just long enough for a thought to enter Jack's mind. The thought was that Julie Wyatt's daughter Connie was due to give birth to a baby boy, and Cooper had a new job to do.

"Well, damn! And double damn!"

Cooper barked. Jack swore later, when he repeated the story to Nikki, that the big dog was grinning at him and he actually **got it.** And he did.

Jack looked up to see Harry putting on

his heavy jacket. "Gotta go, Jack. Yoko is staying here. She said she needs some alone time. Cooper is in a hurry. By the way, I forgot to tell you, Julie Wyatt's daughter Connie is due to have her baby tomorrow if things go off on schedule."

"Yeah, I know," Jack said. "Cooper just told me. Let's not either of us go there, Harry, okay?"

"My thoughts exactly," Harry said.

Cooper barked.

"Need any help with his gear?"

"Nah, I got it. Enjoy your vacation, Jack. You earned it."

"Yeah, yeah. Listen, if you need me, call, and I'm on the next plane, okay?"

"Yep."

"You're in charge of the BOLO deal."

"Yep."

"See ya, Harry."

"Yep."

Chapter 1

Myra Rutledge tamped down the soft, rich soil around the little clump of begonias she'd planted. The last one. She looked up at the gray thunderclouds overhead. **Ah,** she thought, **just in time.** The skies would open up very soon and bring the famous April showers, so she wouldn't have to drag out the garden hose to water the plants she'd worked at planting all morning. She stripped off her gardening gloves, gathered up all her gardening equipment, and dumped it unceremoniously into her special battery-operated wheelbarrow just as the dogs came on the run, yipping and yapping, the joyous sounds indicating that company was coming up the driveway. She corrected her thought. Company wasn't just **coming** up the driveway. The company was blazing a tire-burning streak, and then said company came to a screeching halt. The dogs howled as one.

Countess Anna de Silva had arrived! The way she always did, smoking hot. Myra laughed in spite of herself.

"Ah, communing with Mother Nature, I see. You do know that it's so much simpler to just call a florist and have them deliver flowers, Myra, do you not? And think of the wear and tear you'd save on your knees, not to mention your fingernails." Annie waved her hands to display her own fresh French manicure to make her point.

"Just in time for lunch. I hope you brought something. If you didn't, it's either cheese sandwiches or peanut butter and jelly. I like digging in the earth. I like planting some little seedling and watching it grow. But there is a lot to be said for ordering flowers from a florist. Come along, my friend, and I'll make us some coffee. You look upset, Annie. Is something wrong? Oops. Here comes the rain!"

The dogs beelined through the open door, with Myra and Annie following close behind.

"The sun will be out soon. The weatherman said it was going to be a splash-and-dash kind of day," Annie said fretfully as she sat down to watch Myra wash her hands and prepare the coffeepot.

"I can multitask, Annie. That means I can make coffee and listen at the same time. Spit it out. What's troubling you?"

Annie drummed her fingers on the scarred old oak table that had belonged to Myra's great-grandmother. In the center was a fresh bunch of the first spring daffodils in a nest of greenery. She thought they looked pretty and springy. She liked Myra's kitchen, with all the red brick, the hanging green plants, and the kitchen fireplace. Her own kitchen was almost identical, but for some reason, she liked Myra's better. Maybe because Myra came with the kitchen. Someday, but not today, she was going to try to figure out how many wonderful hours she had spent over the years in this very kitchen.

"Well?"

"Myra, do you remember that talk we had once about dreams and what they meant?"

"I do, but only vaguely. It's our subconscious at work. Didn't we check it out on the Net at the time? Why? Are you having bad dreams?"

"Not bad dreams. Normally, I don't remember them when I wake up, but I've had the same dream with slight variations three times in the past three weeks. I'm thinking it must mean something."

Myra poured coffee, wondering where this was all going. "And . . ."

Annie reached for the coffee cup. "There was nothing special about the dreams. They weren't alarming in any way. In the first one, Dominic, my husband, was showing me around this special island. It was magnificent, by the way. In the dream, he told me that he never wanted to live there. He just wanted to prove that he was wealthy enough to buy a . . . He called it a palace. He also told me that one hundred of the richest people in the world owned palaces on Spyder Island. All of them men. He thought that was funny. In the dream, it made me angry."

Myra eyed her friend over the rim of her coffee cup. "And the second dream?"

"I was there in the palace alone. I went

after . . . after Dom and . . . after Dom and the . . . the children died in that boating accident. The lawyers said I had to go there, take pictures, bring back any and all papers that were there. There weren't any, by the way. In real life, I stayed one day. I didn't sleep there. In the dream, I think I was there for some time. In the dream, I drove around and took pictures of the island. It's truly a beautiful place. In a Stepford kind of way. Everything was pruned, and not so much as a palm frond was out of place. The houses, or palaces, as Dom called them, were pristine, not a flake of peeling paint, which is unusual considering how hot the sun is. The island is thirty square miles. I think I read somewhere that it's as big as Guam."

"Who does it belong to?" Myra asked.

"You mean like the U.S. or the Brits or maybe even the Dutch? I don't have a clue. To the owners, I guess. Of which I am one, I suppose. The island has its own police department, its own city hall, judges, and the like, but all of that is on the north end of the island. The south end is where the billionaires have homes. Strictly residential. I never cared enough to look into it. I guess maybe I should have. I just know you have to be a billionaire many times over to be allowed to own property there."

"And the third dream?"

"We were all there. In the dream, I think we'd just arrived. You were walking down the steps of the Gulfstream with me. The girls and the guys were already on the tarmac, waiting for us to deplane. There were four Land Rovers waiting to take us to the . . . the palace. We were all angry, snapping and snarling at each other. In the dream, I started to cry. Then you started to cry, and I woke up."

"Let me take a wild guess here, Annie. You want to pack us all up and go to Spyder Island. Is that what you're thinking?" Myra asked.

"That about sums it up, Myra. I know it means something. I haven't thought about Spyder Island in years. Probably from the day I visited that place. I just blocked it out of my mind. To me, it didn't even exist anymore, until those three dreams. Before you can ask, my business manager takes care of all that stuff. I think it's a tax write-off. I never cared enough to ask."

"There's something else, isn't there? What **didn't** you tell me, Annie?"

Annie got up off her chair and walked over to the kitchen sink, where she stared out at the falling spring rain. "It has nothing to do with me personally, but last night, on the evening news, I saw something that brought me up short."

Myra got up to pour more coffee. She tried to remember if she herself had watched the late-night news. She had started to but had fallen asleep after the weatherman had pronounced today would be an April splash-and-dash day. "I had the news on but fell asleep. What did you see that bothered you, Annie?"

Annie ignored the cup that Myra had refilled. "Over the past few weeks, I'm sure you heard about the couple with the adopted twins whose biological mother and her family are trying to take back. Do you remember seeing it, Myra?"

"Yes. Yes. I do. The children look like little cherubs. The parents were so distraught because the biological mother has money to fight for them. The adoptive parents are just making ends meet and are relying on friends and free legal counsel to help them. Oh, Annie, wouldn't that be awful if they have to give up those beautiful little children?"

"The birth mother comes from Spyder Island, Myra. Her father is probably one of the richest men in the world."

"So what! The adoption was legal, wasn't it?"

"Yes, but the birth mother and her parents are trying to overturn it, saying she was a drug addict and not in her right mind when she signed the papers. By the way, according to the news, the biological mother never told her parents she'd given birth to the twins and given them up for adoption until several months ago, and the only reason she told them then was that she was in a terrible car accident that left her paralyzed from the waist down. I guess when the doctors took her medical history, she told them about the birth and the adoption, and the parents saw the records or the doctors told them about it. The moment the doctors released the mother of the twins, her parents whisked her back to Spyder Island."

"And this is where we come in, eh? You want us all to go to Spyder Island and take up this cause. How am I doing so far, Annie?"

"Spot on." Annie smiled. "Can you think of anything better?"

"Can't say that I can, my friend. By the same token, we could hire Lizzie Fox to take over the adoptive parents' case, pay the fees ourselves, and give those billion-aires a run for their money. If we did that, we wouldn't have to go to Spyder Island. What's your feeling on someone snatch-ing those twins? The biological mom's parents could pay someone to do that, you know."

"I do know that. I was thinking of hiring Avery Snowden and his people to keep an eye on the adoptive parents and the kids," Annie said.

"Good thinking. Ideally speaking, half of us should go to Spyder Island, and the other half should stay here and keep tabs on the family. Safety in numbers. I'm getting ex-cited here, Annie. Now, where do the adop-tive parents live?"

"When they first adopted, they lived in Miami. The birth mother was going to the University of South Florida. Then the family moved to Maryland because of the adoptive dad's job. Then, when this stuff all hit, they moved again, to New Jer-sey. They are in hiding as we speak. Nei-ther the local nor the national news is giving out their location, but that's easy enough to find out," Annie said.

Myra clapped her hands in glee. "Oh, Annie, I do think we are back in business. And the timing couldn't be more perfect. Nikki and Alexis are back from their year's leave of absence. Kathryn has been in town since her accident. I don't think that titanium bar they had to put in her leg will slow her down. We can help her with her physical therapy or bring a therapist with us. With Lily in her special school, that frees Yoko up to join us. Except for Isabelle, we have a full court." Myra winced then. "That leaves Maggie. Either she will go with us in Isabelle's place or we go one short. Maggie, I think, will opt to stay here with the guys. I don't know why I say that. I just do. Besides, someone has to run the paper. And let's not forget young Dennis. Our first and second string is more than intact. Tell me what you're thinking, Annie."

"I'm thinking we need a lot more information. Information we can gather on our own over the next few days. Then I say we invite everyone out here for a barbecue over the weekend and present our next mission. We're both thinking they will all jump at the chance to get back into action, but we could be wrong. Until then, I say we keep it close to our vest and start gathering information. I will contact Snowden but not Lizzie, at least not yet."

"That works for me," Myra said happily. "So, do you want a sandwich or not?"

"Not. Let's go into town and get a really nice lunch to celebrate our new mission. We can bring something back for dinner, then work through the evening. It's stopped raining, and the sun will be out soon. Let's do it, Myra."

"Okay, but first I have to change my clothes. Call Avery while I do that, okay?"

Annie nodded, the cell phone already in her hand. She looked up at Myra. "What about Pearl and Nellie?"

"Second string. They stay here with the guys. It's too hard to count on either of them. Pearl is knee-deep in her underground railroad, and Nellie is with Elias 24/7 because of his Alzheimer's. The only one I left out is Jack Sparrow, who is now the new director of the FBI and is number one on my speed dial. The fact that we have really not used our special gold shields is giving me confidence. You, Annie?"

"You know it. I think we are golden. So, we'll put it to the test and see what happens. Hurry up. My stomach is growling."

"Ten minutes."

Myra was as good as her word. Nine minutes later, she was standing in the kitchen in a rust-colored pantsuit, her hair brushed back. She wore her heirloom pearls like a badge of honor. While Annie gathered up her light jacket, Myra handed out dog treats and a list of instructions, which went in one dog ear and out the other. "No messes!" she said as she slung her purse over her shoulder. Lady barked happily and went back to her chew bone.

Sunday, Myra said, was a gift from the gods. She waved her arms about to indicate the beautiful spring day. The trees were in leaf, and while the tiny leaves were no bigger than four-leaf clovers, they were green and would grow at the speed of light and shade the many-tiered deck where she was hosting her family.

The skies were blue, the clouds were pristine white, little dots here and there, and the sun was golden as it warmed the beds of daffodils, lily of the valley, and many other beautifully colored spring flowers that turned the garden into a vibrant rainbow of color.

"It's so peaceful out here," Annie murmured. "In an hour, it will be a zoo, with everyone talking and laughing. And that's a good thing. I need some excitement right now. I am excited, Myra. I can see you are, too. You actually look dreamy."

Myra smiled. "Actually, Annie, I was thinking about Charles there for a minute. We used to sit out here on pretty spring mornings and have our coffee and a sweet roll." Myra sighed and turned around. To Annie's surprise, Myra's eyes were dry, not even a hint of the tears Annie had expected. "I'm okay, Annie. Don't look at me like that. Memories are a wonderful thing, even when they're sad memories."

"I think today will be a new memory. Young Dennis volunteered to do all the barbecuing. He said he has his grandfather's secret recipe for the spareribs. That young man has turned into a real gem, hasn't he, Myra?"

"Indeed he has. Do we know any more about Kathryn and her accident? They, meaning she and Bert, have kept that pretty close to the vest these past few months. I

have to say, Annie, I was more than a little
miffed at that. Then Kathryn told him, according to what Yoko told me . . . Kathryn
said she was coming here, to her own
house, so she could be closer to **her family.** They had a fight but have since made
up. Ah, these young people. We both know
Bert wanted to be the one to take care of
her. She wanted to come home. End of
story."

"She said she's doing well, that the therapy is working. She'll be able to drive on
her own in a few weeks. She can be a bear
at times. There is no doubt about it. I truly
think she is the most fiercely independent
woman I have ever met in my whole life. I'm
not saying that's a bad thing, Myra, but
sometimes we all need someone, a little
help, if nothing more than a hug and a
smile."

"I guess she thinks the same thing, or
else she wouldn't have come back home.
She feels better around her family. To me,
that says it all where Kathryn is concerned.
She'll be fine, Annie."

"And then there's Alexis. I have to laugh
every time I think of Joseph Espinosa stand-

ing up for himself. He was always such a pushover where Alexis was concerned. Oh, he loves her heart and soul, but he drew his line in the sand on New Year's, when Alexis returned and thought he would rush right to her. Instead, he told her he had promised to take his mother and sisters to New York to see in the New Year, and he wasn't about to break that promise. Nikki told me that Alexis cried for days, believing, wrongly, that Joseph was done with her. They're working on their relationship. Our birds are all safe in their nests, and their lives will be whatever they make of them. Life is all about learning lessons. Don't you agree?"

"I do, Annie. I do. Some of those lessons are more painful than others, sad to say. Now, if we could just figure out things with Isabelle, I'd say we're golden. I do not see that happening anytime soon, however."

Annie shrugged. "The only two we haven't touched on are Nikki and Maggie." She eyed Myra to see if she was hiding any secrets from her.

Myra shrugged in return. "I know what you know, Annie. They were originally go-

ing to go away for a whole year. I'm referring to Nikki and Jack. But after three and
a half months of togetherness, they decided
to come home and paint their house, do
some gardening, and go on side trips of a
few days each. Nikki is ecstatic that she
pulled off those two class-action suits she
had going on. The third one is being han-
dled by the firm, but the last thing she said
to me was that the defendants were about
to cave because of her two previous wins.
She's still talking about selling the firm. Will
she do it? I'm not sure.

"Alexis and Joseph's time in Argentina
was about like Nikki and Jack's. Three and
a half months, and they were ready to come
home. We're a full house minus Isabelle
and Charles, but we have added two new
players to our little group, young Dennis and
Jack Sparrow. Perhaps if we don't think too
hard about Charles and Isabelle, we can
make it all work."

Annie quirked an eyebrow. "Maggie?" It
wasn't a statement; it was a question.

"I wish I had the answer. I imagine today
will give us her answer. She's back with Ted.
That in itself makes me happy, because I

truly believe the two of them were meant for each other. What time is it? Should we turn the grill on?"

Annie looked down at her watch, a Mickey Mouse watch with huge numbers that she'd won in Las Vegas and that covered half her arm. "I'd say so. Don't get up. I'll do it. We're good here. Everything is ready. Want something to drink? Iced tea?"

"Sure. And let's have a cigarette, too."

"Ooh, you're being decadent, Myra. I like that. Be right back."

Inside, Annie quickly poured the tea and set the glasses on a tray. She then rummaged in all the kitchen drawers until she found a pack of cigarettes, which had probably been in the drawer forever, and added it to the tray. She scampered over to the kitchen window so that she could observe her oldest, best, and dearest friend in the whole world. And right now that oldest, best, and dearest friend was hurting. Badly. She was missing her husband, Charles, and remembering things that were better left alone. She watched as Myra swiped at her eyes, then yanked at the pearls around her neck. She scowled at what she was seeing, and for one brief minute she wished Charles Martin was standing in front of her so she could plug him right between his eyes.

Annie reached for the tray and tried to erase the vision behind her eyelids. What good was a dead Charles Martin? What good was a live Charles Martin? She couldn't come up with an answer.

"What took you so long?" Myra sniffed.

"Well, Miss Smart-Ass, I was watching you cry through the kitchen window, and I spent all that time trying to figure out how I could plug Charles right between the eyes. That's what took me so long. You happy now?"

Myra laughed. "Annie, Annie, whatever would I do without you? I'm allowed my little pity parties from time to time. Today, in all its perfection, is one of those days. Plus, our girls and boys will be here soon. Like old times, minus Charles. I did love him, you know. I'm not sure what I feel these days. Can we drop this now and have a cigarette?"

The two women sat and coughed, hacked, and sputtered as they attempted to blow smoke rings, which the dogs tried to catch.

"These really are an abomination, Myra. No wonder people die from them. Do you want another one?"

"Sure." Myra laughed. "Only because the dogs love chasing the smoke rings."

"The tea is good," Annie said.

"Is that your idea of small talk, Annie? A diversion? To take me away from my thoughts?"

"Yep."

"Okay, it worked. Can we move on here? How excited are you that we're all going to be going to Spyder Island?"

"I am. I think we need to do some PR work, to let the people on the island know I am arriving with a full retinue. My own plane, my own yacht to follow. Maybe on the yacht, I'm not sure about that yet. The **only woman** to own property on Spyder Island. Then we sit back, ignore any and all invitations, which will most assuredly come our way, and let things develop. Yes, I am excited. I think in my other life, Myra, I could have been an actress. By the way, we're taking the dogs, right?"

"Yes. We'll call them guard dogs."

Annie looked over at the pups and at Lady. They were all sound asleep. Some guard dogs! She started to laugh and couldn't stop.

Chapter 2

"I don't know about you, Annie, but today I am a happy camper," Myra said as she pointed at the boisterous group on her terrace. "All our chicks are here in the nest. They look happy and are enjoying each other. It's been too long since we were all together. Sometimes I feel like our little family is slipping away from us." Her voice was so fretful sounding that Annie patted her shoulder and clucked her tongue like a mother hen.

"Time doesn't stand still. You know that, Myra. We have to take each day as it comes and work from there. And as much as I hate to have to say this, we're all getting older. I'm not saying we still don't have some spit and vinegar left in us—we do—but we might need to add a couple of shots of that fine old Kentucky bourbon you keep locked up in the cellar. Tell me again why you're saving it."

Myra laughed. "I'd tell you if I could remember. It was Charles who came by it somehow and said we needed to save it for a special occasion. I seem to recall his saying we'd know when it was time to break out a bottle. Do you remember his saying that, Annie?"

"You see, that's the thing. Why save it? What if there are no special moments, or if there are, and we miss them? What then? I say we either break it out after we eat, or we save it till everyone is gone. And then you and I get tanked. I think we're overdue for a two-person party. Agree?"

Myra fingered her pearls. She really hated waking up with a hangover, but the bourbon **was** smooth. She nodded vigorously.

"Attagirl, Myra. Okay, let's get this food out there to the tables. The boys are beginning to look mighty hungry."

Myra walked over to the sink to wash her hands. She looked out the garden window, as she always did when she washed her hands. Soap and all, her hands flew to her mouth when she saw a vision in white on the little knoll at the end of the garden. Her spirit daughter. A second vision appeared. Then two visions. The second figure was Annie's spirit daughter. Her voice strangled, she gasped for Annie to join her and pointed at the knoll. Annie dropped the cheese platter in her hands, and the cheese balls rolled across the floor, but not so fast that the dogs couldn't catch them.

"Look, Annie. The girls are dancing. It's almost as if there were a flagpole out there. Remember the year we put up a maypole and decorated it with ribbons and flowers? Oh, Annie, look how beautiful our daughters are! Look at their lovely smiles. Oh, dear God, they're blowing us kisses. They know we're here! Oh, Annie!"

Annie reached out to Myra with a death grip and held her tight. Somehow, she managed to blow a kiss to the dancing girls. Myra did the same.

"Remember the time we were standing here, and they appeared, wearing those cherry-red coats with the white fur collars? They were little then. They were on the knoll then, too, and it was snowing. Oh, God, Annie, I don't understand this. They were little girls then. Now they're seventeen. I know they're seventeen, because I remember those dresses."

"I wish they'd come closer," Annie whispered in a hoarse voice.

"The knoll was their favorite spot. They had tea parties there, they played games, and there was that maypole. Then there was the time they wanted to sleep in a tent on the knoll. We put up the tent, and we were worried sick they'd be afraid during the night, so you and I hid in the woods to watch over them."

"We spied on them, Myra. And we fell asleep before they did. We did hear some of their girlish secrets, which we never divulged."

"They knew. They were always one step ahead of us, Annie."

The spirit daughters stood still, blew kisses, then waved. Myra's hand flew to her cheek. As did Annie's hand.

"I felt it! Did you feel it, Myra? Mother of

God, what does it mean? Is it an omen of some kind?"

"I don't know, Annie. I don't know!" Her hand still on her cheek, Myra looked around in a daze at the dogs, who were staring up at her and wondering if more cheese balls would fall their way.

"Hey, need any help in here?" Alexis called from the doorway. "Dennis said the steaks are ready to come off the grill."

"We're good, Alexis. I dropped the cheese platter. It just slipped out of my hands. We'll be out in a minute. You can take that bowl of potato salad if you want while Myra and I clean up the mess on the floor," Annie mumbled.

Alexis gave both women a sharp look but didn't say anything. She took the bowl of potato salad and went outside.

"Later, when we hit that bottle of bourbon, we can talk about this. Okay, Annie?"

"Absolutely. I saw them. You saw them. That makes it as real as the last time."

Myra swept the bits of pottery into the dustpan Annie was holding. "Oh, that was real, all right. I just want to know why our girls appeared to us today, when we're having this little party and the meeting afterward. I think it means something. My daughter told me when I needed her the most, she would be here for me. Maybe she thinks I need her today. You, too, Annie. We can dwell on this later. Now we need to attend to our family and enjoy the party. Smile, Annie. We just had a miracle. It was, you know."

Annie stared out the window. "I could stand here all day, Myra, and wait for them to come back. I really want to do that. I want to feast my eyes on those lovely young girls until my eyes fall out of their sockets. It's what I want. But I know it won't happen, so grab that basket of rolls, and I'll take this special apple-cabbage coleslaw, and we can get this party under way."

"I hear you, Annie." Myra took one last look out the kitchen window before she joined Annie at the kitchen door. There was a smile on her face, which made Annie laugh out loud. "If that's all we get, so be it. I'll take it."

"Amen!"

The party, as Myra called it, went on for three hours. They were family bringing each other up to date; they were friends sharing events and happenings some had been privy to while others had been unable to attend. There was laughter, backslapping, and, of course, beaucoup congratulations to Jack Sparrow for his new job as director of the FBI. Compliments flowed freely on Dennis's barbecuing expertise, to which he said, "You can't go wrong with Kobe beef." The dogs all agreed and chowed down on the many leftovers.

Much was made of Kathryn's horrendous highway accident and the titanium bar in her leg. While Kathryn tried to play it down, Bert wouldn't allow it, and he went through all the details of her operation and recovery.

Kathryn's voice was fierce when she warned everyone not to feel sorry for her, saying she would drive an eighteen-wheeler again, though not for a while.

From there, the conversation drifted to Nikki and Jack's four-month island vacation and Espinosa and Alexis's vacation in Argentina.

When the conversation turned to Yoko and Harry, the mood became somber, until Harry whipped out his camcorder and played the last video Lily had sent.

"She's happy. That's the important thing," Yoko said. "In four months' time, she's speaking Chinese and Japanese like they are her first languages. She adores her masters. She's ahead in her martial arts class. 'A natural,' her master said. We do miss her."

"Doesn't she miss you? She's so . . . little . . . so young," Nikki said.

Harry grinned. "Funny you should ask. I asked her during our last Skype viewing if she missed her mom and me, and without missing a beat, she said no! Yoko and I cried, but then she said, 'Oh, Daddy, I can't miss you. All I have to do is close my eyes, and I can see you and Mummy. You are always with me.'"

"That is so sweet," Maggie said, tears in her eyes.

"Did you tell Lily we are all going to go see her in November, when it's visiting day?" Annie asked.

"Lily knows that Harry and I are going, but, no, we didn't tell her about the rest of you. We wanted it to be a surprise. You know how Lily loves all of you."

"We're all going to China in November?" Dennis said. "Wow! I've never been out of

the country and never farther than New York and Maryland. Wow!"

Annie looked around to see how much of a detail they needed to clear off the terrace. "Let's get to it. Everyone who ate has to help clean up." The group fell to it, and within twenty minutes, there was no sign a party had ever taken place.

"I think it's time for business," Myra said. She held up her hand. "We have what Annie and I think is one of our most important missions to date just waiting for our brand of justice. It more or less fell into our laps. So, without further ado, let's go down to the war room and run it all up the flagpole."

The newbies, Sparrow and Dennis, watched in fascination as Myra pressed the carved rose on the massive bookshelf that would swing open and lead the way to the catacombs under the ancient farmhouse. "Careful, everyone. There's moss on these old stone steps," Myra called over her shoulder. "Don't worry. The door will close by itself once the last person is on the landing."

"Cool," Dennis said as he tried to appear as nonchalant as the others. He hoped he didn't do something stupid to give himself

away. He so wished he was suave and debonair like Jack and Bert. At times even Ted had a way about him that Dennis envied.

As Myra led the way down the long tunnel, she tapped at the silver bells, tarnished now, but their sound was as pure as the day she'd hung them for her daughter and friends so they wouldn't get lost when they played in the tunnels.

Jack Sparrow grinned to himself. "Let me guess. The bells are so you don't get lost, right?"

"Yes," Annie called out. "Our children used to play down here. It's always been a secret. Isabelle is the one who designed the war room when we first . . . ah . . . went into business. The war room itself is climate-controlled. We even have a dungeon, which we've used on occasion. You know, when we have to lock someone up until we decide what to do with them."

Sparrow didn't know, but he could guess. Christ on a raft, if the bureau could only see him now. Part and party to wreaking havoc, and he was going to cover it up. The thought pleased him to no end. Sometimes justice needed a little push, and at other times an

outright onslaught, and these people were just the ones to do it. He realized at that moment that he felt as giddy as the young kid behind him.

The massive door leading into the war room opened slowly on its well-oiled hinges. Lights came on automatically. A soft whirring sound could be heard overhead from the ventilation system. The group trooped into the room.

"I love this room. It reminds me of the control room at the Kennedy Space Center," Abner Tookus chortled as he ran up the three steps that took him to Charles's area. He started to press buttons. The giant plasma screen lit up, and Lady Justice gazed down on the little group. As one, they all saluted her.

"It looks different in here," Maggie said, looking around.

"It is different. We replaced the old oak table with this table, which we had Avery Snowden's people build for us. They did it down here. They used old lumber from out in the barn. Look," Myra said as she pressed a button on the side of the table. The center of the table parted, and the leaves that were stacked underneath popped up, then slid into place, creating seating space for eighteen people.

"That's amazing," Jack said as he looked at the mechanism that made it all happen. "Whoever crafted this could make a killing in the furniture business."

"The shoe box is still there," Kathryn said, a smile on her face. "I so clearly remember the day it was my turn to pick our next mission."

The others agreed, smiles on their faces as they, too, remembered the early days here in the war room, where they waited with bated breath for Charles to outline the newest mission's protocol.

Almost in unison, all eyes rose to the dais, where Abner stood, awaiting instructions.

The boys waited as the girls pulled out their chairs, and then they all sat down at the long, beautiful table with the grungy, years-old shoe box in the center.

"We do have a certain protocol for these meetings, but for the most part, we're fairly informal. Early this morning, Annie and I brought down the folders that she is now passing out to all of you. We spent most of last evening trying to come up with as much information as we could. I'm sorry to say we didn't come up with nearly enough. What we were able to garner, which wasn't much, was found on the Net, then printed out. Annie had some contacts she called to see what information she could gather that way, but again, we came up way short. Having said that, I'm going to have Annie give you what we have in a nutshell. This is her mission, because it was her dreams that started it all. Annie, you have the floor."

Annie looked around, her gaze settling on Jack Sparrow, then on young Dennis. She took them through her three dreams and what little she knew, then sent off a series of pictures to Abner, who made them appear suddenly on the giant plasma screen.

"These are the children in question. They are four-year-old twins. Their names are Daniel and Dona. The names of their parents are Marlo and Alicia Domingo. They're Hispanic." A grainy, less-than-clear picture of the parents appeared on the screen.

"As you can see, the parents are true to their heritage. They're dark-haired and dark-eyed. The children are blond and blue-eyed. Alicia Domingo worked in a private clinic.

She's a nurse. She came to know Betty Smith, aka, Gretchen Spyder, the birth mother, when she came into the clinic for her monthly visits. They struck up a friendship of sorts. Confidences were shared, and Gretchen told Alicia her real identity and swore her to secrecy. Alicia volunteered that she and Marlo could not have children. She says she counseled Gretchen, but in the end, Gretchen wanted no part of motherhood, saying she was going to put the baby up for adoption so her parents wouldn't find out that she had given birth. Gretchen used an assumed name at the clinic and paid for everything in cash.

"As her due date approached, Betty/Gretchen struck a deal, and Alicia and Marlo agreed to adopt the baby she was carrying. The Domingos had the good sense to engage the services of a lawyer. It was all done legally. We got all this from interviews the Domingos gave when trying to fight the girl's parents. Then they ran."

"Where is the birth mother now?" Ted asked.

"According to the news reports, she was in a horrific car accident and is paralyzed from the waist down. She lives in a wheel-

chair at her parents' home on Spyder Island. She is an only child, and the bloodline
stops with her. That's why the parents are
so eager to get their grandchildren."

"Where's the biological father? Does
he even know he's a father? Did he agree
to the adoption, or didn't Betty/Gretchen
tell him? Seems to me that whoever gets to
him first might have a shot at getting the
adoption overturned," Jack said.

Myra looked down at her notes, then over
at Annie. "I didn't see where the Domingos
ever said anything about the biological father. Did you, Annie?"

"No. My guess would be Betty/Gretchen
did not tell the Domingos. Who knows if she
told the father? This all happened during
her senior year at the University of South
Florida. Graduation has come and gone.
It's five years later, and whoever fathered
those children is long gone. The only one
who probably knows where he is now is the
birth mother, and you can bet your last dollar she's not telling Mummy and Daddy,"
Annie said.

"What did Avery Snowden say? Is he going to protect the Domingos, or is he going
to do a snatch and grab?" Maggie asked.

"A snatch and grab, after he explains what we're prepared to do for them. For now, Avery is going to turn the family over to Pearl Barnes, who will put them in her underground railroad. When we go to Spyder Island, we're taking Avery and his crew with us."

Nikki weighed in. "I thought you said you didn't get much information? This is a whole bucketful. Imagine what we're going to get when we turn Abner loose. So when is the snatch and grab going down?"

"As soon as Avery locates the family. He anticipates that will be no later than noon tomorrow. He understands that time is of the essence," Annie said.

"When do we leave for Spyder Island?" Alexis asked.

"The minute we get all our ducks in a row," Myra said smartly.

There was excitement in Maggie's voice when she asked, "What's our game plan?"

"I thought you would never ask!" Annie chortled. "Tell them, Myra."

"Our initial thoughts were that Ted, Maggie, Joseph, and Dennis would check out Gretchen Spyder's college years. That might entail a trip to the university to talk to her professors and advisers. Checking the yearbooks for special friends, locating them, and getting them to talk. Someone out there knows who the biological father is besides Gretchen Spyder. We want to know everything there is to know about her four years of college.

"Abner will do his financial digging on the family and Gretchen to see if there are trust funds and all that goes with that. He will also do a financial workup on the Domingos.

"Jack, you and Harry are up for Spyder Island. I'm thinking that Mr. Sparrow will be able to help you. Bert, you are odd man out and are needed back in Vegas, with the understanding that if things get dicey, you can be here in four hours. Does all of this work for everyone?" Myra asked.

"Who goes to Spyder Island?" Dennis asked.

"Just us girls at first. The following day, Mr. Snowden and his team will arrive. The minute you all have the information you are assigned to procure, you will also join us. The primary thing right now is securing the Domingos so we don't have to worry about them. Any questions?" Annie asked.

No one had any questions.

"Okay, then read the information in the folders in front of you to make sure I didn't leave anything out. We'll have a question-and-answer session, and if we're good, we'll terminate this meeting and go forward."

"When do you want us to head to Florida?" Maggie asked.

"ASAP. Try for a flight first thing in the morning. You have my permission to fly first class," Annie said generously. "Follow and go wherever your leads take you. Just try for results quickly. Colleges and universities usually have five-year reunions. Find out if Gretchen's class had theirs or if it is up and coming. It might be this spring, next month to be precise."

Ted looked up and said, "We have four seats on the six-thirty flight out of Reagan National in the morning. Time for us to hit the road and pack some bags. Unless you need us for something."

"Go ahead," Myra said. "Check in with us by the end of the day."

One by one, the others gathered up their belongings, checked to make sure nothing was left behind. Then they followed the reporters back to the main part of the house.

The good-byes were affectionate and

loud, with kisses and hugs, some back-slapping, and then the big old farmhouse was quiet, with only the dogs snorting and yelping.

"Annie, I'll take the dogs out. You go down to the cellar and get that bourbon. I'm so ready to sample it, it's making me crazy."

"I just love it when you come up with a plan, Myra."

"Me, too, Annie. Especially when we both know this kind of plan means we're both going to have hangovers in the morning."

"You had to say that, didn't you?"

Myra giggled as she led the dogs out into the star-filled night.

Chapter 3

Myra looked at Annie and laughed out loud. "You look like a punk rocker with your hair standing on end like that. The kids today pay out big bucks to get a hairdo like that. I know, I know. I don't look any better." She continued to laugh as she measured coffee into the wire basket.

"It's true, Annie. We are getting older. Look at that bourbon bottle. All we could drink was a quarter of it before we fell asleep. I don't feel all that bad now that I've brushed my teeth. How about you?"

Annie picked up the bourbon bottle and measured it with her fingers before she placed it in the cabinet next to the refrigerator. "We'll just save this for when we return from Spyder Island. I think we were so wired up yesterday with the kids being here, the party atmosphere, **our sighting,** and the plans we made that we were just too tired."

Myra smoothed down her own unruly hair and stared across the table at her best friend in the whole world. "I'm thinking, Annie, that we should do a little PR for our upcoming trip to Spyder Island. Like some Associated Press gossip. What do you think?"

Annie grinned. "You mean like Countess Anna de Silva, the second richest woman in the world, is going to take up residency on Spyder Island to write her memoirs? She will be arriving with a party of . . . say, twenty in her private Gulfstream on such and such a date. When this reporter caught up with the reclusive countess, she would neither confirm nor deny. That kind of PR?"

"Well, there you have it. Maggie and Ted couldn't have written it better. It might need some tweaking, but I like it just fine. As long as you leave the date of your arrival up in the air. Send the kids a text and tell them to get on it ASAP."

While Myra poured coffee, Annie's fingers flew over the keys. "Done!"

"Ooh, I forgot something. Make mention that you are the **only** woman to own property on that prestigious island. Tell them to play up that male-only angle. That should put the Spyders' knickers in a knot."

Annie's fingers again flew over the keys. "I'm getting really good at this. Dennis showed me how to use my thumbs more than my fingers. I really love that kid. Okay, done! Now what?"

Myra shrugged. "Why do I have to come up with all the ideas? You own the place. You've been there. Tell me what you think. As young Dennis would say, 'This is your gig, Annie. The rest of us are just along for the ride.'"

Annie propped her elbows on the table and stared across it. "I blocked all of that out of my mind, Myra. I'm flying blind here. I know that Angus Spyder III is a son of a bitch. He rules the island with fear and an iron fist, just the way his father and his grandfather did before him. Dominic told me that when he bought into it all. He's all about being the richest and the most powerful person in the world. According to him. I don't even know if that's true or if he was just bragging. I think Abner will be able to tell us if it's true or not."

"Want some toast?"

Annie shook her head.

"Where do you think your fortune ranks compared to his? Do you have any idea?"

Annie shook her head again.

"Well, can you find out? Can you call that guy you're always snapping and snarling at on the phone and ask him?"

"I can." Annie squinted to see the clock on the Wolf range. "It's early. I'll call him and wake him up. I just love doing that."

Myra popped two pieces of bread into the toaster and got butter and jam out of the refrigerator. She knew Annie would eat a slice if it was put in front of her. It was all she could do not to laugh out loud as she listened to Annie on the phone. Her eyeballs stood at attention when she heard Annie say, "Well, that better not be true, Conrad. I want you to head to the office right now and send me everything that will back up what you just told me. And. Do. Not. Fudge. The. Numbers."

"What?" Myra demanded.

Annie banged her fist on the table. "Myra, how would you like to lend me some money?"

Myra threw her hands in the air. "Did I just hear you ask me to lend you some money?"

"Yes, you did. It appears, Myra, I say 'appears,' that Angus Spyder has more money than I do. Of course, Conrad could be wrong, and I did wake him up. But on the off chance he's right, I cannot go to Spyder Island unless I'm richer than he is. I know that sounds petty, but we're playing in the big leagues here. Let's just say it's a woman thing. You understand that, right, Myra?"

"Oh, yes, indeedy, I do. How much?"

"Half a billion," Annie said, without batting an eyelash.

"Okay," Myra said, also without batting an eyelash.

"We'll let Conrad and your guy Henry handle the details, but you will have to call Henry. I think your positions in that oil company and Google will do the job. You okay with that? I'll pay you a handsome rate of interest. Short term. Ooh, Angus is not going to like this one little bit."

"What rate of interest?" Myra asked craftily.

"Well, with the economy the way it is and the low interest rates . . ."

"Get off it, Annie. How much?"

"I was thinking 5 percent."

"Wrong. Ten, or it's no deal."

"Myra, you drive a hard bargain. Ten, it is. Shall we shake on it?"

"Nah, my arthritis in my right hand is kicking up this morning. Your word is good enough for me. Send a text to Henry and pretend to be me. My password is 'Annie,' if he asks."

"Oh, Myra, that's so sweet of you to use my name as your password. Okay, I'm doing it," Annie said happily.

"I'm going to take a shower now. When you're done with Henry, call Abner and see what, if anything, he's come up with. He works through the night."

Annie hummed under her breath as she tapped at the keys. She could feel an adrenaline rush coming on. Life on the wild side. She hated to admit it, but she lived for moments like this. **This** was why she got up in the mornings.

Knowing she would have to wait a few

minutes for incoming texts, Annie looked at the near-empty coffeepot. Ah, caffeine and an adrenaline rush all at the same time. Life could not get any better.

She rinsed the pot, threw away the grounds, and prepared a new pot. By the time it finished dripping, Myra would be back, and there should be a blizzard of incoming texts. She rubbed her hands in glee as she walked over to the kitchen window to look out at the knoll. There was nothing to be seen except green grass and the last little bit of the early morning fog drifting away. It was fog, wasn't it? She leaned closer to the window to be sure. Just fog. Her disappointment was so keen, she didn't notice Myra come up behind her. She did feel her comforting hand on her shoulder, however. She whirled around. "I was hoping . . . It was just the last of the low-lying fog."

"I know, Annie. I know. We had yesterday, so we have to be grateful for that. Now," Myra said, leading Annie back to the table, "what do you have?"

Annie's eyes scanned the texts. "We are good to go. And you're making yourself a nice piece of change. Officially, I am now,

as of"—she looked at the clock—"this moment, richer than Angus Spyder. Thanks to
you, my dear friend."

"Should you forward that information to
Dennis to relay to the Associated Press?"
Myra asked as she tried not to giggle at the
expression on Annie's face.

"I just did. I am getting sooo good at this,
Myra. Reminds me of my safecracking
days. I didn't think I'd ever master that, but
I did, didn't I? Now if I lose my thumbs, I am
out of luck."

The two old friends cackled in glee at
what they'd just accomplished.

Annie headed for the second floor, leaving Myra alone with her thoughts, her cell
phone, and her cup of coffee. Annie was
back in thirty minutes, smelling of warm
sunshine and fragrant flowers.

"Now what?"

"It's like the Army, Annie. Hurry up and
wait. Sooner or later, the kids will get back
to us. I'm all for stirring up some trouble, but
I can't come up with anything. You got any
ideas?"

No sooner were the words out of Myra's
mouth than Annie's cell chirped to life. She
clicked it on, identified herself, then waited

for the person on the other end to speak. She wiggled her eyebrows at Myra, a wicked grin stretching across her face. "Well, what can I do for you this early in the morning, Mr. Carlisle of the Associated Press?"

Myra clapped her hand to her mouth so she wouldn't laugh. Young Dennis worked fast. Still and all, any news on Countess de Silva **was** important.

"You want me to confirm my upcoming trip to Spyder Island. My goodness, however did you come by that information? I do so try to keep a low profile.

"Yes, after all these years, I am considering taking up residency there. At least for a little while." Annie listened again and responded to whatever it was that she heard. "I do seem to recall hearing that no females owned homes on the island. Whoever it was who said that obviously didn't check the records, since I've owned the property for over twenty years, and I can assure you that at no point during that time have I been of the male persuasion. No, of course it doesn't bother me to live in a man's world. I plan to change all that with my trip to the island. We women do have our place in the world now, don't we? An island makes no difference. An island, no matter how prestigious, is still part of the world.

"No, I don't have a definite arrival date as yet. A woman in my position has many affairs to be taken care of before she can . . . let's say, even make a trip to the hairdresser. Oh, yes, I travel with a full staff. I think it's safe to say there will be more than twenty of us and, of course, my personal security detail."

Annie went silent as she rolled her eyes, which meant another question was in the offing. "Mr. Carlisle, I never discuss my personal finances, especially on the phone. I personally do not know anything about Angus Spyder. We . . . ah . . . do not travel in the same social circles. I know nothing of his holdings."

Annie winked at Myra and said in a lilting voice, "Oh, I absolutely do think my net worth exceeds that of Mr. Spyder. That's as much as I'm willing to say. Now, if you'll excuse me, Mr. Carlisle, I have a meeting that I must attend. It was nice speaking with you."

Annie broke the connection, then banged her fist on the old, scarred oak table. "How'd I do, Myra?"

"That was just perfect. You did good. I think that will hit the financial networks at the speed of light, which tells me that Mr. Angus Spyder is probably right now checking whatever he can where you are concerned. You need to give young Dennis another raise. Oh, I forgot. It's not like he needs one. Did he ever accept the last one?"

Annie shook her head. "Now what do we do?"

"Play on the computer, make plans for when we get to Spyder Island. Unless you want to go over to Nellie's to see how she's doing. We can take the golf cart. Or we could go into town and have a nice lunch. All the wheels are in motion, so we just have to wait it out."

"I just took a shower, so gardening is out. I'm not hungry, so that leaves Nellie. Let's do it. I'm driving."

Maggie swiped at her forehead. "I didn't expect it to be so hot here in Miami at this time of year. Nice campus. Bet it's great going to school here in the winter, with all the sunshine and these gorgeous palm trees."

Ted parked the rental car in visitor parking, and the foursome got out.

"This is where we separate," Maggie said. "Dennis, you head for administration. Get what you can on Gretchen Spyder. Ted, you and Espinosa ferret out her guidance counselors and a few of her professors, and I'll take on some of the professors myself. It's eleven o'clock. Let's meet back here at the car at two thirty and compare notes. We might hit it lucky first shot out of the gate and be able to take a late flight back to Washington tonight. If not, we'll have to find a hotel and go at it again tomorrow. Any questions, advice, whatever? No! Okay, see ya later. Oh, Espinosa, take pictures of everything and everyone."

"Yes, Mother," Espinosa drawled.

Dennis sauntered off with no game plan in mind. He let his mind go back to his days in college. It seemed like a hundred years ago. He looked around, stopped a student in shorts and flip-flops with a backpack, and asked for directions. He listened intently and set off. The kid had given precise instructions. Maggie was right. It was hot as hell, and he was wearing long pants and a long-sleeved shirt.

Inside the building, Dennis looked at the different signs and followed the directions to the place he wanted. To his surprise, no one was standing in line to be waited on, and there were two students behind the counter, one tapping on a computer and the other one copying a pile of papers. The girl doing the copying stopped and walked up to the counter.

"How can I help you?" she asked.

Dennis went into the spiel that he'd come up with on the fly from the moment the back-packing student had given him directions until he walked through the doors. He lowered his voice and said, "Gee, I sure hope you can help me. My cousin attended college here five years ago, and she . . . she disappeared. My aunt and uncle asked me to come here to see if the university could help us in any way. I know five years is a long time, but they've exhausted every other avenue. You're our last resort. Her name is Gretchen Spyder. She was an honor student." He lowered his voice to a whisper and said, "We think white slavers snatched her."

"Oh, my goodness. I'd like to help, but you know the privacy laws and all. I can't. Did you try the dean?"

"They don't care. All they care about is money. My cousin was just a name with a tuition bill. Are you here on a scholarship?"

The young student smiled. "I wish. I have some aid, and I work two jobs. My parents help a little, but basically, I'm on my own."

"Do you get a break?"

"I do," the girl said, looking up at the clock. "And believe it or not, it starts right now. Why do you ask?"

"Walk outside with me. I want to tell you something, but I don't want anyone else to hear, okay?"

"Sure. Hey, Sara. I'm taking my break now."

The girl at the computer waved her hand to show she'd heard.

Outside, with students going every which way, Dennis led the girl to a bench and sat down. "Listen, I'm going to lay my cards on the table, because I don't like to lie, and I know you're not the type to fall for a lie. I'll give you ten thousand dollars cash if you can get me Gretchen Spyder's records. I need them, like, instantly. No one will ever know you gave them to me. I know you can lose your job, but if that were to happen, all you have to do is call me, and I'll take care of it for you. I can't be any more blunt than that. Will you help me?"

The girl looked at him with wide blue eyes. "That wasn't true what you said about the white slavers, was it?"

"No. It was a lie. I can't tell you the reason, but it's very important. I know you don't know me, and that's a good thing. Sometimes you have to take people on trust. Do I look trustworthy to you?" Dennis almost choked when she nodded.

"Ten thousand dollars is a lot of money. So is ten years in jail." The girl, whose name tag said she was BETSY AMES, let her mind race. He did look trustworthy. **Ten grand. A fortune.** She could buy some new shorts, a few new tops, eat something besides mac and cheese or peanut butter and jelly for a change. Maybe get a manicure and a pedicure, just to see what it felt like. Maybe even get a haircut and maybe have some highlights put in. But then that would eat into the ten grand. "Make it twelve, and you have a deal. But . . . but I want your assurances that nothing bad is going to happen to Gretchen whatever you said her last name is."

Dennis made the sign of the cross and nodded solemnly. "You have my word, Miss Ames. How long will it take you to get all that?"

"A few hours, depending on how busy it is. This time of the year, things are really slow, so I think by two I should have it all. Meet me at the Keg. Ask anyone, and they can tell you where it is. Find the bookstore and buy a black school backpack. Put the money in it, and I'll put the files in mine. We meet up, have a coffee, and then you take my pack, and I take yours. Deal?"

"You sound like you've done this before," Dennis huffed.

"No. I just watch a lot of TV because I don't have the money to hang out at night with the girls. That's how they do it on TV. You okay with that? By the way, what's your name?"

"Do you really want to know, Miss Ames?"

"Actually, Mr. No Name, I don't. I'll see you at the Keg at two. If I'm not there, that means I got caught."

Dennis felt guilty for all of a minute. He knew if that happened, he'd man up and take the blame. "Make sure that doesn't happen," he snapped. "Hey, where's the nearest bank? And the bookstore?"

"Right off campus. You can walk to both of them from here." Betsy Ames started rattling off the turns he needed to take before she sprinted for the door.

Dennis watched her go, not knowing what he felt. Ted would say, "It's all about the mission. Don't second-guess yourself. Do what has to be done, and we'll deal with the fallout, if there is any, later on."

First, Dennis headed for the bookstore, where he bought a black backpack with the school's logo on the front. From there he headed to the First Citizens Bank, where it took him forty minutes to get the twelve thousand dollars in cash.

His job completed, Dennis stopped at a hotdog stand, bought one with the works, along with a ginger ale, carried them over to a patch of grass, sat down, and ate while his thoughts wandered all over the place. He finished his food and soda and decided to text the others to brag that he'd gotten what he came for. Well, almost. Two o'clock would tell the tale if Betsy Ames came through for him. He crossed his fingers the way he had when he was a kid.

He watched the students, marveling at how they were dressed. Back in the day, he'd been a neat freak, wearing pressed khakis and a collared shirt. He definitely would not fit in here. Not only that, he was **old** compared to these kids, some on in-line skates and skateboards as they tooled along to their classes.

Well, there was old, and then there was old.

Chapter 4

Maggie finished up her conversation with Mona Appleby, Gretchen Spyder's class adviser, feeling dejected. While Appleby vaguely remembered Gretchen Spyder, she had nothing good or bad to say, other than that she seemed to be a loner, and she went on to say she didn't know why she thought that. Blank wall.

Maggie walked out into the warm Florida sunshine, wondering if she could ever live with perpetual sunshine and warm, muggy air. She definitely didn't like being cold, but she did love the change of seasons. No, she decided, Florida, the Sunshine State, was not for her.

Maggie stopped a student and asked for directions to the library. Maybe she could find Gretchen's yearbook and make some headway there. She looked down to read the incoming text from Dennis. The kid did have a way about him. Maybe he had gotten everything they would need, and she and Ted and Espinosa were spinning their wheels. Still, one could never have too much information. She stopped under a luscious-looking palm tree and sent off a text saying that she had bombed out with Spyder's adviser and was headed to the library in search of Spyder's senior yearbook.

As Maggie proceeded along the walkways, she, like Dennis, recalled her own college days and how carefree she'd been back then. A melancholy feeling washed over her as she stared at students, some in clusters, others alone, some laughing, some texting, while others looked somber, their thoughts miles away. Or they were thinking about the summer that was ahead of them. Sand and ocean, balmy breezes while soaking up the rays, or dreading their nine-to-five summer jobs, if they were lucky enough to find one. She herself had worked every summer of her life since the age of sixteen. Come to think of it, she'd never really done much in life except work.

Maggie stopped short when she realized she had arrived at the library. How imposing it was. She loved libraries, always had, always would. She loved books. Period. She couldn't help but wonder what would happen to libraries now with the new digital age. Would they become extinct at some point, replaced with computers and all the gadgets on the market? Well, there wasn't anything she could do about it, so she might just as well enjoy her little visit and soak up the atmosphere while she could.

Ten minutes later, with the help of the reference librarian, Maggie had Gretchen Spyder's senior yearbook in front of her. It took her another fifteen minutes to find the picture she wanted to compare with the one Ted had found somewhere and printed out for all of them.

Gretchen Spyder was a beautiful young woman. She had a pretty smile, but even in the black-and-white photo, Maggie sensed that she had sad eyes. One could smile, but if the smile didn't reach the eyes, it wasn't a real smile. It really was true. **The eyes are the mirror of one's soul,** she thought, **especially in this case.** This girl, Maggie decided in a nanosecond, had an unhappy soul.

Maggie flipped the pages, hoping for some tidbits about the young woman. They were few and far between. Twice, she almost missed a few sentences. Gretchen, it said, liked mango milk shakes. Further on she read that Gretchen liked to dance. The last thing she read was that Gretchen Spyder was going to graduate with a 4.0 GPA. A brainiac for sure. She herself had had a measly 3.2 at the end of her senior year, and that was after pounding the books 24/7. And that was the sum total of Gretchen Spyder's life in her senior yearbook. Maggie sat back and stared off into space. Who were Spyder's friends? Surely, she must have had friends. Who was the father of the twins whom she gave up for adoption? How was Maggie going to find all that out?

Maggie brought herself back into focus, whipped out her cell, and sent off a text to Myra, asking if Avery Snowden had located the Domingos and relocated them. The answering text was almost immediate, saying

Annie was on the phone with Snowden, and he was transporting the Domingos to a safer location so that Nellie could take over. Maggie responded by asking Myra to find out if the Domingos knew any of Gretchen's friends or if they had a clue as to who the biological father was. Myra assured her that she would get back to her the moment she had any more news.

Maggie sat quietly soaking up the library's atmosphere. She had to leave, but she didn't want to. How weird was that? She sent off a text to Ted, but there was no reply. Maybe he was talking to some of Gretchen's professors.

Across the campus, Ted was winding down his conversation with Gretchen Spyder's political science professor. "One last question, Professor Atkins. Do you remember any of Ms. Spyder's friends? Maybe a boyfriend? Anyone she was close to, hung out with?"

The professor, a roly-poly ball of a man, frowned. "Tell me again why you're asking me all these questions."

Ted made the instant decision to stick with the bogus story they'd all come up with,

which was that Gretchen Spyder had disappeared, and they, along with the family,
were trying to find her. He hoped that the
professor was a true academic and wasn't
interested in gossip or watching the news.
"We're trying to help the family locate her."

The professor hiked his tortoiseshell
glasses up higher on the bridge of his nose.
"She tutored two of my students, Faye Was-
serman and Gina Gilbert. I think she was
friendly with Gina on a social level. She was
a great tutor. Actually, Gretchen was brilliant. I convinced her to go for her master's
after graduation. As to a boyfriend, I can't
help you there. Gina lives right here in Miami. She teaches at one of the high schools.
I just ran into her a month or so ago at a
restaurant. We talked for about fifteen minutes, but that was it. I can give you her
phone number if you like. When we parted,
we exchanged numbers."

"That would be very helpful, Professor,"
Ted said, trying to keep the elation out of
his voice. "Would you happen to know if Ms.
Spyder was close to any of her other professors?"

"I do know the answer to that question,
and the answer is, 'No, she wasn't.' I know

this because on more than one occasion I mentioned her name and how impressed I was with her, and they just shrugged it off as another overly bright student, which is kind of surprising since there aren't all that many of them." He grinned and rolled his eyes at what he considered his little joke.

"Here it is," Professor Atkins said, handing over a Post-it note. "I hope you find her. Give her my regards if you do."

Ted assured the professor he would do just that. They shook hands all around, and then Espinosa asked Professor Atkins to pose with Ted for a picture. The professor obliged.

Then they were on the way back to visitor parking to wait for Maggie and Dennis. The time was 1:48 P.M. An incoming text from Dennis said he was going to be about twenty minutes late since he had to meet his **source** at the local campus watering hole. Ted laughed out loud. **Source.** The kid was into the spy game for sure.

"Now what?" Espinosa asked as he wiped sweat from his brow.

"We stand here and ogle the coeds and envy those buff studs and make a vow to get in shape so we can look like them. Not.

Oops, here comes Maggie, so I guess we aren't going to be ogling any coeds, after all. Is it my imagination, or are the girls' shorts getting shorter?"

Espinosa laughed out loud. "I think that's a question you should ask Maggie. She's kind of an expert. If you're afraid, I can ask her for you."

"Do it, and you're dead meat!"

Espinosa continued to cackle and doubled over when Maggie asked what was so funny. Ted turned white as Espinosa gasped for breath. "I think Ted just had a vision of himself on a skateboard out of control."

"I don't think that's funny, Joe. First of all, Ted would never be dumb enough to get on a skateboard. Would you, honey?"

"Of course not," Ted said, color coming back to his cheeks.

"I think I have something, guys. A name of Spyder's friend. At least a friend in the sense that Spyder tutored her during their senior year. Her name is Gina Gilbert. I'm going to send her a text and ask if we can meet her at three thirty, when school lets out. She teaches right here at a high school in Miami. It's called New World School of the Arts. It's located on NE Second Avenue.

Espinosa, track it and see how far away we are while I text Ms. Gilbert," Maggie said.

"I'm on it."

Maggie sent off her text. "Even if she doesn't respond, we're going to go there. Uh-oh, here's an incoming text from Myra. Oh, poop. She said the Domingos never really knew anything about Gretchen's private life. She said she knew there was a guy in the picture, because Gretchen was pregnant. Duh. Alicia Domingo said one time she heard her on her cell phone, talking to someone she thinks was named Zack. Myra says the little family is now safe and sound and for us not to worry about them, thanks to Pearl."

"Yeah, well, that's easier said than done," Espinosa said. "If Spyder's parents are as wealthy as we've been led to believe, then they have the juice to hire the best of the best to find the Domingos and the biological father. So don't go counting your chickens before they hatch."

"Well, aren't you doom and gloom?" Ted sputtered.

"Snowden is the best of the best. Otherwise, Charles would never have brought him aboard. He's always come through for us. Pearl's underground railroad is secure. It's the father who is worrying me. We need to get to him first. Cross your fingers that Ms. Gilbert will have some insight on who he is and his whereabouts. I wonder if he was in her senior class or maybe going for his master's. I didn't see anyone named Zack in her senior yearbook. I think it would have jumped out at me, or at least registered, as Zack is not an ordinary name. I'm betting he was a graduate student. What time is it?" Maggie asked.

Espinosa looked at his watch. "I do believe it is 2:25. The kid is five minutes late."

Ted grinned. "Here he comes now, and he's carrying a black backpack. He didn't have that when he started out. I'm thinking he's got something for us."

"How come you don't have the car running with the A/C?" Dennis said, opening the door and climbing inside. "Damn, it's hot. I got **stuff.** Boy, do I have stuff. And it cost me only twelve grand! I offered ten, but she held me up for twelve. She had me over a barrel, but she could have gotten fired, so I agreed to the amount. Don't worry. It's my money. I found a bank and didn't have any trouble. Then I met her at the Keg, I gave her the money, and she gave me all of Gretchen Spyder's records. I haven't really read any of it. Just glanced through to make sure I wasn't buying a pig in a poke. It's all here," Dennis said breathlessly.

Maggie, Ted, and Espinosa squawked in unison. "What!"

"Think about it, guys! If she got caught, she could have gotten fired. She needs the money. She's pretty much on her own, working two jobs and going to school. How else did you think we could do it? Look, it's done. I got the goods, so to speak. And as soon as I cool off, I'll tell you **exactly** what we have. Where are we going now?"

"To New World School of the Arts. Ted got the name of a friend of Spyder's who teaches there. Maggie sent a text to her, saying we need to meet," Espinosa said.

"And Myra said Snowden has the Domingos, and they're safe. They think maybe the father's name might be Zack. No one knows for sure. We're hoping the Gilbert woman might have some information or can back that up," Ted said.

"Can we stop somewhere for something cold to drink?" Dennis asked.

"We have some time to kill. Sure. First fast-food place we come to. We want to be on time so Gilbert doesn't leave when school lets out," Ted said.

"You know what? We're going to have to wait on the contents of this backpack. I get carsick when I try to read in a moving car," Dennis groused.

"Well, I don't," Maggie said, snatching the backpack from Dennis's lap. She rifled through the files and muttered to herself as she ran her fingers down the pages. "The girl is smart. Basically, a straight A student. Four-point-oh all the way. We now have her home address on Spyder Island, her Social Security number, and I guess this last address is the one where she had an apartment. I think I heard someone say that after her freshman year of living in the dorm, she moved off campus to her own apartment," Maggie said.

Ted pulled into a place called the Taco Shell, drove around to the drive-through, and ordered four large Sprites to go. "Fill them full of ice, please. On second thought, make that five," Ted said, knowing that Dennis would finish the first one in one large gulp. Which he did.

They were back on the highway and arrived at New World School of the Arts by 3:15. They exited the rental and beelined to the main building, where Maggie fired off a text, informing Gina Gilbert they were in the lobby and would wait for her.

And wait they did, for a full thirty minutes, before Gina Gilbert made her appearance. They knew it was her because she kept looking around, presumably for a woman, as it was Maggie who had contacted her.

Maggie stood up and said, "Ms. Gilbert? Maggie Spritzer. These are my colleagues. Is there someplace where we can go to talk? We're here about an old friend of yours, Gretchen Spyder."

"Really! That is a name from my past. We lost touch after graduation. Is she in some kind of trouble?"

"We don't know. She disappeared. Let me introduce you to my colleagues. This is Ted Robinson, Joe Espinosa, and Dennis West."

Hands were shaken, and then Gina

Gilbert led the party over to a corner, where there was a cluster of club chairs. "What is it you think I can help you with?"

Gina Gilbert was tall and thin. There was nothing fashionable about her at all. She had the early earmarks of becoming a spinster. She wore granny glasses, her hair was in a bun, and she wore serviceable shoes. If it were winter, she would be dressed in tweeds, but since it was spring, she wore blue-and-white seersucker.

"Were you good friends or acquaintances?" Maggie asked.

"Maybe a little of both. Gretchen wasn't someone you got close to. She never opened up and let you see who she was. I know this sounds corny, but she was deep. She hardly ever smiled. I thought she was brilliant. She tutored me. I wouldn't have graduated without her. I had a bad case of mono my senior year and got severely behind. She was a godsend. No one came to her graduation. Did you know that? My parents invited her to go out to dinner with us, but she declined. She never went home in the summers. She didn't get a job, either. I don't know what she did during summer break."

"Did she ever confide in you, share secrets, anything like that?" Dennis asked.

"Good Lord, no. That girl was buttoned up tight."

"Did she have a boyfriend?" Maggie asked.

"I'm not sure. I think so. A few days after graduation, I was packing up my stuff and getting ready to drive home. I was loading up my car in the driveway, and I saw her with this guy. She was driving a BMW convertible, and he was seated on the passenger side. I waved, she waved, and that was it. I knew the guy. He was finishing up his master's. Let me think. . . . His name was . . . Zack Phillips. He had a younger brother who attended the very school where we're now talking in. The brother graduated and is attending Duke University. That's so strange that I remember all that. I'm just not sure Zack Phillips was what you'd call a boyfriend or just someone she was giving a ride to."

"Any other friends?" Ted asked.

"Not the kind you sit up and talk all night with. At least that I knew of. I think I was the closest thing to a friend she had. I don't know why that was. She was certainly pretty enough to have boys all around her, but that wasn't the way it was. One day I felt bold and said to her, 'What are you looking for in life, Gretchen?' And she said, 'Myself.' Other than what I've told you, I really don't know anything. How could she just disappear? Are the authorities looking for her? Where are her parents? She does have parents, doesn't she?"

"We're looking for answers, too. Thanks for helping us," Maggie said.

"I'm sorry I wasn't more help. I hope you find her. I'm sorry, but I have a four-thirty meeting, and I don't want to be late."

Everyone smiled. They shook hands again. The foursome watched as Gina Gilbert trotted off in her sensible shoes and blue-and-white seersucker suit.

Ted held the door for the others.

"Now what?" Dennis asked.

"Espinosa, Google Zack Phillips. If he lives here in Florida, we're staying. If he lives out of state, we're going home tonight," Maggie said.

Five minutes later, Dennis bellowed, "There is a Zack Phillips who lives in Jacksonville, Florida. We could drive there, but it will take us quite a while, or we could fly."

"See if you can come up with a phone number or address. If you can't, call Snowden or Abner and see what they come up with. We'll head for the airport and take it from there," Maggie said.

Chapter 5

Nikki looked at her luncheon table and smiled. She did love to set a pretty table, and today was no exception. She had invited the Sisters for a hastily called lunch, then had rushed around like a chicken losing its feathers to make sure all was as good as she could make it. Her favorite dishes with the blue pansies on them. A lovely three-tier blueberry candle centerpiece with baby's breath nestled among the candles. It smelled heavenly. The dishes she'd ordered from a specialty house came with matching place mats and silverware. She smiled to herself as she remembered how she'd enticed Jack with this very table arrangement. She'd served him prime rib that melted in his mouth, apple-pecan gravy, mashed potatoes with just a hint of garlic, fresh string beans with slivered almonds and a light balsamic dressing, a garden salad, and fresh yeast rolls that she'd made herself. She'd ended the meal with a berry cobbler and fresh whipped cream and hazelnut coffee.

Nikki grinned then as she remembered how she'd had to help Jack up off his chair. She knew in that instant that she had him nailed for a lifetime.

Today's hasty luncheon was a tad different, but only because it was a last-minute affair. She was serving tuna sandwiches on toast, along with a vegetable-and-cheese platter and, for dessert, Twinkies. And, of course, the hazelnut coffee. The girls wouldn't mind. She was sure of it. They would be more interested in the why of the luncheon as opposed to the food. Then she remembered Kathryn's appetite. Well, maybe Kathryn would eat two sandwiches. In the end, she was sure she wouldn't care.

Nikki looked at the clock on the range just as the doorbell rang. Her face lit up as she ran to the door. Even though the girls had seen each other at Myra's just the day before, it was like old home week as the Sisters trooped in, one after the other.

Nikki smacked her hands together, saying, "Good, good. We're all here! Let's eat and get that over with so we can **talk**."

Alexis looked around, frowning. "We're all here?" It was a question, not a statement. Then she looked at the table in the kitchen, which was set for four. The frown deepened. "I realize Maggie left for Florida this morning, and Isabelle is . . . what and where she is . . . whatever. But what about Myra and Annie? This is their gig. Annie's, to be precise."

Nikki motioned for the Sisters to sit down. She pushed bread down into the six-slice toaster. "I know, I know. I just want to go over something with all of you, and if we're all in agreement, we can go out to the farm and talk it through with Myra and Annie."

"This does sound mysterious," Yoko said. The sparkle in her eyes said it all as far as the others were concerned. Yoko, like Harry, rarely if ever showed excitement about anything.

"Then let's get to it. I need to sit down,

anyway. My therapist worked me hard this morning. Before you can ask, I'm good," Kathryn said as she flopped down on one of the captain's chairs.

"Do you need to prop your leg up, Kathryn? I can get a footstool for you," Nikki said, one eye on Kathryn and one eye on the toaster.

"Nope. I'm good. Really, I am."

Alexis poured the coffee into the delicate pansy-patterned cups, while Yoko passed around the cheese-and-vegetable platter.

Nikki set the sandwiches in the middle of the table while she made a second batch.

"Are we allowed to talk business while we eat?" Yoko queried. "You know Charles's rule."

"Here's the thing," Nikki bubbled as she sat down and picked up a sandwich. "Charles isn't here, so let's be wicked and go for it."

Alexis bit into a crunchy pickle. "This is your show, Nikki. Talk to us."

Nikki leaned into the table, the sandwich in her hand forgotten for the moment. She took a deep breath and exhaled slowly. "Last night I couldn't sleep, so I got up and came downstairs and spent the balance of the night on the computer. Something was off yesterday at the farm. Something someone said that nagged at me at the time, but I couldn't come up with what it was. Just the thought of the Domingos possibly losing their adopted children made me crazy. They did everything by the book. They had a lawyer who crossed all his t's and dotted all his i's, and then along comes the richest guy in the world, who suddenly wants those two little kids and will stop at nothing to get them. I **think** I know now what it is, but I'm not sure. I called all of you because when we brainstorm it, you might come up with the same thing I did.

"There is nothing, and I mean absolutely nothing, to be found on that billionaire Angus Spyder. No pictures, nothing that I could find. That's not to say there aren't some out there that someone like Abner can find. In the back of my mind I know his name. More the Angus part, as opposed to the Spyder part. Think, girls. Do you ever recall hearing that name?"

Kathryn stopped chewing long enough to stare off into space. "Sort of. It's vague."

Alexis shook her head and finished the pickle in her hand.

"Nothing is ringing a bell," Yoko said.

"Think security, the way the man lives on that island. The secrecy. Why doesn't he allow himself to be photographed? They say he is the most reclusive man in the world and also the richest."

"Not true," Alexis said, reaching for another pickle. "Annie is richer than he is. She said so yesterday. I grant you, you said, 'Man,' but Annie trumped him."

"Be that as it may. I did find out that Angus Spyder has Spyder Island sealed off. His own security matches or even exceeds that of the White House. He uses retired SEALs and Delta Force guys, and that constitutes a small army. That was right there on the Internet for the whole world to see, assuming the whole world would even want to see it. The question is, where did he come by this elite little army of his? Being the richest man in the world, do you put an ad in the local paper? Do you call the different branches of the government and ask for a list of their retirees? Advertise in those mercenary magazines?"

"Oh my God! I think I know where you're

going with this, Nikki. It makes sense now."
Kathryn slapped at her forehead in disbe-
lief.

Alexis looked at Yoko like they were the
two dummies in the room. They spoke in
unison. "What? Who?"

"The one that got away. The only time we
failed in one of our missions. Think!" Kathryn said.

Alexis and Yoko hung their heads in
shame as they again muttered in unison,
"Hank Jellicoe"!

"Wait just a damn minute here. We didn't
fail. We caught the guy, and Avery Snowden
let him get away. There's no blame attached
to us on this. Lay it all on Snowden's doorstep, where it belongs. We delivered, and
in spades," Yoko shrilled.

"True. It still doesn't change anything.
The bastard got away. Now does it make
sense to all of you? That's why I didn't invite Myra and Annie. I wanted us to work
through it so we could go back to them with
it all laid out. Look, I'm not saying I'm right,
but nothing else makes sense. Jellicoe had
all the right sources. Even when he cut and
ran, he still had safe houses all over the
world, and he had a small following that was

intensely loyal to him. He had to know sooner or later that someone would rat him out for money, and that's when he went to ground, or **island,** if you prefer.

"If his company did do the security for Spyder Island, why wouldn't he go there and have that same security, along with the richest man in the world, to protect him? He takes his loyal guys, the ones he trusts implicitly, knowing Spyder Island is his only safe haven. Turnabout is fair play. Win-win for Spyder and Jellicoe."

"This has to mean we get another crack at that bastard," Kathryn said, menace ringing in her voice.

Nikki pushed a cherry tomato around on her plate with her index finger. "Maybe yes, maybe no. Myra and Annie tipped their hand, in my opinion. It's out there now that she's going to be going to Spyder Island. Of course, Spyder and his people don't know the why of it. They can't know we know about the twins and the adoptive family. But having said that, it has been all over the news. Jellicoe is one smart man. He'll be on it like fleas on a dog. He's vain and cocky enough to think we won't figure out he's part of anything. The other plus is that

Annie has owned that property for over twenty years. That's all a part of the record. I wanted to delve into anything that pertained to Jellicoe, but my eyes were closing."

"I think that if we alert Abner, Myra, and Annie when we get out to the farm to look into all things Jellicoe, we might find some answers. Instead of concentrating on Angus Spyder, we need to concentrate on Jellicoe. The first time around, he underestimated us, and we caught him fair and square. He won't let that happen a second time. We delivered, and Snowden dropped the ball," Kathryn snarled before she bit into her sandwich. "Man, I hate that man. To this day, I still have nightmares about him."

"One small army versus us. Is that what you're saying?" Yoko asked.

"That's what I'm saying," Nikki said. "We might have taken a sabbatical, so to speak, but now we're back! I think we're up to it, don't you, girls?"

"Oh yeah," Kathryn drawled as she reached for her second sandwich. "Good tuna, Nikki." Kathryn bit into the second sandwich before she fixed her steely gaze on Yoko and said, "If you were a betting woman, who would you put your money on?"

Yoko giggled. "Such a silly question, Kathryn. On us, of course."

Kathryn pretended to wipe sweat off her brow. "Whew. You had me worried there for a minute. The part I like best is that this time, we won't let that bastard get away. You haven't said anything, Alexis. Do you have doubts?"

Alexis grinned. "Not even one. I'm just thinking about what we can do to that guy once we get our hands on him. I can't tell you how much sleep I lost over that failed mission. Like Kathryn, I still have bad dreams about him from time to time. I just hope he knows or finds out we're coming for him and his boss."

Nikki clenched her hand into a tight fist and brought it down on the cherry tomato on her plate. "We'll squash him this time. Oh, girls, we are back in business! I can't tell you how happy this all makes me. I have to be honest. I've dreamed of this moment, begged Myra and Annie in my dreams to call on us. Let's face it. We were born to right the wrongs of the world!"

"Hear! Hear!" Alexis chortled. "I can't wait to bring my red bag of tricks out of retirement. One last comment. Do you think we should try reaching Isabelle or go in one short?"

"Well, there is Maggie, who could take up her spot," Yoko said.

"She might be needed on the outside. Our security blanket. I think Annie and Myra had it right when they said they didn't want all of us on the island at the same time. At least at first. Too much could go wrong. As to Isabelle . . . I don't know what to say. The last few times I tried to call her, the calls just went to voice mail. Then there's Abner. I'm speaking off the top of my head here when I say maybe we should just let sleeping dogs lie for now," Nikki said. "Or we could vote on it."

"I think we need to be fair where she's concerned. I say we call. If we can't get through, we'll know we tried," Yoko said.

Alexis agreed.

Kathryn shrugged.

"Okay, I'll try to call her," Nikki said, reaching into her pocket for her cell phone. She scrolled down and hit the number five on her speed dial. "It's dinnertime over there right now."

The Sisters watched as Nikki's shoulders slumped. She mouthed the words "It's going to voice mail." She drew a deep breath and left a detailed message, ending with, "Give one of us a call if you think you want to be part of this, Isabelle. It goes without saying, we all miss you."

Nikki placed her cell phone back in her pocket and gazed at the women seated around the table. "Let's clean up this mess and head out to the farm, unless you guys have something else you have to do this afternoon."

The women hopped to it and, within minutes, were ready to head out to Pinewood, delighted smiles on all their faces.

An hour later, Nikki drove through the gates as she blasted the horn to announce their arrival. Myra and Annie, along with all the dogs, appeared out of nowhere, shouting happily at the unannounced visit. The hugs and kisses and laughter led them all to the terrace, where Myra poured ice-cold lemonade into frosty glasses.

"This is so like old times." Annie laughed.

"There are no words to tell you all how much I missed all of this," she said, waving her arms about. "You know, the excitement, the adrenaline rush, the danger, the plotting, the scheming, and making it all come together just the way we planned. Except for that one time."

"And that's exactly why we're here, Annie," Nikki said. She quickly reiterated what she'd told the girls earlier. "Think of it as a twofer. We take down Jellicoe, get that skunk Spyder to lay off the Domingos. We can do it! We just have one small worry, and that's that you two tipped your hand by announcing your arrival. But, hey, I think maybe we can make that work to our advantage. I say we hit the war room and let it rip."

The mad scramble through the house, with the dogs yipping at their heels, made Myra double over laughing. "Nikki is right. We were born to do this."

"I can't remember the last time I was this happy. We are back in business, girls! And I, for one, love the feeling." Annie grinned from ear to ear.

"I can't wait to kick some ass," said

Kathryn, always the most outspoken of the group.

"This is the place. I guess the studio is in the back," Ted said, looking at the brochure he held in his hand. "Zack Phillips School of Dance. Look. There's the sign! Okay, guys, let's see what this Mr. Zack Phillips has to say." He moved forward, the others trailing behind as he meandered down a flagstone walkway that led to the dance studio.

The building behind the main house looked like it had been added recently. It was all glass and steel, with a modern look and feel to it. Inside, it was all lines and angles, again stark. A man seated at a desk at the far corner of the entryway looked up and said, "Can I help you? We're closed right now, but I never turn anyone away. What we can't do today, we can always do tomorrow."

He's a good-looking guy, Maggie thought. He looked muscular and in robust shape.

Ted made the introductions and went into his spiel. The others watched Phillips closely to see what his reaction was. Annoyance.

"Again? I've had three different people here asking me the same questions. If this keeps up, I might be able to sell my DNA for a profit. Here it is, the hair from my head, the root still attached," Phillips said, pulling a small sealed Baggie out of one of his desk drawers. "I'm going to tell you the same thing I told them. Gretchen Spyder and I were friends. She really liked to dance. I teach dancing. There's nothing more to tell you other than that I haven't seen her or had any communication with her for years."

"Sure there is," Maggie said quietly as she rummaged in her backpack for her special gold shield. She held it up like a beacon. "There's some serious juice behind this shield, so it might be a good idea to tell us what you **didn't** tell those other people. Let's start over. My name is Maggie Spritzer. Talk to me," she said, slipping the gold shield back into her backpack.

"Okay, okay. Gretchen was a good friend. A really good friend. No, not that kind of friend. I'm gay, and I have a partner, so get that look off your faces. She lent me the money to start this studio, as long as she could come and dance to her heart's delight. Sometimes she'd come in the middle of the night and dance until dawn. By herself. Yes, she had a lover. Sometimes she brought him here. Actually, it was like every other week, when her security, her handler, whoever the hell the guy was, rotated. She had an arrangement with the off-week guy so he wouldn't report to her parents what she was doing. I guess she paid him more to keep her secret than her daddy was paying him. Whatever it was, it worked. For her. The guy's name was Greg Albright.

"It all came to a crashing end when Gretchen came here one night and told me she was pregnant. She was so hysterical, I didn't know what to do for her, so I just let her cry and tried to comfort her. She asked me to talk to Greg and to tell him she went away and wouldn't be coming back. She took a new apartment and hid out until it was time to give birth, at which point she gave the baby up for adoption."

"Correction," Dennis said. "Gretchen Spyder gave birth to twins."

"Really? I didn't know that." Phillips shrugged. "I never saw her again. But she did something very generous. She canceled the loan she had with me. I own the studio free and clear, thanks to Gretchen."

"Did you know about her accident?" Maggie asked.

"No. What accident? Is she okay? What happened?"

Maggie spelled it out for Phillips. "They say she's in a wheelchair and might never walk again. We really don't know much more than that. Are you saying Greg Albright doesn't know about the pregnancy?"

"Well, I know that Gretchen didn't tell him, and I sure as hell didn't tell him. If he found out, he found out from someone else. Oh, there is one other thing. Gretchen said Greg wouldn't accept a simple 'Gretchen is going away' excuse, that he'd try to find her, so she came up with a story and gave me a hundred thousand dollars in American Express traveler's checks made out in his name to give to him along with the story that he was to go to London, England, out to the countryside, and buy a little cottage with a lot of flowers, and she'd join him in a year. She left a letter for him, too. He took it all and left. And I've never heard from him since. I just assumed that Gretchen joined him at some point, since I never heard from her again, either."

"And you didn't tell any of that to the other people who came here, snooping around?" Espinosa said.

"Look, I might not be the sharpest tool in the shed, but I can read people. What those guys wanted did not bode well for Gretchen. They looked like trained military, and I could tell that two of them were packing heat by the cut of their jackets. I think I pulled it off, because no one ever came back, and that was almost four years ago."

"Do you have any way at all of tracking down Albright?" Maggie asked.

"No. Sorry."

"Do you know where Gretchen met Albright? Did anyone but you know about him?"

"Her secret bodyguard, I suppose, but like I said, she paid him well not to squeal on her. I suppose he could be turned. Money talks and bullshit walks. We all know that. The guy might be afraid to open his mouth for fear Gretchen's father would fire him. She told me one time after too much wine that her father, and these are her words, not mine, was meaner than cat shit. She said he was a cruel man. Having said all that, there is nothing more I can tell you. She never said where she met Greg. I know they loved each other. I wish you could have seen her dance. She was a natural. She just glowed when she was free to be the dancer in her. It's hard to accept that she won't dance again. She was a good friend. A really good friend."

Maggie pulled a business card out of her backpack. "If you hear anything that will help us, please call. If anyone comes back, asking questions, be sure to let us know. We're trying to help."

Zack Phillips got up and walked around the desk to shake hands with the little group. "If I hear anything, I'll be in touch. If you talk to Gretchen, give her my regards."

"We'll do that, Mr. Phillips," Maggie said.

Outside in the balmy evening air, Maggie looked at the others and said, "Are you all thinking what I'm thinking?"

Ted and Espinosa grinned and said in unison, "Isabelle."

"Oh, yeah. C'mon. Let's grab something to eat, head to the hotel, and call it a night. We're outta here at six in the morning, and it's a forty-minute ride to the airport," Maggie said.

"We did good today, didn't we, guys?" Dennis said.

Espinosa clapped Dennis on the back. "Real good, kid. Real good."

Chapter 6

Zack Phillips watched the sun creeping over the horizon. He'd barely slept, tossing and turning all night long. He'd talked last night's situation over with his partner ad nauseam until he thought he would go out of his mind with the lack of any solution. His first loyalty was to Gretchen Spyder. She'd trusted him to do what she asked, and he'd failed her. Because . . . because . . . he'd thought Greg Albright had a right to know the secret he'd been entrusted to keep. He felt guilty as hell now. "A guy thing," his partner had said. Bullshit! What could be worse than a man waiting for the love of his life to show up and being left hanging. With no explanation. And the baby. Twins. He needed to tell Greg that, too. Right or wrong, he had to live with what he'd done. And now he was going to compound the problem.

Zack hitched up his sweatpants. Normally, he was out running at this time of the morning, but today he could barely place one foot in front of the other, much less run his usual five miles. All the lies he'd told lately were starting to eat at him. His placid life was now full of stress and intrigue. His guests last night had seemed the best so far, but he was still glad he had held back. At the present time, he didn't trust anyone. Hell, he couldn't even trust himself. He'd betrayed his best friend. What did that say about him? Not much, that was for damn sure.

"Crap!" It was an explosive sound. So loud, his cat hissed his disapproval and flew out of the room.

Zack rummaged in one of the kitchen drawers for the prepaid cell phone he'd bought at Target a few months ago. He'd used it only three times, and that was to call Greg Albright in England. It took only one meeting with the gun-toting visitors to tell him they were more than capable of checking the calls he made on his own cell phone or any other cell phone that used a SIM card, like a TracFone.

He didn't watch **Law & Order** on TV for nothing. He knew how it all worked. Even though he'd done his best to stay under the radar, he was absolutely positive that he was under surveillance. Too many strange faces around, too many times that the hair on the back of his neck warned him things weren't normal. So he took a deep breath and hit the only programmed number on the prepaid burn phone. He thought he'd been clever when he asked the mother of one of his students to pick up the phone. He'd given her cash, and she'd done as he asked and brought the phone to him before class.

"Greg, it's Zack. Listen, I had another batch of visitors last night. I think you need to relocate, and just to be on the safe side, I'd get some new identity cards if you can. This thing seems to be heating up. Look, they found me, not that I'm that hard to find, but sooner or later, someone is going to tie you to me. There's only so much I can do. And before you can ask, no, I have not been able to get in touch with Gretchen. So, are you going to take my advice?"

Zack listened to the voice on the other end of the phone. His stomach roiled at the torment he was hearing. "Greg, you're the father of the twins. Gretchen's father wants your kids to carry on his bloodline. With you in his corner, he can get the kids, and the Domingos lose. You lose, too. Trust me on that. Is that what you want? I know you didn't know any of this when you did what Gretchen asked you to do. I think now that she was trying to protect you from her father the only way she knew how. She wasn't counting on being in that killer accident.

"The good news is she never told her father about you. I don't know this for a fact, but I would guess that she probably said something like she had too much to drink and had a one-night stand. Something like that. Otherwise, they would already have you in their hot little hands. Do not forget for one minute that he's the richest man in the world, or at least that's what he says. Money is power. If he wants you, you're his. That's the bottom line. Run, buddy, as far and as fast as you can. If you need me to do anything, call only this number. Let's set a time for calls. Let's say, nine o'clock my time. I'm usually home by then. Good luck, buddy."

When the phone was shoved back into the kitchen drawer, Zack realized he didn't feel one bit better. He immediately took it out and shoved it down in the bottom of a box of cornflakes. If anything, that made him feel even worse. He poured himself a cup of coffee and drank it as he paced the spacious kitchen. Then he poured a refill as he thought about the people who had visited him last night. There was something different about them, as opposed to the gun-toting jerks who had confronted him earlier. The foursome seemed like they were on the Domingos' side, and rightly so. It would be cruel to rip the twins away from the only parents they had ever known. And yet they seemed genuinely concerned about Gretchen Spyder. He didn't know if he was glad or not that he'd opted not to tell them more about Greg Albright.

Zack's shoulders slumped as he made his way to the second floor. He needed to get a move on since he had an aerobics class for a group of senior citizens at eight thirty, followed by a class in ballroom dancing for the same group of seniors. He always enjoyed the classes with the oldsters, all of whom claimed to have two left feet. Which, he'd come to find out, was true. Secretly, he thought some of them came just for the coffee and doughnuts and the socializing. Whatever, he had to get a move on. He crossed his fingers the way he had when he was a child in the hope that things would go well in regard to Gretchen Spyder and the Domingo family. And, of course, Greg Albright.

Maggie Spritzer was a whirlwind as she raced through her duties as editor in chief of the **Washington Post.** She delegated tasks, signed her name a dozen different places, scanned the morning's front page, and nodded in approval. As an afterthought as she munched on a banana, she watered the plants in her office. And all this was done while she was still wearing her rain gear. She opened the door to check on the boys, who were standing in a straight line, their arms crossed over their chests, waiting for her. Their expressions clearly said, "What's taking so long?"

"You guys ready?" Maggie asked breathlessly. "You know, Ted, that was a brilliant idea you had for the front page. Annie is going to love it."

Ted basked in his beloved's praise. "It was Espinosa and Dennis's idea. I just ran with it and wrote it."

"I like the idea of a prize of a Barnes & Noble Nook for the first ten people who can name the woman you wrote about. By the end of the week, Countess Anna de Silva will be a household name. Let's just hope that someone on Spyder Island reads our paper," Maggie said.

"Everyone reads the **Post,**" Dennis said confidently. "I think you can take off your raincoat, Maggie. The sun is out. April showers bring May flowers, and all that." Dennis chortled. "Who's driving?"

"Me," Espinosa said, raising his hand. "Anyone in favor of stopping somewhere for some takeout we can eat in the car on the way out to the farm?"

Settled in the **Post** van, Maggie leaned back and started to talk. "What's your honest opinion of Zack Phillips? We really didn't talk about him last night, and we all slept on the flight home."

"Seemed okay to me," Espinosa said as he hit the highway.

"Something was off-key," Ted said.

"I think he knew something he didn't tell us. I don't think he gave us the full skinny on everything," Dennis said.

"I agree. I think he knows exactly where Greg Albright, the baby daddy, is," Maggie said. "My gut tells me that even if we pulled out his toenails, he won't give it up, either. He's a loyal friend. I understand that and admire him for his loyalty."

"I didn't get that feeling," Espinosa grumbled.

"That's because you don't have a reporter's instincts. Didn't you pick up anything with your photographer's eye?" Ted demanded.

"No, I didn't," Espinosa grumbled again as he turned on his blinker to hit a burger house that claimed to have the best hamburgers in the state of Virginia. They loaded up with killer fries, burgers, and fruit pies and added diet sodas to make up for their fat intake.

The foursome ate with gusto. Bad manners or not, they kept up a running conversation about what was going on, with Dennis asking for explicit clarification as to why they were so interested in a man like Angus Spyder when it was the Domingos they should be concentrating on.

"Listen to me carefully, kid," Ted said. "It all ties together. The girl, the birth mother named Gretchen Spyder, who, by the way, is an only child, was sent to Florida to go to college. She had bodyguards. Because her daddy is who he is. I'm sure she had a list of do's and don'ts a mile long. She wasn't to mix with others, just go to classes and behave herself. Which I guess she did until she met Greg Albright. She somehow managed to convince one of her bodyguards to cut her some slack. She probably paid him a fortune, but I don't know that for sure. Then she finds herself in the family way. I'm thinking she panicked and made arrangements to give the baby up for adoption.

"We have to assume both bodyguards knew of her condition, and again, we have to assume that she paid bodyguard number two to keep quiet, even though it was bodyguard number one who had allowed the dirty deed to take place. It all worked, and Daddy and Mummy were none the

wiser until she was in a car accident several years later. You know hospitals ask a
lot of questions before they admit you. It
came out that she had given birth to a child.
Just part of the questionnaire. Her family is
notified because she is seriously injured.
Her daddy sends someone to take her back
to Spyder Island."

Ted turned to Maggie and said, "We
should have checked the hospitals to see
what we could find out."

"Yeah, I thought about that last night, so
I called Abner and asked him to hack into
the hospital records to see what he could
find out. Someone signed her out. Her daddy's goon squad. Imagine that. He couldn't
even come to the mainland to see his
daughter. What kind of father is that? And
where's the mother in all of this?"

"We should be trying to find the two bodyguards," Dennis said.

The others laughed.

"Kid, they are long gone," Ted said.
"Maybe even dead, for all we know. People
like Angus Spyder do not tolerate mistakes
or betrayal. The daughter is probably locked
up in some dungeon for bringing disgrace
to the family. Yet he wants those kids. Go

figure. The man doesn't give a hoot in hell that he'll be ripping those twins away from the only parents they've ever known or that the adoption was perfectly legal. They're his blood, and he wants them. Unless he can find the birth daddy. That would be our guy Greg Albright, who supposedly resides in England these days. And that is the end of the story as we know it at this point in time."

Dennis leaned forward. "So you're saying no matter what we do, he's going to get those kids."

"Unless we stop him," Maggie said as she licked at her fingers. "We can do that, you know. Stop him, that is. If you don't believe that, then you don't belong in this group, Dennis."

Dennis snorted. "This whole thing sounds like some bizarre fairy tale. Us and what army?"

"No army, kid. Just us." Ted laughed. "Obviously, you need to read up on the vigilantes. Have you already forgotten what happened with the crooked judges? Or the crooked developer who had been your benefactors' childhood friend? And while you're at it, remember who our newest best friend is. Jack Sparrow. That army enough for you, kid?"

Maggie waved off the conversation like it was too stupid to discuss any further. "Ted, what is your gut telling you? Mine is telling me, we're missing something or we've over-looked something." Maggie's tone of voice was so fretful, Dennis sat up straight and stared at her. He'd learned over time to pay attention to Ted's and Maggie's reporter's instincts.

"Like what?" Dennis demanded.

"I don't know. That's the problem. Ted, am I right or not?"

"No, you're right. When my left eyelid twitches, that means I'm missing something, and it's been twitching like crazy since yesterday. Don't sweat it. Sooner or later it will come to one of us. It always does," Ted said.

"Let's hope it's sooner rather than later," Maggie groused. She hated it when she couldn't get a handle on something. And her middle name was **not** Patience.

The rest of the trip out to the farm was made in silence. Espinosa, always a careful driver, kept his eyes on the road and his thoughts on Alexis, while Ted, Maggie, and Dennis tapped out text messages.

"Wow! Look! The parking lot is full," Dennis said as Espinosa pulled alongside Alexis's car. "Everyone is here, it looks like."

"Nope! Just the girls! Something's going on," Maggie said, eyeing the cars. "Park this van already, Espinosa, so we can find out what's going on. Damn, I hope we didn't miss anything." Maggie was out of the van the minute Espinosa brought it to a full stop.

Inside the kitchen the women went through their little war dance, with hugs and kisses, questions and offers of coffee. The guys stood like dummies in the doorway, waiting for the five-minute festivities to be over. As one, they shrugged and accepted Myra's offer of coffee.

"We have news, and I'm sure you have news, so let's decide if it's war-room worthy or if we can do it all here at the kitchen table," Kathryn said.

"I think the kitchen table will work, because we're all kitchen-table people," Alexis said as she moved her chair closer to Espinosa's. She reached for his hand, not caring if anyone saw the little byplay or not. No one cared.

"Go first, Maggie," Annie said.

Maggie related the past day's events,

with Ted and Dennis adding bits and pieces. She ended with, "The trip was a success, but we don't really have that much more than we did before. Ted and I both agree that Zack Phillips didn't give us the full skinny on the biological father. Here's the thing, though. Ted and I both feel—and I admit, it's our reporter's gut instinct here—that we are missing something. Can't put my finger on it, but it is nagging me."

The women at the table laughed.

"We know what it is. Nikki came up with it earlier. We all missed it, too," Yoko said.

"What?" the four new arrivals asked as one.

All eyes turned to Nikki. "You ready for this?" she asked.

The four new arrivals nodded.

"Think Hank Jellicoe!" Nikki exclaimed.

"Oh my God!" The words ripped out of Maggie's mouth like gunshots.

"Son of a bitch!" Ted blurted.

Espinosa was befuddled enough to take his hand out of Alexis's and throw his arms up in the air at the fact that he, too, had missed it.

"Who is Hank Jellicoe?" Dennis demanded.

"Before your time, kid. A really bad dude," Ted responded. "Just follow along, and you'll catch up."

The conversation ramped up, with everyone throwing out ideas and suggestions. Observations that might or might not mean something were offered up at the speed of light. Then they all wound down at the same time, with Alexis saying, "Now we wait."

Ted decided to move on to his article in the morning paper and Annie's take on it.

"I thought you did a super job. It would be nice if we knew if Angus Spyder reads the **Post.** I'm not sure about my becoming a household name, however," Annie said, laughing.

"Types like Angus Spyder read every newspaper on the market. That's how they stay ahead of the game, or at least that is what they want us to believe. The object of the five-day series of articles is to let him know how rich you are and that your wealth exceeds his. The philanthropic part will make him nuts because his type doesn't believe in giving or sharing. All they believe in is 'Gimme more, more, more' and how to accumulate even greater wealth. I think it's safe to say the man doesn't have a generous bone in his body," Ted said.

Maggie's cell chirped to life. She clicked it on, announced herself, then mouthed the word "Abner." She listened as she scribbled notes on a pad next to Myra's phone on the counter. The others could hear her say, "Uh-huh. Yep. Sure. Oh. Good work, Abby. Thanks."

"What?" the group asked as one.

"We now have the name of the orthopedic surgeon who worked on Gretchen Spyder. He's in Miami. Abner's hacking also gave him the name of the ob-gyn who delivered the twins. Abby said there is a note on Gretchen's chart that the surgeon didn't want Gretchen transported out of the hospital. Seems that the four people who came to get her convinced him otherwise, and he did sign off on her being moved, but only under protest. The hospital lawyers got involved and made the four men, each and every one of them, take full responsibility for Gretchen and agree that if something went awry, they could not come back and retaliate against Miami General. They all signed off on the agreement, and Gretchen Spyder was taken to one of those medical planes, never to be seen or heard from again. End of that story right there."

"I don't think there's any point in going to Miami to talk with the surgeon. He won't tell us anything, because of the privacy laws. Keep his name and phone number, just in case. Also the ob-gyn's," Myra said.

The others agreed.

"Now what?" Yoko asked.

"Like I said before, now we wait," Alexis intoned as she reached for Espinosa's hand under the table.

Chapter 7

Isabelle Flanders stood at the window of her London flat and looked out at the heavy spring rain. Normally, she liked a nice rainy day, but that was back in the day when her life was normal, which it decidedly was not anymore. She wanted to cry at her circumstances, but she bit down on her bottom lip so she wouldn't. Big girls didn't cry, especially when the reason they were crying in the first place was their own fault.

She was **sooo** done with England. She hoped she would never have to set foot on these shores again. What had seemed like a dream come true had turned into a nightmare. Not that the nightmare was her own fault. She should have bailed out months ago, gone home, and begged Abner's forgiveness—and the girls', too. But, no, stubborn mule that she was, she'd had to hunker down and not give in. Giving in was a sign of weakness. **Crap!**

Like it was her fault the financial people behind the building of the new age city ran out of money. Or so they said. Was it her fault they didn't pay their contractors? How could all this happen when the consortium responsible said they had the queen's backing? The queen's backing to her meant the queen's money was being used. Unless it was all a lie, and she couldn't prove whether it was or it wasn't. And then there were those weird new people who had marched in and taken over. Just like that. The Brits were a tight-lipped lot, for sure, especially when it came to confiding in a Yank from across the pond.

Two months ago, her paycheck had been returned for insufficient funds. She was told to resubmit it. It was paid, and it was the last check she'd gotten. The very next day, when she reported to work, the building site was deserted, and a barricade was set in place. There was no way she could even get onto the site. She'd called every name she had stored in her phone, but no one had answered. Even if she were stupid, which she wasn't, she should have known that it was the end of the road, and that the new age city, her dream, was already crumbling to ashes as far as she was concerned.

Why she'd stayed on in this tiny London flat was beyond her. She turned when she heard the cell phone on the table, where she'd left it, ring. She walked over, but before she could answer it, the call went to voice mail. She waited, then clicked it on. **Maggie! Well, damn!** She listened to the message five times before she flopped down on a worn sofa that came with the rented flat. The ad in the paper had said elegant furnished flat. It was so far from elegant, she wanted to cry all over again.

Isabelle walked over to the tiny foyer, where her five bags were waiting to be taken down to her rental car for her trip home. Going home with her tail between her legs. **How humiliating.** As she stared at her bags, she wondered if her husband, Abner, would ever forgive her. Would the girls forgive her? She rather thought she would fare better with the girls than with her husband. She wondered if she was capable of begging her husband to take her back. She winced at the thought. Better to think about the message Maggie had left for her. She headed back to the living room to call Maggie.

A needle in a haystack. Didn't Maggie know how big the English countryside was? How was she going to find an American who bought a cottage four years ago in the English countryside? How? Maybe . . . She had made some contacts while she'd been here, like . . . Arnold Biberman. One of the biggest Realtors in London. She'd even had dinner with him, because he'd wanted to pick her brain on the new age city and to see if he could get an exclusive rental agreement. Now that the entire project was down the drain, she wondered if he would even talk to her. She hadn't exactly given a promise, but she had alluded to the fact that she would do her best to help him out because she liked him. Well, it was worth a try. If she struck pay dirt by some wild stretch of the imagination, she wouldn't be going back home empty-handed.

Isabelle scrolled through her contact list and pressed in the digits for Biberman's number. She was surprised when he answered the phone himself. She identified herself, said why she was calling.

"It's kind of urgent, Arnold. I'm leaving for the States tomorrow. By the way, this flat will be available for rental at noon tomorrow. I've cleaned it up, and it looks better than the day I moved in. So, can you help me or not?" She listened. "That's fine, Arnold. I'm not leaving till tomorrow. Like you said, it might be easier than we think, since not that many Americans buy cottages in the English countryside. Call me when and if you find something." She listened again and then said, "Of course I'll miss all of you. I won't miss your weather, though." She forced a laugh she didn't feel and broke the connection.

Back in the foyer, Isabelle rummaged in one of her bags for her laptop, yanked it out, and carried it over to the small table in the living room. She booted it up and typed in the name Greg Albright. Two hours later, she closed up the laptop and walked out to the mini kitchen to make a pot of coffee that she didn't really want or even need. She almost dropped the wire basket when her cell phone buzzed to life.

"You actually found the needle in the haystack?" Isabelle said in wonder. "Amazing. And you have a phone number! Glory be! Of course I want it. And directions to the cottage. Arnold, you never cease to amaze me. The next time I find myself on your shores, I will spring for the biggest dinner you have ever had in your life. Seriously, thank you."

"Ah!" Did she dare call Greg Albright, or should she head out to the cottage? Even with the bad weather, it shouldn't take her more than an hour each way. She didn't have anything else to do to while away the hours until the crack of dawn, when she would leave for the airport. She ran to her bags and rummaged again for her rain gear. Five minutes later, she was out of the flat and down at the parking area, map in hand. She closed her eyes and relished the adrenaline rush seeping through her. Damn if she wasn't excited. Very excited.

Ninety minutes later, Isabelle pulled onto the gravel driveway of a small cottage. She opened the car door and stepped out onto the driveway. It was hard to see details through the rain, but it looked enticing. A smattering of spring flowers were already blooming; others, just poking through the soft, loamy earth. The shade trees were starting to bud, and a few were already in full leaf. She peered through the rain to see that the cottage looked to be in good repair. It looked quaint, with its Dutch doors and heavy black hardware in the back, probably the kitchen area. She particularly liked the diamond-paned windows. From where she was standing, she could see that the porch was tiny, just barely big enough to hold two caned rocking chairs.

She ambled along a well-manicured walkway of colored flagstones bordered by bright yellow daffodils to a pristine white front door. She gave the knocker a resounding bang and stood back. When there was no response, she banged it again, then a third time. Finally, the door opened to reveal a tall, muscular man with a deep frown on his face.

Before Isabelle could utter a word, he said, "Whatever you're selling, I don't want or need. I didn't invite you here, so please turn around and leave."

"Will you please listen to me, Mr. Albright? Please. Then if you don't like what I'm telling you, I'll walk away, but at least listen. I'm an American, like you. In fact, I'm returning to the States tomorrow morning. A friend asked me to check on you. It's rather complicated, and you really need to speak to the people who asked me to find you. It's about . . . Gretchen Spyder."

The man's face lit up like a football field at night. "Gretchen! Why didn't you say so? Come in, come in."

"I thought I just did. Tell you about Gretchen, that is."

"Right, right. Please come into the parlor and sit. Tea, coffee?"

"Thank you, no. I hate tea, and I'm coffeed out."

Isabelle looked around. It was a pretty little place, with chintz-covered furniture, a wood-burning fireplace. The tables looked like they were handmade and sturdy. There was no clutter. A man's place. But definitely homey. And yet it felt empty to Isabelle. It smelled good, though, like he had cooked something earlier or something was baking.

"Tell me about Gretchen," Albright said with a catch in his voice.

"I can't tell you anything. But I can call the person who asked me to find you, and she can answer all your questions."

Albright rubbed his hands through his thick hair, his eyes alight with something Isabelle couldn't define. Love maybe.

Isabelle punched in the numbers for Maggie, and when Maggie came on the phone, Isabelle grinned at the exuberant greeting. "Whoa! Listen, I'm sitting in Mr. Albright's living room, as we speak. He has questions that I can't answer. I'm going to turn him over to you." Isabelle handed the phone to Albright, who walked away toward his kitchen. She could hear him talking, but not distinctly. She walked over to the window to stare out at the rain. It hadn't let up at all.

Isabelle felt twitchy, nervous. Maybe she should have eaten something. What was Maggie telling Albright? She knew enough background now to worry that things were going to escalate fast. If she had found this guy, someone else could find him just as easily, if all that Maggie had said was spot-on. She clenched her fists and unclenched them.

Isabelle felt his presence before he spoke. She whirled around and was stunned at the tortured look on the young man's face. He returned her cell phone to her. She waited.

Albright rubbed his hands across his face, then through his hair. "I don't know what to say. I feel like I've been kicked in the gut by a mule. I just recently learned that I'm a father, the father of twins. I had no idea, no clue. I hadn't even known Gretchen was pregnant until a friend, Zack back in the States, told me. I don't understand why she didn't tell me. It all makes sense now.

"I don't know what to do. The lady on the phone—she said her name was Maggie Spritzer—suggested I return to the States tomorrow with you. She said if you found me, then Gretchen's father's people will find me. She explained as much as she knew about what's going on. Jesus, all this time I've been sitting here like an idiot, waiting for Gretchen to come and knock on my door. Talk about being a fool!"

"I'm just the messenger, Mr. Albright. I know Maggie very well. If her advice is for you to return with me, it would be wise to do just that. From what I'm told about him, Mr. Spyder, Gretchen's father is . . . an un-savory character, to put it mildly. And that despite the fact, or maybe because, he is either the richest or at least one of the rich-est people in the world. He wants those children. And from what I understand, when that man wants something, he's going to get it, no matter what. Nothing will stand in his way. Your children are safe, with parents who love them. I get it that you didn't know until very recently, and that alone might give you grounds to fight for them on your own, but do you really want to disrupt those children's lives and rip them away from the only parents they've ever known?

"Gretchen herself is the one you need to speak with. I don't know how you can make that happen. I truly don't. If her father finds you, he will dangle you as bait for his daughter and use you for his own ends, getting possession of those children. And that is exactly what they would become, his possessions. You know her better than I do. What will she do?"

Albright shrugged. "I thought I knew her. I loved her. I still love her. I never understood why she didn't get in touch or join me, the way she promised. Now that you and Zack have told me about her accident, I don't feel quite as much a fool. She loved me. She did. She never talked much about her family. She did say one time that she wanted to get as far away from her father as she could. But then she went on to say there was no place on earth that he couldn't find her. I hate to admit this, but I thought she was being overly dramatic.

"She did tell me to buy this place under an assumed name, but things didn't work out with that plan. The Brits are a cautious lot. So I guess you are right in that respect. Buying it under my own name with Gretchen's money was a mistake. Since Zack called, I have been trying to adjust to the fact that I have two children, twins."

"You really don't, Mr. Albright. The children are no longer yours or Gretchen's. I suppose a case might be made for you since you did not know about them and did not agree to their being adopted, but I'm no lawyer. Right now, the children are all that matter. The Domingos have your children, and it was all done legally. The fact that their mother lied is going to be a problem, and you are now part of that problem. I'm sure, considering the circumstances, that if things can be worked out, the Domingos would let you be part of the twins' life. Gretchen, too, if she wants. Not so Gretchen's father. So, what are you going to do?"

"I don't know. Sit here and think. That

Maggie person gave me her number to call
if I decide to head back to the States. She
warned me that the airports are probably
on alert, should my name pop up. She
said that's how much clout Gretchen's father has. I don't know the first thing about
how to go about getting a bogus identity.
Do you?"

Isabelle laughed. She couldn't remember
when she had last laughed. "As a matter of
fact, I do. Let me make a phone call."

Albright stared at Isabelle like she'd
sprouted horns, then shook his head and
shrugged.

Isabelle walked over to the window and
made her call to Avery Snowden. She talked
quickly, explaining the situation, then motioned that she needed a pen and paper.
Albright tripped over his own feet in his
haste to get them to her. Isabelle scribbled
furiously. "And the amount?" She listened
and nodded before she broke the connection.

"Do you have a car, Mr. Albright? If you
do, is it in your name?"

"I do, and it's parked in back of the house.
Yes, it's in my name. The garage is full of
stuff."

"Go to this address in London, and the people there will do what needs to be done. It's going to take roughly two days, give or take. You'll need to make some alterations to your physical features, and they will help you with that. All this will be paid for by our people, as well as your airline ticket. Once you arrive at that location, you are not to leave until your new identity is totally in place. If you have a bank account, close it out and take the money in cash. Do not use a credit card. Sell your car and take that money in cash also. You will leave all that money with the people who are helping you. When you arrive Stateside, the money will be given back to you in dollars as opposed to pounds. You will lose a bit in the exchange, but that's the cost of doing business."

"This is so . . . so . . . cloak and dagger-ish. I feel like I'm in a spy movie or something."

Isabelle quirked an eyebrow but didn't say anything.

"It's mostly Gretchen's money. I didn't spend any of it except for the house. What will happen to it?"

"I don't know. Right now, that is not important. Do you have a job?"

"I do medical billing for a group of doctors in London. It's all done here. On weekends I do gardening for some elderly people."

"No loose ends. Notify everyone that you have a family emergency and need to leave for . . . wherever. I don't think I would say the good old USA. Maybe France or Belgium. Depending, of course, on whatever you may have said to them in the past concerning your background. Okay, we're done here, then, right? If so, I'll leave you to take care of your personal business.

"One more thing. I think that if I were you, I would wipe this place down and not leave any telltale signs that you were ever here. Take all your personal belongings. I can't stress enough the importance of your doing as I say."

"Is my life in danger, Miss Flanders?"

"I don't know the answer to that question, Mr. Albright. If you want me to guess, then I would say yes."

"From Gretchen's father?" Albright's eyes were round as saucers. "You make him sound like a devil."

"Sound? My mistake. He **is** the devil. Whatever you do, don't forget that. If there's nothing else, I'll be on my way."

Albright rubbed his hands together as he walked Isabelle to the door. "Will I ever see you again? Do you have any idea how I can get word to Gretchen?"

"I think you can count on seeing me again at some point. Let's both hope it is under more favorable circumstances. As to Gretchen, I'm sorry, but I don't have a clue. Perhaps when you return Stateside, our people can help you with that. Nice meeting you, Mr. Albright."

"Whom do you mean when you say 'Our people'?"

"I think it's better that you don't know right now. Good luck, Mr. Albright." With that said, Isabelle pulled the hood up on her rain slicker and ran for her car. She suddenly felt so alive, she thought about singing. Instead, she turned over the engine and cranked up the radio.

Homeward bound.

Chapter 8

Isabelle Flanders staggered under the weight of her heavy shoulder bag as she walked through the concourse at Dulles Airport. She was beyond tired, beyond exhausted. She hadn't slept a wink the night before the flight, and she'd been unable to sleep during the flight across the Atlantic. Her mind buzzed and whirled with what would happen when her feet touched down on American soil. She wished now she'd put together a game plan, but game plans were for people who had missions and a course to follow. All she was doing was putting one foot in front of the other. If she had a plan, it was to pick up all her luggage, go through customs, find a cab, and head to the nearest hotel. Tomorrow was another day. Tomorrow she'd make a plan.

Forty minutes later, with a porter behind her and her five bags loaded on a dolly, Isabelle headed for the taxi line, only to be stopped by people calling her name. She whirled around to see her Sisters running toward her, their faces wreathed in smiles. Maggie was the first to reach her and grabbed her in a viselike bear hug. The others crowded around, to the amusement of other travelers. They were all laughing and crying, rubbing her back, and mouthing words she would only later remember.

"We'll take it from here," Nikki said, tipping the porter and wheeling the dolly with Isabelle's luggage around. "Maggie has the **Post** van parked in the garage. C'mon, everyone. Shake it. We have some celebrating to do."

Isabelle laughed and cried, her exhaustion gone. She was home. Her Sisters had forgiven her, and she was back in the fold. "Where are we going?" she managed to ask.

"For the moment, to Maggie's house,"

Kathryn said. "Damn, girl, it's so good to see you."

Alexis dabbed at her eyes. "We're all together again. This is so perfect. We all missed you. Are you okay? You are staying this time, right? You aren't going back? Does Abner know you're here?"

Isabelle beamed happily. "I've never been better, now that you're all here. I am staying. I will never, as in never, go back there. I . . . um . . . didn't tell Abner. I need to . . . work on that. I can use all the advice you guys care to give me. I love this sunshine. I couldn't wait to get back here. Girls, we need to talk."

"Until we can't talk anymore. We have all day. We'll order in and have a regular gabfest, like we used to. We have a new mission, and we were all worried that we were going to have to go in one short. Now that you're here, it's working out perfectly," Yoko said as she stroked Isabelle's back. "We missed you."

"I feel like we're whole again," Kathryn said jubilantly.

"You can stay with me, Isabelle, for as long as you want. Or if you want to go to the farm, that's okay, too. This is just temporary, until you and Abner . . . you know . . . patch it all up. No sense looking for a house or an apartment and making an unnecessary move. You okay with that?" Maggie said.

"I am."

"What about Ted?" Nikki asked, a wicked gleam in her eye.

"Ted . . . ah . . . has visiting privileges. He doesn't live with me," Maggie said defensively. The girls hooted as Maggie's face turned pink.

Forty minutes later, Maggie pulled the van to the curb directly in front of her house. "By the way, I have a roommate. I found this cat shivering on my doorstep one day some months ago. I took him in, and he's my new best friend. I call him Hero. I think he saved my sanity the day he found me. Like I always say, everything happens for a reason."

The girls piled out of the van and shared in carrying Isabelle's luggage up the four steps that led to Maggie's front door.

"Just leave it all in the foyer until Isabelle decides what she wants to do. Ah, look, here's my little love," Maggie said, bending over to pick up the now-plump cat, who purred her happy song as she looked inquisitively at all the strange faces that were oohing and aahing over her.

"Coffee?" Nikki asked.

"Round table with coffee sounds like a plan," Kathryn said.

While Maggie washed her hands, Alexis made coffee, and Yoko put water on to boil for her special blend of tea, which Maggie kept stocked. Kathryn got out cups, while Nikki rummaged in the refrigerator for the cream. As always, when the girls were together, everything was a team effort.

Coffee cups in hand, they all looked at one another. "Talk to us, Isabelle," Kathryn said.

Isabelle did. For fifteen minutes. "End of story. The new age city is down the tubes. Someone else has taken it over. I'm home, I need a job, and if I'm lucky, I just might get my husband to forgive me. There's nothing more to tell. My dream of building a new age city is crumbling to ashes as we speak. I can't dwell on that now. That part of my life is over. Your turn. I want to hear everything, so start from the moment I left. By the way, has anyone heard anything from Charles, or is he still among the missing?"

"Nada on Charles," Yoko said. "I think we

should let Maggie tell you what's going on. It is Annie's mission. She's the one who got us motivated to take it on. So, Maggie, speak up."

Stroking the snoozing cat in her lap, Maggie ran through the past week's activities. If she left something out, one of the other girls filled in the blanks, and Maggie moved on. She finished up with, "Right now, we're waiting to hear from Avery Snowden on this Albright guy, and Abner . . . ah . . . Abner is trying to hack into the hospital where Gretchen Spyder was taken after her accident to see what he can garner. We've already learned who the doctor was and decided that it's a dead end. To save us another trip to Florida. I seriously doubt that any other doctors or nurses will give up anything, even with a subpoena. We kicked around the idea of having Jack Sparrow get us some federal subpoenas but are in a holding pattern right now in that regard."

"When is the trip to Spyder Island?" Isabelle asked. "What are you going to do with Greg Albright once he gets here?"

"Soon, I think. Myra and Annie think just us girls should go, and then a few days later we'll have the boys arrive. As to Greg Albright, my thoughts would be to take him with us to Spyder Island. You know that old saying 'Hide in plain sight.' Well, I think that will work for us where he is concerned. The planning is all still a work in progress," Nikki said.

Kathryn leaned into the table and said, "I have a thought. Shouldn't we know before we go in who owns all those resort homes on the island, and won't it be to our advantage to know how many of those homes are occupied or are just being used as vacation getaways?"

"Good point! And we have to make some decisions where Hank Jellicoe is concerned. Thinking and guessing he's there isn't good enough. We need proof that he's there," Yoko said.

"And you're right," Maggie said. "That's another job for Abner. I think we're snowing him under, but I also know he works best under pressure. Who wants to call him?"

All eyes turned to Isabelle, whose face drained of all color. She shook her head. "I'm not ready to. . . . I have to make my case in my own mind. Maggie, I think you're our best shot when it comes to Abner. By the way, how are you so free now, when you're the **Post**'s EIC?"

"I have a stand-in, a guy who would kill for my job. His name is Liam Eisling, and Annie okayed it. I'm back to being an investigative reporter. Okay, I'll call him. Oops, Avery is sending me a text." Maggie's eyes raked over the words. "Aha, our Mr. Greg Albright is good to go and will be on the first flight out of London the day after tomorrow. Sooner, if at all possible. Avery is sending me a picture of what he looks like now. Oh, and his new identity says his name is Stephen Wolansky. He is listed as a rookie agent of the FBI. Snowden said his creds are A1. That means even with close scrutiny someone won't pick up anything amiss, so I would imagine Jack Sparrow helped out there quite a bit. Okay, here comes the picture. Isabelle, what do you think, since you met him? Does he look anything like Greg Albright?"

"Good Lord, no! If I were face-to-face with him, I would swear that I had never seen him before. Greg Albright was . . . is a very good-looking young guy. Buff. Clothes fit him well. Really a nice guy. Sad, though. He truly loved Gretchen Spyder. Still does.

This guy, Stephen Wolansky, looks kind of nerdy and yet sharp somehow. They, whoever they are, did a remarkable job."

"Snowden is going to pick him up at the airport when he arrives and take him out to the farm," Maggie said as she read off a second text that came through.

"Well, then, that's one loose end tied up tight with a nice big bow," Nikki said happily. "What's next on our agenda?"

"I think we should all head out to the farm and let Isabelle give Myra and Annie a big surprise." Alexis giggled.

"Let's do it, then," Kathryn said as she got up stiffly and worked her leg until she felt comfortable enough to put her full weight on it. "It's such a beautiful day, so who in their right mind would want to stay inside?"

"Not me, that's for sure," Isabelle said. "I've dreamed about a day like this for weeks. I can't remember the last time I saw the sun."

"Okay, then, let me fill Hero's bowl and get him settled. Then we can head out. Isabelle, do you think you might want to spend a day or so at the farm? If so, take what you need from your luggage."

Ten minutes later, the **Post** van was on the road and headed toward Pinewood.

Jack Emery was working on his "honey-do list," which Nikki had left for him, when his cell phone rang. "Hey, Abner. How's it going?" He listened, then laughed as he laid his paintbrush across the can of paint and leaned back against the back-porch pillar. "You should be on top of the world with Isabelle back." The silence on the other end of the phone made Jack stand bolt upright. "Oh, crap. You didn't know? Is that what you're not saying? The girls went to the airport to pick her up. It's a long story. I don't know why I just assumed you knew. Actually, I thought that was why you were calling me.

"Well, as I understand it, Maggie called Isabelle in England and asked her to see if there was any way she could track down Gretchen Spyder's baby daddy, and it worked out that she knew a Realtor, one with whom she'd dealt during the construction of the new age city, and she enlisted his help. Not that many Americans buy cottages in the English countryside. Long story short, she not only found the guy, but Nikki just texted me that he's due to arrive here the day after tomorrow, and Snowden is picking him up at the airport and taking him to the farm. Snowden got him a new identity."

Jack listened, then said, "How the hell should I know? The guy's a spook. He's got all kinds of sources. Anyway, the guy will arrive here, and the way Nik tells me via a text is that the guy will go on the first plane to Spyder Island with the girls. Hiding in plain sight, so to speak."

Cyrus nudged Jack's leg and dropped the ball he had in his mouth in front of Jack. Jack dutifully picked it up and threw it, and Cyrus raced off. "So why did you call? What's up? Tell me you need me to come to wherever you are, because I don't want to paint this damn porch railing." Jack listened, waiting for the invitation to visit Abner's loft. "Okay, I'm on my way."

Jack slammed the lid on the paint can, stomped it down with his foot. He dropped the brush in a coffee can that held turpentine. He whistled for Cyrus, who stopped chasing the ball and came on the run. Man and dog barreled through the house as though they were being chased by a team of man-eating lions. While Jack washed his hands and changed into a pair of old, worn, clean jeans, Cyrus gathered up his toys to take with him.

"One toy, Cyrus! And you didn't make your bed. Nikki is going to have a fit when she sees how sloppy you're getting."

The big shepherd, his head down, headed for his plush bed. He tugged at the blanket until the bed was covered.

"I see some wrinkles there, buddy."

Cyrus yipped, which meant "Take it or leave it."

Jack laughed. "Okay, let's go. Hey, you really want to take that duck? Go with the elephant. If you forget it, I'm not going back for it, and I don't care how much you whine because you can't sleep without it. Make up your mind."

The shepherd did his dance around his bed before he dropped his beloved duck with half a beak and only one ear on his bed. He picked up a stuffed elephant by its trunk, his second favorite toy, and raced out of the room.

"Okay, let's go!"

In the car, Jack hit his speed dial to call Ted. "Where are you guys? I'm headed to

Abner's loft. Meet me there. I think he has something." He hit a second button, and Harry's surly voice came through as he announced his own name. "I know it's you, Harry, and you know it's me by the caller ID. I'm headed to Abner's loft. Can you meet me there? Ted, Espinosa, and Dennis are on the way. I think Abner has something. By the way, in case you don't know it, Isabelle is back, and she's with the girls, heading out to the farm."

He listened to Harry expound on business, the state of the economy, the weather, and the price of gasoline before he wound down, saying he would make it but would be a little late as he had twenty more minutes to run on his current class of ladies from the mayor's office, who loved to torture him. Jack was stunned at how fast Harry, always a man of few words, was talking. He grinned to himself at the vision of Harry with the mayor's office ladies who were trying to learn martial arts.

Forty-five minutes later, the guys were gathered around Abner's dining-room table. At the moment, instead of looking pleased with himself, Abner looked meaner than a junkyard dog, and he let it show. He looked at his friends and snarled, "Okay, let's hear it and get it out of the way. I hate advice, but I know we aren't going to get anywhere until you tell me what I should and shouldn't do in regard to the return of my wife. Spit it out, boys."

"I don't think I'm in any position to offer marital advice, but you need to think about the other ladies offering your wife advice. It's you against **them.** I don't think I would have the nerve or the guts to go up against those women. I've . . . uh . . . heard some pretty wild stories. So I'm going to pass on offering advice," Dennis said in a squeaky voice. He sat up straighter and squared his shoulders when he saw Harry glaring at him.

"The kid is right. You're doomed, Abner. It's all about Isabelle. Either you accept that she's back, kiss and make up, or you go ahead and file for divorce," Ted said. "Didn't you learn anything from me and Maggie and Joe here and Alexis?"

"Who said anything about a divorce?" Abner yelled.

"That's what happens when two people go their separate ways, even if it's just a relationship and not marriage. You cut your losses and move on," Espinosa said.

All eyes turned to Jack. Cyrus reared up and yipped, just to remind people he was in the room. "I know you all think I'm an authority on women—"

Ted interrupted Jack. "We think that only because you jammed that nugget of information down our throats. Either you are or you aren't. Which is it?"

Ted's voice was so testy, Jack frowned. "Well, Mr. Investigative Reporter, I see your knickers are in a knot, and would it be because Isabelle, Mrs. Isabelle Tookus, is going to be staying at Maggie's house, which means you won't be staying there? Ah, I see I hit it right."

Jack went on. "Okay, Abner, this is my advice. Take it or leave it. When we leave here, we'll be heading out to the farm, and Isabelle will be there, so gird yourself for a meeting. It will be whatever you make it. Invite her out to dinner, and talk like two civilized people who love each other. Forgiveness is a virtue, Abner. In other words, don't cut off your nose to spite your face and chalk it up to your making a statement."

"Yeah, don't do or say anything you'll regret," Dennis said. "You can't take back ugly words once they're said out loud. Women, I'm told, and I can't verify this, have memories like elephants and **never** forget." Dennis beamed when he saw Harry give him a nod of approval.

Abner looked around at his friends. "Duly noted. Now, do you all want to hear what I've found?"

"Well, yeah. Isn't that why we're here? Let's hear it, Mr. Computer Man," Jack said.

Chapter 9

Abner flexed his fingers, took a deep breath, and stared at his guests, who were looking at him in awe, absolutely convinced that he had something very big to report. Of course, the maniacal look in his eye totally confirmed what they were all thinking.

Abner pinwheeled his arms and smacked his hands together in glee. "This guy is so damn rich, I got dizzy just looking at the numbers. He's got some sharp people taking care of business, too. I can't wait to give it all away. The short version is this guy is a billionaire, like, a thousand times over. That might be a slight exaggeration, but he could whittle down our national debt in the blink of an eye. We might want to think about that when it comes time to settle up. Or maybe bail out Texas!"

"We knew Spyder was rich. Is that all you got?" Ted demanded.

"Patience, patience, my friend. As you can see by the way I look, I have been on the computer for over thirty-six hours, with no sleep and very little nourishment. When I saw what I saw, I just kept at it, and this is what I found. Gather close, boys."

"Jesus, Abner, will you just spit it out? We're flying blind here," Jack said.

Abner took one look at Harry's unhappy face and started talking. Being the subject of an attack by the world's leading martial arts master held no appeal to him.

"Okay, okay, I was able to find out the ownership of all the properties on Spyder Island. Except one. Annie was right when she said the richest people on earth own those properties. At first, I thought it was an empty house. But then I started checking the utility and tax bills. They're paid in cash. That means green money. There is no name on the utility or tax bills. Just the address. The bills are paid January second each year and are paid for a full year. For the last seven or eight years. What do you think of that?"

"And that means what?" Harry demanded, his tone surly.

"Think about it, Harry. How long ago did Hank Jellicoe slip out of the net? Same time frame, if I'm not mistaken. Jellicoe's company, Global something or other . . . The exact name eludes me at the moment, but he and his company did the security for Spyder Island. Back in the day, that is. Fast-forward or go backward to that time, and that's when the security changed to a company called Spyder Island Security. I don't think you need to be a rocket scientist to figure all that out. Right, guys?"

Jack stroked his chin, deep in thought. "Let's run this up the flagpole here. Do we handle this ourselves, or do we tell Jack Sparrow at the FBI? What a coup that would be for Sparrow if he could bring him in. What jurisdiction is Spyder Island in? Is it part of the United States or not? And if it isn't, does that mean the CIA would be the U.S. agency to involve if we don't take care of it ourselves?

"That would make me very unhappy,

since the spooks over there hate us. And they hate the FBI even more. Is that who we're going to have to go up against? If it's the FBI's jurisdiction, it would solidify Sparrow's position as the new director like nothing else. The CIA, as I said, is a whole other can of worms."

Abner shrugged his shoulders. "That, Jack, is not my field of expertise."

"The girls are not going to like that scenario no matter how you slice it. Jellicoe has always been a sore point with them. They had him fair and square, and Snowden dropped the ball. Snowden's pants will be on fire where Jellicoe is concerned, but he's smart enough not to make waves or challenge Annie, since she's the one who pays his bills. More or less. Less meaning we pay him out of the mission funds," Ted said.

"No, they're not going to like it one little bit," Jack said.

Cyrus reared up and let loose with a loud bark to second Jack's declaration.

"You got anything else?" Harry asked.

"I do. Spyder Island has its own airport. There are three Sikorsky helicopters and a Gulfstream and a Learjet parked at the hangar this very moment. From time to time, when one of the owners shows up, room is made available for his private plane. It appears to be unusual for all the houses, palaces, estates, or whatever you want to call them, to be inhabited. I'm going by the utility bills. Especially the electricity and the usage. What it looks like to me is that only two of the houses are used on a full-time basis. Spyder's and the supposedly empty one. I take that to mean that the old saying 'The man is an island unto himself' is probably true.

"That's pretty much it, other than I hacked into the records of that Florida hospital and didn't find out much. I copied Gretchen Spyder's medical records. Medical legalese. All bills were paid in cash. She was airlifted via a medical transport plane against the doctor's wishes. Someone signed off on the airlift, but the signature is not legible. There was a handwritten note in the margin, by the doctor, which said that Gretchen did not want to leave and had to be heavily medicated. And underneath that little blurb, two nurses added their names. I think it's called CYA."

"Meaning 'covering their asses,'" Dennis chirped.

"Correct." Abner grinned.

"Well, then, if there's nothing else, let's head out to the farm. You printed all this out, right, Abner?" Jack asked.

"It's all there in the box. Take it with you. I need to take a shower and get a few hours' sleep. I'll meet you all out there later, if that's okay," Abner said anxiously.

"That'll work," Harry said, picking up the box and settling it on his shoulders. "You guys go in the van. I'll leave the box for you to load into it. I'll follow on my Ducati. I need to stop by the dojo first."

Jack and Cyrus were the last to leave. Jack turned to Abner and said, "You did good, Abner. Thanks. Uh . . . hey, listen, I know you're shook up about Isabelle. Don't be. I know this is going to sound strange coming from me, but follow your heart. If it feels right, go for it. If not, no harm, no foul. See ya!"

Cyrus let loose with a series of short barks, then ran over to Abner and put his paws on his shoulders to show his approval.

Abner burst out laughing. "This dog is something else, Jack."

"Yeah, and he can make his bed, fold the towels, and answer the phone, too. Well, what he does is knock the receiver off the cradle and bark. See ya."

Abner was still laughing when he headed for the shower. **Go with your heart. Sounds good,** he said to himself. **Sounds really good.**

There were cookies, all manner of snacks, and ice-cold tea and lemonade on the deck when the boys arrived. As always, there was the backslapping, the hugs, and the smiles. And, of course, laughter. Isabelle tried not to look past the sea of human flesh to see if her husband was with the group. Her shoulders sagged, until Espinosa whispered in her ear that Abner had been working 24/7 for the past two days and would be out later, after he got a few hours' sleep and cleaned up. Isabelle smiled up into Espinosa's eyes and patted his back. Nothing more needed to be said.

The group, the gals versus the guys, shared their information.

"So now what?" Jack asked.

All eyes turned to Annie. "Like I'm the sole authority here?" she snapped. "Let's hear some ideas. I'll start it off. I think we girls should head out first and take

Mr. Albright, or Mr. Wolansky, as he is now known, with us the day after tomorrow. Two days later, you boys will follow. We'll go in my Gulfstream, and Dennis can have you all ferried in on the Welmed Gulfstream that came with his inheritance. That's for starters.

"There is no housekeeping staff at the island house, so we'll all have to do the work ourselves. It's been closed up for over twenty years, but it has been maintained by my business manager. He told me earlier that the pool is being drained, cleaned, and refilled. Actually, he's there now with his people, seeing to everything. When I say 'His people,' I think those people actually work for Avery Snowden. Once they leave, which is tomorrow, we are on our own. They will make just enough of a fuss so that we're taken seriously when we arrive."

"We have to finish your interviews, Annie. With a picture of you in your tiara." Ted grinned. "Dennis is going to write the article today, and it will run in the morning edition. The AP will pick it up, and Mr. Angus Spyder will see it no matter what paper he reads online. And, hopefully, Mr. Henry 'Call Me Hank' Jellicoe will also see it."

"That all worries me," Nikki said as she nibbled on a nail.

"We're tipping our hand," Kathryn grumbled as she massaged the calf of her leg.

"It's the only way," Myra said. "Hank Jellicoe fell into our laps. We can't change our plans at this stage. Let's all think of him as a bonus. Short of driving around the island with a bullhorn, announcing our arrival, this works best. Will the man dive for cover? I think not. He'll try to take us down. The vigilantes have been a sore point with him from the day we caught him. He wants us as bad as we want him. Don't forget that superior male force he's got by working for Spyder. All those mercenaries. I think it's safe to say there is a price on our heads even now, and we haven't even gotten there yet."

Dennis's eyes popped wide. "You mean like a bounty on our heads? Do we need guns or something? A rocket launcher? How are we going to go up against an army of mercenaries?"

Harry fixed his gaze on Dennis and cleared his throat.

Dennis eyeballed him for a nanosecond as he recalled the brutal punishment his body had endured under Harry's tutelage to earn his colored belt. "We're up to it because each of us is our own army, right, Harry?"

Harry smiled the special evil smile that drove fear into the hearts of those seeing it.

"Who needs an army when you have a Harry Wong on your side?" Jack said.

The others all agreed. Harry bowed low at the praise. Yoko clapped the loudest and winked at her husband. Everyone in the room was well aware that Yoko could wipe up the floor with Harry. And Harry was no exception.

Dennis leaned back and closed his eyes as he tried to plot out a scenario where he was his own army and was going after all the Spyder Island badasses and **winning.**

"I think we should adjourn to the war room, where we can view maps of the island and all this paperwork you brought with you. By the time we get off the plane, I want all of us to know the island like the backs of our hands. Know it well enough that we won't get lost in the dark or, worse yet, blindsided. Do you all understand what I'm saying?" Annie said.

The others nodded their understanding.

Nikki led the way to the living room and the bookcase that would, with the press of a button, lead them to the catacombs beneath the old farmhouse.

"Abner isn't here yet," Dennis said.

"No, but Cyrus is. He knows how to push the right button. So does Lady. Not to worry. Abner will find us," Jack said.

Jack rummaged in Myra's tiny kitchen office for the papers she'd sent him upstairs to fetch. He looked up when he saw the dogs streak past him to the door. Ah, Abner had arrived. He unlocked the door, slid the security bolt, and opened the door wide. He waited while Abner tussled with all the dogs for a few minutes before he commented on his friend's appearance.

"You didn't sleep, did you? You spent your time picking just the right outfit to impress Isabelle and standing in front of a mirror, rehearsing what you plan to say when you're eyeball to eyeball. Right?"

Abner shifted from one foot to the other. "Damn, Ted was right. You do know everything, don't you? What did I do to give it away?"

"You look like shit, that's why. Any other

time, you would have arrived here in your worn-out jeans with the holes in the knees, that ratty Duke University T-shirt, and boat shoes. Look at you. Pressed khakis, white button-down shirt, sleeves rolled just so, fresh from the dry cleaners, no less, and your Brooks Brothers loafers. How'm I doing so far, Abner? Oh, and you smell good, too."

"Eat shit, Jack. So what?" Abner said, going into a defensive mode.

"That's Harry's line, Abner. He says that to me all the time. Listen to me. This is what you're going to do when we get back downstairs. You are going to walk right by Isabelle, and I'll tell you where she's seated so you can get a good frontal view. You strut in there like you're king of the road and say to her, 'Lookin' good, Izz,' and keep right on going to take Charles's place on the dais. I gotta tell you, she does look good, thinner and a little tired looking, but still good.

"Now, that's my advice. You gotta know the girls are giving Isabelle advice, too, so bear that in mind. If she winks at you, just grin. If she smiles, nod. Don't give an inch until you feel comfortable with the situation. I know you want to grab her and kiss her till her teeth rattle or chew her clothes off, but you **cannot** do that. You didn't do anything wrong. Isabelle abandoned you in favor of her career. You are not chopped liver, Abner. You getting all this now, or are you going to screw it up?"

Cyrus nipped at Abner's leg, a warning that he had better not screw it up. Lady dribbled on the Brooks Brothers loafers to show she was also in agreement.

"**I am not going to screw it up, Jack.** If I do, you can shoot me."

Jack snorted. "Don't think I won't. Okay, take deep breaths and let's move. Remember, you're king of the road. You and you alone. No one else. Focus. Keep taking deep breaths."

"**I got it, Jack!**" Abner said through clenched teeth. He knew he was lying, and he knew that Jack knew he was lying. **Shit!**

Five minutes later, Jack yelled, "Coming through. And Abner is here!" He saw it all in a nanosecond: Isabelle sat up straighter, and the girls all focused on her as Alexis nudged her slightly, probably as a reminder to do whatever they had told her to do. If he saw it all, then dumb-ass Abner should have seen it, too.

Jack sucked in a deep breath just as Abner said, "Lookin' good, Izz," as his long legs carried him across the room and up the two steps to the dais like he belonged. Jack wanted to hug him. Especially when he saw the stunned looks of surprise on all the women's faces. Evidently, Abner saw the same looks, because he was grinning from ear to ear.

"Score one for the Gipper," Jack muttered under his breath. He turned to see his wife glaring at him. Ooh, this wasn't over. Somehow, someway, those women were going to make him pay for this one up for the man that he'd just pulled off.

Sensing the tension in the room, Myra took control of the meeting, which hadn't really been a meeting thus far, but a gabfest. "Time to get back to work here, boys and girls. Let's review your assignments and get this show on the road. When we step onto that plane for Spyder Island, I want us all on the same page. Who wants to go first?"

Dennis raised his hand. "I should. I think. If Annie's last interview will be the lead story in tomorrow's paper, then we need to get it started right now. Espinosa is going to be

taking pictures." He looked at Annie and demanded, "Where's your tiara?"

"At home, in my jewelry box. I suppose
you're going to tell me we need to go there
so I can gussy up."

Dennis nodded as Espinosa gathered up
his gear.

"Okay, that's working for everyone. Next!"
Myra said.

Alexis raised her hand. "I'm trying to get
my red bag of tricks filled. Charles . . .
um . . . used to do that. It's going to take me
the rest of the day to get up to snuff. There's
no way I'm going to Spyder Island without
my bag." To make her point, she whipped
out a list that was as long as her arm. "I
don't even know if I'm going to be able to
get everything I need by overnight delivery.
And before any of you ask, no, you can't
help me. This is something I have to do myself."

"Duly noted, dear," Myra said generously
as she recalled how many times Alexis had
saved the day with her red bag of tricks.

Nikki raised her hand. "I'm on Jellicoe.
Jack is with me on this. I have a few ave-
nues I want to explore, and Jack can help
because he was there at the end."

Maggie went next. "I, along with Ted, am on Gretchen Spyder. Something has been nagging at me, but I can't put my finger on it. We're going to try to get a fix on her from the day she dropped out of the womb. There has to be someone, somewhere, who can help us out here. When it comes right down to it, we really don't know anything about her except for her college years."

"All right, dear. That works. Kathryn?"

"I'm on the wife and mother with Yoko. She wasn't hatched from an egg. Somewhere there is a record of where she came from. We need Abner to point us in the right direction."

Myra nodded.

All eyes turned to Isabelle. In a firm but steady voice, Isabelle said loud enough for Abner to hear, "I thought maybe I could help Abner, if he wants some extra help."

"Sure," Abner bellowed from the dais, where he was busy clicking away at one of the computers.

"And they lived happily ever after," Jack muttered under his breath.

"Guess I'm odd man out," Harry said.

"Oh, no, dear. I am assigning you to Avery Snowden. If he gives you any trouble, you have my permission to . . . um . . . take him out," Myra said.

Harry grinned his special evil grin. He loved to torment Avery Snowden, and here he was, actually being given permission to take his sorry ass out. He could do that blindfolded with his hands tied behind his back. Oh, life was looking better and better.

"What are you going to do, Myra?" Nikki asked.

"I am going to get in touch with Mr. Sparrow. Then I am going to call Mr. Snowden to arrange a phone call with the Domingos. My intuition is telling me that the wife knows something about Gretchen Spyder. I'm not saying she deliberately withheld anything, but I think she might know something and not even realize she knows it, because she didn't think it was important at the time. One woman to another, one mother to another mother, might bring us some bit of news. It's just a thought but worth playing out at the moment.

"Do any of you have any questions? No. All right, then, let's get to work. We have less than forty-eight hours till we leave for Spyder Island. And don't forget, Stephen Wolansky, the baby daddy, will be arriving shortly. Let's get to it, boys and girls."

Chapter 10

The young woman in the wheelchair turned her head when she heard her name being called. She knew she should smile or at least make the effort to smile, but that was precisely the problem. It took effort—a great deal of effort. Why couldn't everyone just leave her alone? She'd come out here to the garden to be by herself so she could read the book in her lap. She'd been reading the same book for over a year now, and if pressed, she couldn't give the name of the book or the author's name if her life depended on it. Once upon a time she had loved to read, had always had her nose in a book. Because . . . by reading she could escape into a make-believe world. Anything, anything at all, was better than the real world in which she lived, then as well as now.

"Good morning, Mother," Gretchen Spyder mumbled. "Do you want something?" How cold that sounded. Like she cared.

"Yes, I do want something, Gretchen. I want my daughter."

"You sure have a funny way of showing up and asking for strange things. Unless you are blind, I am right in front of your eyes. Did **he** send you out here? Of course he did. Such a stupid question. You never have a thought, an action of your own, just **his.** You're like a puppet on a string that he jerks when it suits **him.** I wish you'd stop pretending, Mother. I wouldn't put it past you to be wired for sound. Or maybe the bushes and flowers are wired so **he** can hear our conversation. Meaning, of course, that you are merely doing what **he** told you to do. After all, you never do anything else."

Felicia Spyder's eyes narrowed slightly as she stared at her beautiful daughter. "You're talking nonsense, Gretchen. Your father didn't send me out here to talk to you. I came out here because I thought we should talk."

"Nonsense? Don't you mean bullshit, Mother? Stop referring to your husband as my father. He's a sperm donor. He's never been a father to me, just like you've never been a mother to me. Ooh, did that little barb hit home, Mommie Dearest?"

"I hate it when you talk like that, Gretchen. There's no need to be vulgar. You were raised better than that."

"Cut the crap, Mother. I'm not buying into that garbage any more now than I did when I was growing up in this hellacious place. You want to talk! Okay, let's talk. Get me the hell off this frigging island and back to Miami, where I can get that operation that will allow me to walk again. Can you do that for me, for your daughter, who you profess to love and adore? Or won't you do it, because you fear that monster you married the way I fear him? Which is it, Mother?"

"Gretchen . . ."

"Don't you 'Gretchen' me, you worthless piece of crud. And I sure as hell don't want to hear the story again about how that monster pulled you out of the gutter when you were just a wee lass of thirteen and saved your life back in Russia. I'd rather hear about Goldilocks and the Three Bears, or Rumpelstiltskin, if you are going to tell fairy tales. Why won't you admit you're nothing but his slave, his whore? Surely you know about all those women who come here in the middle of the night to service him. He's a pig. He's the ugliest man in the world on the outside, and even uglier on the inside. All the money in the world can't change that. He's still a pig."

Gretchen laughed then, an unholy sound that reverberated around the garden, when she saw her mother look around fearfully to see if anyone had heard her outburst.

In the blink of an eye, Gretchen pressed the controls on her wheelchair and swung it around till she was facing her mother. As always, she was stunned at her mother's beauty, at her fashion sense, at how impeccably made up she always was. And she smelled like the very garden she was sitting in.

"Tell you what, Mommie Dearest. Go to that pig and ask him if you and I can go on a mother-daughter trip. Pick a place. Or let the pig pick a place. What do you think the son of a bitch will say?"

"Gretchen . . ."

"Go back to the house, Mother. Isn't it time for you to change your clothes? You do that three times a day because that's one of his rules. Just like he tells you what to eat and when to eat it. All those designer clothes, all those jewels wasted on the servants and **him.** Oh, and **his** goon squad. I've seen them ogling you. **He** gets a perverse sense of pleasure out of that. Then again, maybe you like it. Someone appreciating your fashion sense, your beauty."

Felicia got up from the spindly little outdoor chair she had been sitting on. She looked down at the wrinkles in her linen dress. That would never do. Gretchen was right; she needed to change her clothes before Angus saw the wrinkles.

There were tears in her eyes when she bent over to peck her daughter on the cheek. She whispered in her ear. "If there were a way to get us both off this island, I would snatch it. It's all I think about, dream about. I'm not giving up, and I don't want you to give up, either. I think I might have a plan. When you feel like it, go online and read about the person who is coming to the island any day now. Let your imagination run wild."

Gretchen soaked up the words like a sponge. It was a game the two of them played, each playing her part to the hilt, with the exception of the whispered words at the end of each meeting.

Gretchen continued in her playacting role. She pressed the controls on the wheelchair and spun around so fast, she almost knocked her mother over. She laughed. "Sorry, Mummy. I don't need to hear you tell me how much you love me, and I sure as hell don't need you to tell me to honor and respect that pig who sired me. Go on. Run back and change your clothes and report in to that sperm-donor pig. Now that you've managed to ruin what looked to be a promising day, I think I'll go play on the computer to while away my hours until it's time for my leg therapy."

Felicia Spyder dabbed at her eyes with a lace-edged hankie that probably cost more than the cook's weekly salary. She ran as fast as her Louboutins could carry her back to the mansion where she lived. She immediately corrected the thought. Where she **existed**.

She hadn't lied to her daughter. She did have a plan. It wasn't exactly a plan, but something close to a plan. If she could just make it work, all her prayers for herself and her daughter would be answered.

A man literally stepped out of the bushes, startling Felicia. "Are you all right, ma'am? Is something wrong?"

Felicia looked up at the man whom she thought of as the warden of Spyder Island. She supposed he was an attractive man and would appeal to certain women, with his hard-muscled body, his high and tight snow-white hair, and his bronzed skin. He carried a gun in a shoulder holster and made no effort to hide it. She knew for a fact he also wore a gun strapped to his ankle. All the guards carried guns and rifles. He gave her the creeps the way he watched her. He was her husband's number one man. If she so much as burped, the man would inform her husband. She didn't know whom she hated more, the man standing next to her or her husband. She knew she had to keep playing the game, because this man had eyes that saw everything.

"I'm fine. Thank you, Mr. Jellicoe. No matter how many times I see my daughter in that wheelchair, it still upsets me. Now, if you'll excuse me."

Hank Jellicoe stepped aside, his demeanor respectful. His eyes told a different story. "I understand that, ma'am."

Almost immediately, the watch on his wrist buzzed. He was being summoned by the man himself. Jellicoe clenched his teeth as he walked down the path that would take him to the annex at the rear of the vast property, where Angus Spyder had a suite of offices. He hated Angus Spyder, but he was indebted to him, and if nothing else, he did have his own code of ethics and was loyal. To a point. And Spyder paid him so well, he was a millionaire a hundred times over.

Trouble was brewing. He could sense it, smell it. The big question now was, was Angus Spyder picking up on his apprehension?

Hank Jellicoe took a deep breath, held it, then let it out with a loud **swoosh** of sound.

He knocked on the stout mahogany door, which even a rocket launcher couldn't penetrate, and waited. He'd learned early on never to take liberties where his employer was concerned. You knocked. If there was no answer, you walked away. Under no circumstances did you **ever** open a door unless you were invited to open it.

As always when he was in the man's presence, he felt intimidated. The only man in the entire universe who could actually intimidate him, and the man knew it and played on it. One of the wealthiest men in the world and also the ugliest. He was a short man and was shaped like a barrel. God had not been kind when he fashioned his face. It was flat like a shovel. His hair was thick like a bush, kinky yet greasy at the same time. His colorless eyes were deeply set over a forehead that looked like a shelf. His nose was red-veined and bulbous, and his lips were large and blubbery. His teeth were pointy like a dog's. One ear was oversize; the other undersized. A scary-looking individual, to Jellicoe's way of thinking. No way could he comprehend the fact that Felicia had married him, then produced beautiful Gretchen. Both were trophies to Angus Spyder, and he loved nothing more than to show them off.

Spyder favored colorful island wear, Bermuda shorts and flowered button-down shirts. Jellicoe knew for a fact that the man had a closetful of one-of-a-kind Armani and Hugo Boss suits, which he hauled out for special occasions.

"What do you have for me, Hank?"

"Nothing, sir. They were the way they always are. Your wife trying to be nice and your daughter rejecting her pleasantries. All they did was snap and snarl at one another. They acted the same way yesterday and the day before yesterday. Nothing has changed in their relationship."

Spyder nodded, his beady little eyes taking the measure of the man standing in front of him. Whatever he saw satisfied him. He moved on. "Did you read the papers online this morning?"

"I did, sir, and I guess it wasn't a rumor, after all. Countess de Silva will be arriving any day now. With her entourage."

"Were you able to place the listening devices in her home?"

"Of course. In every room and the

garages, too. Also the pool house. Nothing has been overlooked."

"All right then," Spyder said, waving his short, stubby arm, which meant Jellicoe was dismissed. "Oh, one more thing, Mr. Jellicoe. My patience is wearing thin in regards to my grandchildren. You promised results. To date, there have been none. People simply do not disappear into thin air, especially people like the Domingos, dragging along two children. When can I expect some results?"

"Mr. Spyder, we have our best people on it. The family has gone to ground. It is that simple. What that means is they had to have had help from somewhere. The only thing that comes to mind is that a government agency has them under protection. How that happened, if it happened, I can't explain. We are working night and day on it. Sooner or later, we'll catch a break. We always do. Mistakes happen even with the best-laid plans."

"That isn't good enough, Mr. Jellicoe. I want those children. They belong to me. They carry my bloodline. Do I make myself clear?"

"As crystal, Mr. Spyder." The head of

security turned on his heel with an off-hand wave of his own and left the office. Outside, out of view of the man himself, Jellicoe's shoulders sagged. Christ, how he hated the man behind the door. If there was a way to gut the man from his throat to his groin, he'd do it in a heartbeat.

As always, when he left the man's presence, he had these thoughts, and the memories came rushing back. When he'd gotten away from the vigilantes, he'd headed straight here, believing that Angus Spyder would keep him safe. And he had. But he'd had to give up something for the promise of safety. The something that earned Spyder billions of dollars. And he'd just handed it over like it was nothing. But Spyder had hired him to keep the island secure, and he had upheld his end of the bargain. And because of that crazy-ass inbred loyalty, he'd accepted the man's offer. The way he looked at it at the time, his life was worth more to him than what he had been forced to give up. Loyalty to an insane man. How crazy was that? "Pretty damn crazy," he muttered to himself as he squared his shoulders and marched off.

Jellicoe made his rounds, spoke with

several of his top people. Satisfied that all
was well, he headed home to make himself some lunch. He needed to think and
think hard. Trouble was brewing. He'd honed
his gut instincts till they were razor-sharp,
and his gut was screaming loudly to tread
softly but carry a big stick.

Inside the mansion where he lived, Jellicoe headed straight to what he called his
monitoring room. He checked to see what
Gretchen was doing. As always, playing on
the computer. The mother was changing
her earrings and spraying herself with per-
fume. A daily ritual that her husband demanded. All these years of doing the same
thing over and over again had made her
movements robotic. He wished he knew the
real story behind the married couple. And
there was a story. Sooner or later . . .

Jellicoe headed for the kitchen, where he
made himself a ham sandwich on rye bread,
which he washed down with two ice-cold
bottles of beer. One of his rules, a rule that
he broke every single day, was no drinking
on duty. Well, for Christ's sake, he was on
duty twenty-four hours a day, so the rule
simply did not apply to him.

The laptop computer on the kitchen

table beckoned to him. None of Spyder's lapdogs could even come close to figuring out how this particular computer worked, nor would they ever figure it out. On the surface it looked just like any other laptop. But there were layers upon layers of fire-walls, installed by some of the most brilliant minds in the world. It held his life, the key to his life, the key to his future. Right out in plain sight on his kitchen table, which was cluttered with reports, food wrappers, crumbs, and an ashtray full of cigarette butts. He let loose with a bitter laugh. His future. What a laugh that was. Unless . . .

Jellicoe's cell phone buzzed. He clicked it on, listened, then frowned. What the hell difference did it make if Gretchen Spyder was reading about Countess Anna de Silva's visit to the island or not? Obviously, his overexuberant operative thought it was worth mentioning. Because all snitches were rewarded with bonuses at the end of the month. Rule number one with Angus Spyder. "What is she looking at now?" he asked with a bite to his tone.

"She's checking a sale at Nordstrom on shoes that are called Crocs."

"And you think this is noteworthy, Minnelli?"

"The man himself said he wants everything. No matter how silly or inane. You backed it up, boss. She's moved on now to some waitress who was given a hundred-dollar tip by some patron who liked the way she served his table."

"Say good night, Gracie," Jellicoe said, clicking off his cell phone. Why couldn't that ugly bastard just lie down and die? **Only the good die young.** Now where had he heard that old tried-and-true saying? He rather thought there was a song by that title. He slammed his fist down on the table with such force, the ashtray, filled to the brim, dumped its contents out over the table. Another mess to clean up.

Jellicoe reached for his baseball cap, which said SPYDER ISLAND SECURITY on the brim, and mashed it down over his head. He reached for his specially tinted sunglasses, fixed them in place, and left his spartan house. A ten-thousand-square-foot house that had one bed, one foot-locker, one easy chair, one seventy-two-inch television, plus a kitchen table with four chairs. Plus all the monitoring equipment that was a requirement of the job. But that was just the first floor. He hated the place, called it a rat hole in his mind. Hated it almost as much as he hated Angus Spyder.

Outside, in the hot, humid air, Jellicoe let his thoughts go once again to the imminent arrival of Countess Anna de Silva. Then he threw his head back and laughed until he was breathless when he remembered how Angus Spyder had hit the ceiling the morning he'd read in the **Post** that de Silva had more money than he did. He'd screamed at the top of his lungs for his lackeys to explain how that was possible. Shivering and quaking, almost in tears, the team of grown men hired to account for his fortune had suffered through the tirade with the only answer they could give, which was that it was true and that numbers didn't lie. Thirteen minutes later, the nine-man forensic team was being ferried off the island. The following day, a new set of number crunchers arrived. Angus Spyder had not been the same ever since.

He now knew without a shadow of a doubt that the only way to get to Angus Spyder was money. Now, if he could make a plan that worked, he'd be home free, and

Spyder's ugly, evil body would be at the deep end of the ocean. And the Domingo family would remain safe and sound.

Hank Jellicoe now had a new mission in his life.

Chapter 11

Greg Albright, aka Stephen Wolansky, looked around Myra's kitchen at the gaggle of people staring at him. Who were these people? Was he supposed to say something? What? He squared his shoulders, took a deep breath, and plunged right in. "I think you people just kidnapped me. I know what that lady . . . What's her name? Oh, yeah, Isabelle something or other . . . I know what she said to me back in England, but I'm not buying into that crap. Kidnapping is kidnapping, and we're on American soil now. Look at me!" he barked. "I'm not even Greg Albright anymore. I'm some dude named Stephen Wolansky, and I have a badge that says I'm an FBI agent. Okay, folks, you're all under arrest, and I'm outta here!" he said dramatically as he crouched into a shooter's stance, pretending he had a gun.

When no one moved or said anything. Albright sat down hard on one of the kitchen chairs. But he wasn't finished quite yet. He reared back up and barked a second time. "Oh, yeah, now another thing you're telling me is I'm going on yet another vacation, to some goddamn island I never even heard of, where the very rich and famous frolic, and where I might, that's as in might, get to see the woman I love. But that's only if her crazy-ass father doesn't find me first and kill me if I don't sign my kids over to him, kids I didn't even know I had until a few days ago. How am I doing so far, folks?"

"That's pretty accurate up to a point," Annie said. "Knowledge is a powerful thing, Mr. Wolansky. But knowledge that you do not need can also get you into a peck of trouble. It can even get you killed. How'm I doing so far?"

"Why do I feel like I just fell through the rabbit hole?"

"In a manner of speaking, you just did, dear," Myra said. "I know we came at you out of the blue, but someday we're all hoping you will thank us for saving . . ."

"Your sorry ass," said Kathryn, always the most outspoken of the group, finishing what Myra was in the middle of saying.

"You're the **only ones** who are saying my sorry ass needs to be saved. I want to see some **proof.** Another thing, I could go to jail for impersonating an FBI agent. Did any of you think of **that?** Oh, I get it. It's my sorry ass, so it isn't your problem."

Nikki stood up, then leaned over the table to stare at Albright. "I would think you would be a little more grateful to us. You have no idea what could have happened to you without our intervention. You want proof? Okay, here's your proof." She nodded to Myra to produce the proof Albright had requested.

Myra walked over to the little kitchen cubby where she kept her laptop computer, and reached up to the shelf above to remove a cardboard box loaded with all the information they'd gathered to date on Gretchen Spyder, the Domingos, the twins, the lawsuit, and Angus Spyder himself. She plopped it down in front of Albright. "Take your time. The rest of us will be in the dining room, having lunch. Feel free to join us when and if you feel like it."

"He's a wild card," Ted said, after they were all seated around the dining room table.

Always a defender of the underdog, Dennis reached for a ham on rye. "Try putting yourself in his place, Ted. First off the bat, he didn't even know he was a father, much less a father of a set of twins who were given up for adoption without his even knowing about it. So he's in love with a woman who did him dirty. He's still loyal to that love, so how can you blame him for that? In the end, I believe that Gretchen Spyder was trying to protect him and the twins from her evil father. I do believe she would have found a way somehow to join him at some point. Unfortunately, fate intervened, just the way it did with Marie and Sally when they left me their Welmed fortune. If nothing else, I am a believer in faith. You should try it sometime.

"Not only that, the guy is just a regular guy. He's not into all this spook stuff. I bet the closest he's ever been to a cop is for maybe a speeding ticket, and I even doubt that. He strikes me as the kind of guy who obeys the rules and got caught up in something beyond his control. So, let's all ease up on him, okay?"

Dennis looked around when he felt a soft touch on his shoulder. "Well said, kid," Harry murmured loud enough for everyone to hear.

"Let's move on here," Maggie said just as she bit into a pastrami sandwich loaded with so much spicy brown mustard, it oozed out of the sandwich. "Ted and I attacked the infrastructure, what we could find of it for Angus Spyder. The guy wasn't hatched from an egg. Nor was he flown here on a UFO."

While Maggie chewed her way through her sandwich, Ted picked up where she left off. "With Abner's help, we hit cyberland running. Using the word **spy,** we ran through millions of possibilities. But, with Abner's skill, we managed to center on Russia, and that's where we think Angus Spyder was hatched. We found a family named Spyovich that had a boy child named Feodor, who would be around Angus Spyder's age. At some point, Feodor lit out on his own, but we found some pictures a relative posted on Russia's version of Facebook, and I can believe that that guy is as physically ugly as everyone says he is, since the picture we found of him as a kid is even uglier. Obviously, he changed his name along the way. We are still tracking him. We found nothing on the wife, but Russian women are not named Felicia. Nor are Russian men named Angus. Those are Anglo names."

"That's good work," Jack said.

"And we have the sleepless hours to prove it," Maggie snapped. "One thing is for certain. The guy knows how to make a buck and how to hang on to it."

"There is also that little business Jellicoe bragged to Charles about starting up," Ted said. "We have to factor that into this whole mess. Then, when Snowden got lax, Jellicoe just flew the coop and went on the run. We all know about Spyder's Internet launch called Spy Trap. It's the world's largest Internet security firm. I can't prove this, but a thug like Spyder strong-arms his way in the world. He's his own Russian mob. There is no way that Angus Spyder, or Feodor Spyovich, could come up with something as sophisticated as Spy Trap.

"Someone like Jellicoe would have to have been the brains behind that outfit. My personal opinion is that when Jellicoe took off, he went straight to Spyder Island and offered up Spy Trap to Angus Spyder for safety reasons. It was a trade-off, his life for the Internet security firm. Which, by the way, is worth billions upon billions. It's the only thing that makes sense, if we all truly believe Jellicoe is living on Spyder Island."

"I'd stake my life on the premise that that's where Jellicoe is," Nikki announced, venom ringing in her voice.

The others seconded her declaration.

Greg Albright appeared in the doorway, a newspaper clipping in his hand. His eyes were moist; his voice shaky. "These are my children?"

"Yes, they are, Mr. Wolansky," Myra said gently. "Please sit down. Join us for lunch."

His eyes on the clipping, Albright managed to croak out the words, "I'm not hungry. Just like that, she gave them away, my flesh and blood. Her flesh and blood, and she just handed them over to . . . to strangers?"

In a voice as gentle as Myra's, Jack said, "Yes, it would seem so. At first. But the more we learn, the more convinced we are that she did it to protect the children, you, and herself. This is all still a work in progress. Even though you don't believe us right now, we are trying to help you."

Albright looked around at the group seated at the huge dining-room table. "If Gretchen's father is as evil and ruthless as you say he is, what do you"—he waved his arm about to indicate the lot of them—"think you can do? Look at you! A bunch of women, a couple of guys with good intentions. You plan on taking him out? Is that what you're saying? If that's your intention, I applaud your guts."

The women as one stood up and glared at Albright.

"Did you just say, 'A bunch of women'?" Nikki said in a voice that would have frozen milk.

"Yeah, and a couple of guys who want to play cowboys and Indians. None of you are instilling any confidence in me. Plus, I don't want to die. I'm too young to die."

Abner, silent until then, rose very slowly from his seat at the table and said, "Do you know who these women are, Mr. Wolansky? They are not just a **bunch of women.**

They're the **bunch of women** who virtually everyone in this country knew as the vigilantes. We, the guys with good intentions who want to play cowboys and Indians, are their backup." Abner eyeballed the man in front of him and waited for the dawn to break in his eyes. When it did, he almost laughed out loud.

"Holy shit! Gretchen and I used to talk about . . . you . . . I guess. She donated a huge sum of money for something or other that would help you all. I even remember her saying she wished she could hire you. Holy shit! Okayyy, I'm good with all this now. Why didn't you say so in the beginning?"

"You see, here's the thing," Yoko said sweetly. "We don't like to brag." Albright gulped as she flopped down on a chair and reached for a sandwich. "I doubt you have any input, but if you do, we'd like to hear it. Give us the skinny on Gretchen, anything you remember, no matter if it's important or not. We need every scrap of information locked inside your head."

"Well, lady, here's the thing," Albright said, mimicking Yoko. "Gretchen did not talk about her family, other than to say how rich her father was. And she said that only because of her bodyguards and how she had to pay them to look the other way so we could see each other. There was only one time when I really pressed her to talk about her life growing up, her family, and what the future held for us. She got this far-away look in her eye, and she said that if I was going to persist in asking questions, then we would have to break it off. I didn't want that, because I loved her, and I never asked anything again.

"Gretchen wanted so badly to fit in with people, but she knew she didn't. This might sound corny, but she always looked fear-ful to me. The only time she was ever . . . a free spirit, for want of a better term, was when she was dancing. She was a really good dancer."

"Didn't she ever talk about her mother, the lack of siblings?" Kathryn asked.

"She said her mother was beautiful, like a model. Said she went to Europe, to all the fashion shows, and then she laughed, tell-ing me how her mother changed her clothes three times a day, complete with different jewelry, because she had so much. She also said no one ever saw her in all her designer duds except her father, Gretchen herself, and the servants."

"Did you get the feeling there was any kind of closeness, family solidarity, that kind of thing?" Kathryn asked.

Albright rubbed at his temples as he struggled with his memories. Finally, he shook his head. "There was no love in that family, but I think, and this is just my own opinion, there was a lot of fear for both her mother and Gretchen herself."

"And yet Gretchen was allowed to leave the island and attend college in Florida. That does not make sense," Annie said.

"Yes, it does make sense. Gretchen had bodyguards around the clock, two shifts, two men each. Big guys, and they packed heat. They carried their guns in the back of their pants. I saw it myself. When I pointed it out to Gretchen, she said it was her father's paranoia because he was so rich. He thought she might be kidnapped. Now, that's a hoot, isn't it? I'm the one who got kidnapped," Albright said, bitterness ringing in his voice.

"Even with all that, you two managed to carry on an affair right under their noses," Isabelle said skeptically.

"Because Gretchen cut a deal with one of the guards. She paid him a lot of money to look the other way. I don't know about his partner. My guess would be he shared a part of his bribe with him. I do not know that for a fact. What I do know for a fact is I got to see Gretchen only when that one guy was on duty. Between times, we would each go to the library, log on to our computers, and e-mail each other back and forth for hours while we pretended to study. As far as I know, they, her guards, never caught on. Plus, they didn't sit anywhere near either one of us, because they stood out like bumps on a log. We made it work the best we could."

"Did she ever say what nationality she was? Or where all her father's money came from?" Myra asked.

"No, as to nationality, but I think, and this is just a guess on my part, she understood Russian. At least I think it was Russian. Actually, she spoke several languages, because I heard her from time to time cussing in a foreign language when the guards got the best of her. As to the money, I did ask, and she said her father had his fingers into everything. Actually, she didn't refer to him as her father at all. She referred to him as SD. Finally, one day I asked her what the initials stood for, and she laughed till she cried. Sperm donor. She said all he had to do was touch something, and he made billions. She said she suspected most of it was illegal. I kind of laughed at that, but she was serious. She did say that he hit the jackpot, and those were her exact words, when he came out with his Spy Trap cyberthing.

"That's all I know. You can keep me here forever, and I won't be able to tell you another thing. I'm not lying. I'm telling you the truth, the whole truth, and nothing but the truth."

"All right then. I'm sure you're tired from your trip across the pond. Jack, will you show Mr. Wolansky his room upstairs while we finish our preparations for our trip to Spyder Island the day after tomorrow?" Myra said.

"Sure thing. Let's go, Mr. Wolansky."

"I hate that name. Why can't you call me Greg?"

"Because that might put your life in danger, and we don't want that to happen. You need to stop whining and get with the program. You're playing with the big boys now. Shake it, Wolansky. I don't have all day," Jack urged his recalcitrant charge.

Albright eyeballed Jack and offered up his middle finger. Jack laughed all the way to the second floor, where he showed the man his room.

"Are you going to lock me in here?"

"Why would I do a stupid thing like that? The minute this door opens, all six of those dogs downstairs will be on you like the fleas on their back. Nighty night, Mr. Wolansky."

Downstairs and back in the dining room, Jack just shrugged when the others looked at him with questions in their eyes. "He doesn't know what to think or believe, but he wants to see Gretchen again, so he'll do what we tell him to do. Right now, he's thinking he's been thrust into a pit full of alligators."

"What will be will be," Annie said philosophically. "We have a lot to do before we leave for Spyder Island the day after tomorrow. For starters, we have made yet another change, but it all depends on whether Alexis will be able to get us airborne faster. How is it going, dear?" Annie asked.

"We're good, Annie. My last delivery is

due this afternoon, and then the first group is good to go. It's been a bit of a rush, but I think I have it all covered. You might all be going into a nest of vipers, but you'll be carrying a ton of venom of your own."

"Ooh, I do like the way that sounds," Myra cooed.

Chapter 12

The ancient branches of the three-hundred-year-old angel oak outside the Pinewood farmhouse swayed and danced in the pre-dawn breeze. Clouds, dark to the eye, sailed lazily across the velvety night, soon to be erased by the upcoming dawn. Off in the distance, a dog barked, followed by another dog, each canine communicating in its own way to let the world know a new day was about to begin.

Inside the farmhouse, in a darkened bedroom that was older than the angel oak at the side of the house, Myra Rutledge slept peacefully. With the sound of the barking dogs off in the distance, an early morning greeting, Lady and her pups stirred, causing Myra to stir. She opened one eye to squint at the red numerals on the bedside clock: 5:10. She groaned into the pillow. It was too early to get up. She still had an hour and a half of sleep due her. She rolled over just as her room started to grow light. Her head swiveled to the right to see if Lady had somehow turned on the lamp. Such a silly thought. Like that could really happen.

An uneasy feeling started to crawl through her as she watched her bedroom grow lighter and lighter, until she was blinded with the brightest, the most magnificent light she'd ever seen in her life. She tried to shield her eyes from the brightness. In her entire life, she'd never seen such a light. In an instant, she knew that what she was seeing was not of this world. Panic engulfed her. Her tongue grew thick in her mouth, and she started to shake. "No, no, please. I'm not ready. I still have so much to do. Please," she cried.

"Oh, Mummy, no. That's not why I'm here. It's not your time," her spirit daughter responded.

"Barbara! Darling girl, is that you in the

light? I can't see you. Why are you here? You said you come to me only when I need you the most. Something's wrong. What is it?" Myra cried, tears rolling down her cheeks.

"Annie needs you, Mummy. You have to get up and go to her."

Myra could barely get the words past her tongue. "Is it . . . is it Annie's time? Oh, darling girl, please tell me that's not why she needs me." She was getting used to the magnificent light, which was brighter than Broadway and Las Vegas all rolled into one.

"No, Mummy, it's not Annie's time, either. Go to her. Help her."

"I will! I will! Of course I will. Can't you tell me why?" Myra swung her legs over the side of the bed and almost stepped on Lady, who was sleeping soundly now, unaware of the brilliant light and the conversation going on around her.

"Hurry, Mummy."

And then her room was dark again, so dark she had to turn on the bedside lamp. Lady hopped up then, as did her pups. They waited patiently, even though they didn't understand this early morning change in plans, which had Myra throwing on her clothes and slipping into her shoes. Lady trotted over to the bathroom to see if there would be showering, tooth-brushing, or hair combing going on. When it didn't happen, her tail swished as she led her offspring to the door, down the hall, and out to the kitchen door, which Myra unlocked.

"Make it quick, guys! Like, really quick."

The dogs took her at her word and were back inside within eight minutes.

Myra handed out chews, checked the water bowls, and poured out kibble. Then she rummaged around for her purse and car keys. "I'll be back soon."

It was chilly out, and Myra was glad she'd pulled on a fleece sweatshirt, which she'd need to remove later in the day, because the weatherman last night had predicted that the daytime temperatures would be in the seventies, saying the cherry blossoms at the Tidal Basin would be in full bloom with the warm day. Like she gave a hoot right now about cherry blossoms.

Myra drove faster than she'd ever driven in her life, out through the gates, down the gravel road. She knew she took the two doglegs at ninety miles an hour. She screeched to a stop in the parking area out-

side the back of the house, which led to Annie's kitchen. Her eyes registered Annie's
low-slung sports car and a second car,
which she didn't recognize, but a decal on
the plate made her think it was a rental car.
Annie had a guest!

As fast as her legs could carry her, Annie's key in hand, Myra bounded up the
steps that led to a small, closed-in breezeway, which in turn led to Annie's kitchen.
Breathless with all the effort she was ex-
pending, she muttered, "I am so out of
shape and **wayyy** too old for all of this," as
she barreled up the steps to the second
floor. She burst into Annie's bedroom, her
heart thundering in her chest, to see Annie in her Mother Hubbard nightgown sitting on the edge of the bed. "Annie!"

Annie turned, her voice fuzzy, her eyes
not quite focused, and mumbled, "Myra!
What are you doing here? It isn't even light
out yet." She reached up to settle the sparkling tiara a little more firmly on her head.
"Stop looking at me like that, Myra. I always
sleep with my tiara. Where else can I wear
the stupid thing?"

Myra took a deep breath, then another.
Then they were both jabbering at once,

neither of them understanding what the other was saying. A shrill whistle came from the doorway.

"One at a time, ladies!" said Jack Sparrow, director of the FBI. "Better yet, I'm going to go downstairs and make us all some coffee. Please join me as soon as you can." He turned at the door and said, "I'm not much up on ladies' fashions, but is that thing on your head a tiara?"

Myra threw her hands in the air. "It is a tiara. Mr. Sparrow has a point. Now that I see you are okay, I'm going to go downstairs. Make it snappy, Annie. This is way too early in the morning for such shenanigans. You know, I have that same nightgown. Charles always hated it when I wore it. What is **he** doing here?" she hissed.

"Fergus never liked mine, either," Annie snapped as she marched off to the bathroom without answering Myra's question.

Myra stared at the closed bathroom door, trying to decide if she was nuts, if Annie was nuts, or if Jack Sparrow had dropped out of the clouds on his way to the funny farm.

Down in Annie's kitchen, Myra sat down. "Looks like you know your way around the kitchen," Myra said, indicating the coffee canister in Sparrow's hands.

"I do, actually. I'm a fair cook, if I do say so myself. When I got here last night, Annie made coffee. I saw where she kept the canister. Mystery solved."

"I don't know what I'd do without coffee. I'm addicted," Myra mumbled.

"Me, too," Sparrow said, getting light cream out of the refrigerator and the sugar bowl from the cabinet. "You'll have to help me out here. I'm not sure where the napkins are kept."

Myra started to laugh and couldn't stop. "I'm sorry, Mr. Sparrow," she gasped. "Annie uses paper towels. She says napkins are a waste of money. She's frugal like that." She went off into another peal of laughter, and before she knew it, Sparrow was doubled over.

"What's so damn funny?" Annie barked from the doorway.

Myra reached for the paper towels, ripped one off for Sparrow and one for herself before she doubled over herself. "I was just telling Mr. Sparrow how thrifty you are and how you think napkins are a waste of money."

"And that's funny? I don't think so!" Annie reached for a cup and poured coffee, spilling some of it all over the counter. "Why are you here, Myra?" Annie asked as she sat down at the table.

Myra folded her hands on the table and leaned in closer. In a calm, steady voice, she explained what had happened in her bedroom. She fully expected Jack Sparrow to laugh, but he didn't.

Instead, he said, "I believe in stuff like that. Someday when none of us have anything to do, I'll tell you about my own experiences. Which brings us now to the question for Annie as to why she needs you. You have the floor, Countess."

Annie frowned as she tried to think how to put into words what she wanted to say. Myra and Sparrow watched her struggle. Finally, Myra said, "Oh, Annie, just blurt it out. We'll make sense of it, I'm sure."

Annie's frown deepened. There was a tight edge to her tone when she said, "I'm spooked here, and I don't mind admitting it. I also had a dream, the same dream now for four nights. Tonight, though, it was different. I knew it wasn't a dream. **It was real.**" She got up off her chair and started to pace her spacious kitchen, which, as always, was neat as a pin. Annie didn't believe in cooking, as it messed up things. She hated dirtying up her Wolf stove. "Like what you experienced, Myra. I know it was real, just the way you knew what you experienced was real. You also know me well enough to know I do not, as in ever, get spooked."

"You said you had the same dream for four nights. Was it exactly the same dream, or were there some deviations? In other words, define the word exactly," Sparrow said.

Annie squeezed her eyes shut as she allowed her mind to travel back into her dreams. Myra could see how her old friend was struggling. She wanted to hug her, but Sparrow shook his head.

"I was on the mountain. It was a beautiful day. The sun was so warm, and the sky as blue as the sea at the bottom of the mountain. I was watching some men, two men, playing chess, but I couldn't see their faces. Their backs were to me in the dream. There was a pitcher of some kind of drink on the table. I could see the ice cubes in the pitcher. I counted them. There were eleven of them. Both of the men were smoking cigars. It was blue smoke. Cohibas. I don't know how I knew that. The breeze carried the smoke away.

"I was angry in the dream. I asked them how they got onto my balcony, because the cable car wasn't working. Someone from the village was due to repair it. I asked them their names, and neither man answered me. It was like they didn't hear me. I screamed at them, but they still didn't answer me. I went inside, or maybe I was already inside and just looking out the French doors. Anyway, I went to get my gun. I was going to shoot them, but when I got back, they were gone. The pitcher and the chess set were gone, too. And I couldn't smell the cigar smoke. It was the same dream on the other nights except for . . . last night. I'm sure of it."

"How big were they weight wise? Did they wear glasses? I know you said you couldn't see their faces. Why exactly was that?" Sparrow asked.

Annie squeezed her eyes shut again. "One of the men was wearing one of those floppy fishing hats. The other one wore a baseball cap. They wore sandals, cargo pants, and plain white T-shirts. They were in the sun on the balcony. It gets full sun till around four in the afternoon. Oh, they were wearing sunglasses. It was the same dream all three nights. I woke up each time when I had the gun in my hand to shoot them. I was prepared to shoot them."

"Why?" Myra asked softly.

"Because they were on my mountain. That mountain was . . . is . . . sacrosanct. You know that, Myra. Don't you remember how I almost threw you over the side for invading my privacy?"

"You were grieving for your husband and children at that time. I understood. These two men invaded your privacy and usurped what you held sacrosanct. That is not acceptable."

"Damn straight it's not acceptable," Annie snapped.

"Tell us about the dream you had last night. What and how was it different?" Myra asked.

"It was the same two men—I'm sure of it—but it wasn't on my mountain. The reason I know it wasn't my mountain was there were no neighboring mountains to be seen. Plus, from my balcony on the mountain in Spain, I could see the cable-car platform and all the foliage. This place in my dream had palm trees, and it was very windy. Ocean breezes, I assume. This time in my dream I sneaked up on them, and I had my gun. Then I must have made a sound, and both men looked up. I saw them clear as a bell."

Myra gasped. "Did you know them? Did you shoot them?"

"It was Fergus and Charles, and they were at my house on Spyder Island."

"Oh, dear Lord," Myra said as she slumped in her chair. "Tell me you didn't shoot them, Annie."

"I didn't shoot them, because Charles said, 'What took you so long?' and then Fergus said, 'We've been waiting forever for you to spring us out of here.'"

"And you took that to mean . . . what?" Sparrow asked.

Annie started to pace again as she kneaded her hands. "That they are being held prisoner on Spyder Island. Think about it, Myra. It makes sense. I'll bet my tiara that when Charles was whisked away to England by the queen's people, somehow, someway, Angus Spyder was involved in that new age city that was supposed to be built. None of us know what went awry. As Abner told us, Spyder has so many layers of holding companies and shell companies that it's almost impossible to trace down any of it. And don't forget that Spy Trap company he owns.

"And if Hank Jellicoe was on the scene, and they got downwind of Charles, he was fair game. I don't know how Fergus got into the mix. I'm thinking that because he used to work for Scotland Yard, Charles requested his help. I'm just throwing this out there. I could be way off base, but my gut is telling me I'm right. What do you think, Myra?"

"If it weren't for my own—I don't know what to call it—epiphany, encounter, the blinding light, my spirit daughter telling me to get over here, I might question your dream as just a dream. I believe you, Annie." She looked over at Jack Sparrow, who was nodding in agreement.

Myra sighed so deeply that she almost slid off her chair. "That empty house on the island, the one Abner said no one lived in, and yet utility bills are currently being paid on the property . . . Is it too far-fetched to think Fergus and Charles are being held prisoner there?"

Sparrow grimaced. "Why? Why wouldn't Jellicoe, if he's even there, just kill them and be done with them once and for all? What's his game plan?"

"I don't know. Power over them? Back in the day, Charles and Fergus both were top-notch black ops agents," Annie replied. "Humiliation? Jellicoe and Charles were friends at one point during their lives, until Hank Jellicoe went rogue. And, of course, we captured him, or I should say, the vigilantes captured him. Unfortunately, one of Charles's men let him escape. Being caught by a bunch of women had to be humiliating. Some men, and I think Hank Jellicoe comes under the heading of 'some men,' would never be able to live that down. Plus, he is now in exile, so to speak, taking orders from Angus Spyder. This is all guesswork on my part, of course, but I think I'm right, and I have a pretty good track record. What do you think, Myra?"

"I think you are scary right, my friend. That is what I think. Right now, though, there's too much we don't know. Remember now, we're just guessing that Jellicoe is on Spyder Island."

Annie settled the sparkling tiara more

firmly on her head, a sure sign that whatever was to follow would be up to her. She
looked over at Sparrow and said, "We've
had more than our share of false starts here.
We had plan after plan, but in the end none
of them were good enough, so we went
back to the drawing board. It was Alexis
who finally nailed the final plan, the one we
are going with. We all agreed. We are
scheduled to leave for Spyder Island tomorrow. Having said that, our ETD is up in the
air because of several things. Alexis had to
order two cargo planes. She was having
some difficulty, as I understand it, and that's
another reason we might be delayed."

Sparrow jumped in, a smile on his face.
"I got her two C-130s from Andrews Air
Force Base. Actually, I got one from them
and one from Quantico. They will be parked
and ready for takeoff at Dulles the moment
you give the okay."

Annie grinned. "I knew I liked you for a
reason. Nice going. Alexis called me last
night and said that everything we agreed
upon will be arriving at the airport by noon
tomorrow. We can load up and be ready to
go the moment she's satisfied with her plan,
which, by the way, is a really good plan."

"Now might be a good time to share that plan, Countess," Sparrow said, grinning from ear to ear.

Giving her tiara a firm nudge, Annie said, "I think you might be right, Mr. Sparrow. Gather close, children, and listen very carefully."

Myra laughed out loud. This was Annie at her finest. She watched her give the tiara another nudge. She did love her.

Chapter 13

The kitchen and dining room at Pinewood crackled with electricity as the group talked, laughed, and plotted. The adrenaline in the room was at an all-time high as the group prepped for the new mission, which was to get under way in less than thirty-six hours.

Her dream shelved for the time being, Annie let loose with a sharp whistle that brought all the dogs on the run. Not so those in the group, who merely stopped talking to see what was going on.

"War room, everyone!" Annie called. The gang peeled off, with Jack Sparrow in the rear. Annie handed him a picture and said, "I want one of these. How do I get one?"

Sparrow looked down at the picture in his hand and gasped. "Just like that, you want one of **these?**"

"Yep," Annie said. "How do I go about getting one? Can you help me? I'd like it by tomorrow, if possible. Actually, it's not negotiable. I **need** it by tomorrow afternoon."

Sparrow burst out laughing. "Well, now, let's see. I guess I could call one of the Joint Chiefs or maybe someone at the Pentagon and tell them that Countess de Silva wants a Little Bird by tomorrow."

"Is that how it works?"

"**No!** I was making fun of your request. Why in the hell do you want a Little Bird helicopter, and what makes you think that I, of all people, can get you one?"

"That's the way that I want to travel to Spyder Island. I'm going to make a statement. And since you are the director of the FBI, you must have some clout. Use it. Please."

In spite of himself, Sparrow laughed. "Will you be wearing your tiara when you hop off the bird? Do you know anything about he-

licopters? You jump off. You do not deplane."

"You jump, you tuck, and you roll. Yep, I
got it. Of course I'll be wearing my tiara. I
told you, I want to make a statement, and
the tiara is part of it. So, can you get me
one or not?"

"I don't know this for a fact, but I tend to
think the only way you can get one is if some
retired general has one he restored or came
by some other way. I'll make some calls.
What are you willing to pay?"

"Whatever it takes," Annie responded
smartly. "Please don't disappoint me, Mr.
Sparrow. I really have my heart set on flying and deplaning out of one of those."

"Uh, Annie, you don't . . . ah, deplane.
Didn't you hear what I just said? You jump
and hit the ground running. You could lose
your tiara."

"Smart-ass!" Annie snapped. "I still want
one. I'm just having fun with you."

Sparrow had his cell phone in hand as
he shuffled along behind Annie to the secret staircase that led to the underground
dungeon and war room, where a lively dis-
cussion had already begun, with Alexis having the floor. He watched as Annie ran over

to Alexis and whispered in her ear. He grinned when he saw Alexis burst out laughing and give Annie a thumbs-up.

Jack Sparrow was one of those people who could listen, absorb, even comment while texting or mumbling into his phone. He was doing it all at that very moment. Of all the things he'd ever been asked to do in his personal or professional life, this request was the strangest. For some ungodly reason, however, he really did not want to fail Annie. He'd get that damn Little Bird one way or the other. As Annie had pointed out, he was, after all, the director of the goddamn Federal Bureau of Investigation. That had to count for something in this life.

Three hours later, as the meeting droned on, Sparrow finally got a solid lead and followed it up. A group of six army officers, all full-bird colonels and pilots, had in 2004 purchased a Little Bird that was about to be eighty-sixed. They had had it restored and took turns using it for pleasure. It was currently housed in a private hangar in upstate New York. On his third call, Sparrow managed to speak to a retired colonel, Duke Wilson. After Wilson got over the shock of having the FBI director personally call him, things got under way. Sparrow made his offer. He encountered little resistance. Wilson said he would contact the others and get back to him within an hour. Sparrow gave him thirty minutes, but not before Wilson told him the Little Bird wouldn't come cheap. He rattled off some numbers, which Sparrow shot down, then agreed to. He motioned to Annie to see the number on his phone. She nodded.

And the deal was put to bed with the promise that the Little Bird would set down at Dulles International Airport by midmorning of the following day, complete with all the paperwork. Annie then whispered in Sparrow's ear that after she had her fun with the Little Bird, it would be sold to the highest bidder, with the money going to the Wounded Warrior Project. Then he saw her look over at Alexis again and wink. Sparrow was the first to admit he knew almost next to nothing about women, but at that moment he was totally convinced that the two women were plotting something with the Little Bird. He shrugged. There was nothing he could do about whatever it was, and he was smart enough to recognize the fact.

Sparrow crooked a finger in Abner's direction and showed him the screen on his cell phone, which meant he was to wire the funds for the Little Bird to Colonel Wilson ASAP. He nodded and grinned at a mental picture of Annie sitting on the running board of the Little Bird, wearing her tiara and Louboutin shoes with the spike heels. It wasn't that he knew anything about women's fashion, but he recognized the famous name from the chattering women. Obviously, if you wore Louboutin shoes, you were a fashionista. As far as making a statement to one Angus Spyder, he personally didn't think it could get any better than that.

Sparrow got all flustered and turned pink when Annie winked at him and gave him a thumbs-up. He'd come through for her. That was all that mattered. Damn, he felt good. He leaned back and focused on the conversations around him to make sure he wasn't missing anything.

After listening carefully for thirty minutes, Sparrow decided it was time to speak up. He waved his hand for attention. "So far, all I'm hearing is the name Hank Jellicoe. Hank Jellicoe this and Hank Jellicoe that. I thought this mission of yours . . . ours was about

Gretchen Spyder, the children she gave up for adoption, and the adopting Domingo family.

"Mr. Albright, alias Stephen Wolansky, who is the biological father of the adopted twins, twins he knew nothing about, is now an FBI rookie agent with the assignment of seeing to the matter and bringing it to a resolution. I haven't heard anything about how we're going to do any of that. So, is the mission Hank Jellicoe or the Domingos and Gretchen Spyder?"

"Both. They are inextricably intertwined, Mr. Sparrow," Myra said. "Gretchen and the children are our primary concern, but we have to factor in Mr. Jellicoe. And, to be honest, we are trying to be preemptive, because we do not know for certain that he is even on the island. We need to be prepared if he is. Hank Jellicoe is an evil man and will stop at nothing, and I mean nothing, to protect his own skin. He was a hair away from losing it once, and he will never let himself be put in that position again. And this time he has all the might of Angus Spyder and his fortune to back him up. We're just a bunch of women. That is the way he thought of us back then. If you have any advice or ideas, now would be a good time to present them."

"I don't. I just wanted to make sure I understand. I'm still not getting how you think he isn't going to recognize you all. Your pictures were in all the papers. You were all household names."

Myra laughed. "He never met Annie. He never met Abner, Dennis, or Mr. Albright. Alexis is a master at disguise. Trust me when I tell you that that lady has everything under control. As for you, Mr. Sparrow, you will not recognize yourself when she's done with you. Even though you never met either man personally, your picture has obviously been in the papers more than once. We can't risk exposing you. And, by the way, Mr. Snowden just sent me a text assuring us that the Domingos are as safe as safe can be. He does want to know what we want to do about the bugs someone planted in Annie's house. We need to think about that and make a decision."

Sparrow nodded as he sank deep into thought. The meeting went on, notes were taken, and coffee was consumed by the gallon. Myra left twice to see to the dogs and returned immediately both times. He was amazed and stunned at how the group worked together. They could finish each other's sentences, voice each other's thoughts. A well-oiled team. Better than most of his own teams at the bureau, where it was all about ego and whose name went first on the list.

When the group finally wound down, they all looked exhausted, but in a good kind of way. They were pumped and ready to go. Especially the women. Once again, he thought about how little he knew about women. What he did know was that he was looking at one hell of a group of dedicated women who did not know the meaning of the word **failure.** In that one second, he knew this mission would be successful. He felt himself relax and wished he had a dozen teams like this one at the bureau. If only. He didn't give a second thought to breaking the law. Not one nanosecond. Been there, done that.

It was approaching seven o'clock, dusk now, as Pinewood came alive once again. Dennis and Greg Albright had volunteered to barbecue steaks outside on the grill. The women were bustling about in the kitchen, making salads and baking potatoes. A good but plain dinner that would give them all enough sustenance to work through the night so they could leave on schedule. A schedule that had been moved so many times, it was almost as though it would never happen. And then, suddenly, everything was in place, and their estimated time of departure was set for three o'clock the following afternoon.

It was finally happening. There was no backing out now.

It was a pleasant spring evening, not too hot, not too cold. A gentle breeze whispered among the trees. The dogs meandered around the yard, sniffing at all the fresh sprouts appearing like magic. The floodlights, while bright, were angled just so, bathing the entire expanse of lawn in a soft glow of light. As Myra expressed it to the others, and they all agreed, it was a fitting end to an exhausting day.

At some invisible sign that Sparrow missed, a whirlwind ensued. Within minutes, the terrace was free of any signs of dinner. The grill was cleaned and turned off. The dishwasher was loaded and humming. With no leftovers, there was nothing to wrap and refrigerate. The dogs contentedly gnawed on the massive steak bones.

To his amazement, Alexis whistled sharply for instant silence. She had the group's attention immediately. "Listen up, people. We are now in our final phase. So, let's get to it. Nikki and Isabelle are going to be helping me. Otherwise, we'll be here till the cows wander home. Your transformations are going to take all night and into tomorrow. I am going to count myself lucky if we finish on time."

And from there on in, things worked like the final prep before a rocket launch. Sparrow settled back with his iPad and conducted business, then dozed off until his name was called sometime during the middle of the night.

Hours later, just as the sun was rising, Sparrow walked out into the kitchen to see a strange group of people milling about. He had no clue who they were. Feeling stupid and foolish, he asked and was rewarded with gales of laughter. From out of nowhere, one of the strange guests handed him a mirror. For a moment, he found it hard to breathe when he stared at his reflection in the mirror. He looked down at his wrist to see if his arm was his own. His watch was the same; his signet ring was the same. He wondered if he had a new name to go with his new persona.

Jack Emery clapped him on the back, but Jack Emery now looked like a runway model. A **female** runway model. Sparrow almost choked on his own saliva. Ted Robinson now looked like a nerdy female librarian, complete with curly gray hair and granny glasses. Espinosa was an over-the-hill senorita wearing a ton of noisy turquoise jewelry that clanked and tinkled when he moved. They were all wearing high-heeled shoes.

"The guys are now girls, and the girls are now guys. The reason for this is that Jellicoe knows us all quite well. Believe it or not, we used to work for him, as did Bert." Jack motioned to Harry and Yoko, who were dozing. "Mama-san and Papa-san."

Sparrow gasped. Harry and Yoko looked to be a hundred years old to Sparrow's eyes. He looked over his shoulder to see a guy he'd never seen before. A light-skinned black man with a close-cropped head of hair. If his life depended on it, he couldn't have said who he was looking at. Nor could

EYES ONLY   239

he tell who the other two black men were.
He could hardly keep from laughing when
Kathryn, Nikki, and Isabelle started to gig-
gle.

"What I'm seeing is the impossible," Sparrow said. "What and who is Alexis going
as? And where is Myra?"

"Alexis is probably going to be a secret
until the last moment, and she'll probably
do herself, plus Maggie, on the plane. That's
the way it usually works," Nikki said.

Sparrow looked around. Dennis, Abner,
and Albright stood off to the side, more to
show the contrast between all of them than
anything else.

"Okay, okay, I get it, and I am impressed.
I didn't think this was possible, but now I
see that it is. Alexis is a genius. Having said
that, who are we? What names will be on
the flight manifest? You have to know that
is the first thing Spyder will have his people check."

"We all have legends, thanks to you and
to Avery Snowden. All foolproof. The countess always travels with a full retinue of people, staff, friends, relatives. She's eccentric,
so anything goes where she is concerned,"
Nikki said.

Sparrow absorbed all that he was hearing and tried to wrap his mind around how it was all going to go down. He needed to stop the buzzing in his head. He switched topics. "I understand about the Little Bird, but what's going in the two C-130 cargo planes?"

Annie reached for a clipboard, but not before she gave her tiara a jolt. "First of all, a ton of food. Not literally, but a lot of it, plus everything under the sun that can be bottled. Four Range Rovers, seven Harley-Davidson motorcycles, and one special cycle for Harry and Yoko to tool around in. Dennis will serve as their driver. A lot of Abner's equipment. My personal trunks, all of Alexis's stuff for when she has to, you know, **redo** us. That's half a plane right there. And then some jamming devices. Think of it this way. Everything in those two cargo planes is what you would go to war with. We are going to war!"

Sparrow jammed his hands into his pockets so no one would see him cross his fingers. It was so out of the box, he could actually see it working.

Jack chirped up in his new falsetto voice.

"You didn't ask about ammunition or guns or anything, Director. Why is that?"

"Because Harry said, and I believe him, that you are all killing machines. Perhaps the word **killing** isn't the right word. I get the point, however. So we are going in without any kind of hardware?"

"No! We are packing heat. The last time I checked, our firearms were to be packed between the frozen pearl onions and the spaghetti squash in the deep freezer we're taking with us. Myra's pearls are the only thing we're leaving behind us. Dead give-away," Jack deadpanned.

"I'm loving this," Dennis said as he paced frantically. "I didn't think I'd like being a spook, but you know what? I am loving it. The adrenaline rush, the excitement about taking those scumbags down, then, on top of that, giving all their money away and maybe finding Charles and that other guy. Boy, this is living. And the cherry on top is that we will reunite Gretchen and Greg, and everyone will live happily ever after. I'm so excited that I can hardly stand it."

"Time to put a cork in it, kid. We're getting the picture," Ted said.

"Yeah, but, Ted, this is big-time. Not like

Baywater and those two crooked judges, and it isn't like that Bernie Madoff clone caper, either. This is **big.** I can't believe I'm a part of it, and all of us are going to be participating. That's the part I like best. All of us working together."

"Someone give him an Ambien, please," Espinosa said, but not unkindly.

"Okay, I get it. I'm just going to sit here and fantasize. And listen to all of you. I might pick up some tips if it comes to crunch time. Okay, okay, I won't say another word."

"Where is Maggie?" someone asked.

Annie responded. "She's at the airport, overseeing the loading of the cargo planes. Alexis gave Maggie her instructions. She also has some special instructions from me. Right now, she's who she is, Maggie Spritzer, intrepid girl and editor in chief reporter with more guts than all of us put together. She'll get made up on the plane after takeoff."

"I guess we're good to go, then," Abner said. "I sure hope all my equipment is bundled properly. I won't be any good to any of you if it isn't working properly."

"Don't worry, Abner. Maggie will personally see to it all," Annie said cheerfully. "I think I'll make some coffee. Any takers?"

Every hand in the room shot upward. Dennis West's shot up first and was the highest. A sappy smile was spread across his face. He was now officially a spook.

Chapter 14

The monster ship's wheel clock, a true antique, hanging over Myra's kitchen fireplace said the time was 12:02. Myra looked around at the eager, expectant faces and said, "I see no reason to hold to our original departure time since we finished up ahead of schedule." She looked over at Annie and said, "Can you call the pilots and see if we can be wheels up in, say, forty-five minutes?"

"Consider it done," Annie said, moving off to make the call.

"Then let's get ready to move out. Just give me five minutes to go over some last-minute things with the vet assistant who is dog sitting for me until we get back." Myra had had a change of heart in regard to taking Lady and her pups on the trip, hence the dog sitter.

"Jack, does Cyrus have all his gear?" Myra asked as she looked around for the list of instructions she'd typed out earlier for the vet assistant. She found it by her cookbooks. **Charles's cookbooks,** she mused, clarifying the inner thought.

"And then some. I think he snitched a few toys that belong here."

Myra laughed. "They won't be missed, and maybe Cyrus wants a memory of his time here this past week. I'll be with you in a few minutes."

Cyrus slapped one huge paw on Myra's shoulder. He licked her ear, then let loose with a loud bark. His way of saying good-bye.

"I'm coming, too, Cyrus. This isn't good-bye," Myra told him.

Chagrined, the shepherd backed away and looked up at Jack for confirmation.

"Yep, she is coming with us."

Cyrus tilted his head, taking in the words.

He barked twice. Translation, "Okay, then. I'm outta here." He was a black streak going through the door.

Maggie stood back to admire her handiwork. It was impossible not to smile. Then she grinned, and after that, she burst out laughing. Annie's Little Bird was a sight to behold. It had taken her a full hour to spray a special glue that Alexis had given her on the Little Bird, and then she had thrown two full bags of sparkling gems all over the helicopter. It sparkled, it shimmered, and it glowed brighter than the Las Vegas Strip at night.

The chopper pilot looked at her and said, "I sure hope none of my friends see me piloting this pimp chopper."

Maggie laughed even harder. "The countess likes to travel in style," she said to the pilot, whose name was Leroy. "This is style. Don't knock it. See ya, Leroy," Maggie said, moving off to check the two cargo planes one last time.

Maggie strode across the tarmac. She grinned when she saw all the pilots standing around straighten up and stare at her.

She knew they were wondering what the hell was going on. Wondering who Countess de Silva was that she had so much clout she could commandeer two cargo planes and a Little Bird. And the C-130s' cargo had put them all into a tailspin. But like the professionals they were, they asked no questions as they all eyed the sleek silver Gulf-stream that the countess owned, plus its counterpart, owned by some big corporation named Welmed.

"I think we're good to go, gentlemen," Maggie said as she motioned to the **Post** van and two other SUVs, which were approaching at a good clip.

The vehicles stopped; doors opened. Maggie gasped, lost her footing, and went down on one knee as she blinked, trying to absorb what she was seeing. She heard gasps, and she thought she heard a chuckle or two, when Annie stepped out, looking like a harem princess, her tiara sparkling in the early afternoon sunshine. Try as she could, Maggie couldn't figure out who was who as the gang moved toward the portable stairs leading into the Gulfstreams. She held her breath when she saw Annie and the decadent-looking woman next to her,

who she assumed was Myra, approach the
Little Bird, Abner and Dennis in tow.

Maggie waved to the pilots as she
sprinted toward Annie's Gulfstream and
climbed aboard, but not before she turned
around to see Annie's reaction to her handiwork. Annie's arm shot in the air. **Good.**
Annie liked the job she'd done on the Little
Bird. She also wondered if the decorated
version would bring more money when
Annie offered it up for auction, with the
proceeds going to the Wounded Warrior
Project. She shrugged. No matter how you
looked at it, it was win-win.

Fifteen minutes later, the fleet of planes
was airborne, with the Little Bird the last
to leave the ground. The expected time
in flight was four hours and ten minutes.
It could be as little as three hours and
four minutes if the robust tailwinds continued.

The minute Annie's Gulfstream climbed
to a cruising altitude of thirty-one thousand feet, Alexis was up and out of her
seat and ushering Maggie to the back of
the plane, where she would transform her
appearance. The others sat around in the
plush seats, talking and chattering about

everything and nothing. The excitement level was as high as the altitude at which they were flying.

With years of practice under her belt, Felicia Spyder moved about the mansion in what she called her surreptitious mode, which meant she was doing her best to spy on her despicable husband and his good-for-nothing underlings. Sometimes she was successful in hearing a little nugget of information, which she stored away like a squirrel in the hopes that one day she would be rescued, at which point she would share all those nuggets with her saviors.

Felicia looked down at the diamond-crusted watch on her wrist. **Almost four o'clock. Something is going on.** Less than an hour ago, she'd heard the gong sound, calling all security to her husband's suite of offices at the back of the building. Minutes after that, she'd heard seven vehicles leave the compound. Over the years, she'd trained herself to recognize the sound of each and every vehicle.

Seven vehicles, to her mind, meant twenty-one security personnel were on their way to someplace. Her husband was adamant that each vehicle carry three gun-toting guards. With twenty-one missing guards, this would be the perfect time to wander over to Gretchen's room and offer to take her for a ride around the boardwalk. She'd done it before, with little or no opposition, as long as Gretchen continued to play the game. She just hoped that her daughter was as intuitive as she was.

Her stomach a jumble of knots, Felicia made her way down a long, well-lit hallway that had cameras positioned at each end, around a bend, then down another, shorter hallway to an outside breezeway that would take her to her daughter's suite of rooms. Her skin crawled when she considered how many sets of eyes she knew were following her progress.

At the door to her daughter's suite, which was standing open, she trilled a greeting, hoping that when her daughter looked up, she would see something in her eyes and continue to play the game.

"What do you want now?" Gretchen snarled.

"To take you for a walk on the boardwalk. It's beautiful out right now. You need to get away from the computer for a little while. We can feed the gulls, I'll make us a sand castle, and we can pretend you're five years old again. How does that sound?" Felicia asked cheerfully.

"Puhl-eeze. Sand castles, Mommie Dearest! What will the sperm donor say if you get that fancy dress all mucked up? Not that I give a good rat's ass. I was hoping you came here to tell me the bastard had dropped dead."

"Please, dear, don't speak that way about your father. Come along. You can control the chair till we get to the boardwalk."

"Will it do me any good to say no?"

"No, dear. I'm your mother, and I want to take you for a walk. It really is a beautiful day outside. Can I get you something to drink to take with you?"

"No. Let's just get this faux bonding out of the way so I can get back to the computer. There are some new books I want to order." Without another word, Gretchen whirled her chair around and buzzed out the door into the breezeway, which led to the lawn, then to the boardwalk that ran along the oceanfront.

Felicia had to hustle to keep up with the

motorized wheelchair. When she caught up, she whispered, "You're doing good, baby. Keep it up. No one can hear us out here. Something is going on."

"I heard the cars," Gretchen said, her lips barely moving as she slowed the wheelchair so her mother could walk alongside her.

They moved on, their eyes constantly on the lookout for anything out of the ordinary. Paranoid as she was, Felicia felt safe enough to say, "I think we're okay. Oh, my goodness, look at that!" She pointed at the sky.

"What does that mean? Airplanes fly in here all the time," Gretchen said as she adjusted her sunglasses to look upward into the bright blue sky.

"Yes, of course they do. One at a time. Never like this. And there is a helicopter off in the distance. My goodness, it looks like the crown jewels. I didn't know helicopters sparkled like that. I've never even seen one up close. Have you, Gretchen?"

"No, I haven't. Four planes and a helicopter. Those first two are Gulfstreams. I know what they look like. Those other two look like planes the military uses. Don't tell me the sperm donor is calling in reinforcements. For what?"

"I knew today was somehow momentous. It's a good thing the flight pattern is right overhead. Look at that helicopter. That is the strangest flying machine I've ever seen. Look, Gretchen. Two women are sitting on some kind of bench. Oh, my Lord! It's that countess woman. The woman your fa . . . Angus hates. She's wearing a tiara. That must be so exciting! I guess it's our thrill for the day."

"What do you think this means, Mom?" Gretchen hissed.

"I don't know, dear. But whatever it is, I now understand why Angus sent out those seven cars full of security. That tells me he's worried. And yet Mr. Jellicoe didn't take his car. He's still here. I find that very puzzling."

"If we go all the way to the end of the boardwalk, we can see the road leading to the countess's house. There's a snack shop there, and we can get an ice cream or a soda and sit in the shade for a bit. I've come this far before on my own, and no one ever stopped me," Gretchen said.

"I don't have any money on me," Felicia said.

Gretchen laughed. "I have a stash here in the pocket of the chair. You never know who you might get a chance to bribe." She fished around and came up with a ten-dollar bill, which she handed to her mother. "Fifteen minutes, and we should see some action."

Ten minutes later, both mother and daughter were licking strawberry ice-cream cones and appearing like they didn't have a care in the world. Their eyes were sharp and alert as they watched the road to see what was going on.

"I don't know why, but I have a good feeling about this," Felicia whispered. "I know it means something. I just know it."

"I never thought I would agree with you, but I think you're right." To herself, Gretchen thought, hoped, yearned that somehow, someway, Greg had found her and was part of the party, and that they were coming to rescue her. She knew it was a foolish thought, but such thoughts were all that kept her from going insane. If only.

The small island airport, which wasn't that small, looked like a prelude to an armed attack somewhere as the planes settled down smoothly, their engines deafening. The Little Bird hovered, its rotors whirling as its occupants waited for the word to **jump.**

Annie shouted to be heard over the noise of the planes' engines and the rotors overhead. What she was screaming, which no one could hear, was, "Who are those people on the ground? This wind is playing hell with my tiara."

And then her own crew members were right below, their heads and shoulders bent to form a blanket of sorts for the two women to **deplane.** Annie gave a thumbs-up and jumped the second she released the harness that was holding her in place. Strong arms caught her, and she was finally standing firmly on the ground in her Louboutin shoes. Myra was next.

"Thank God my wig didn't come off with all this wind," Myra said, once her feet were planted on terra firma. "I have to say, Annie, that was a thrill a minute, and you finally outdid yourself. The only thing left for you to do is shoot that damn gun you carry on your backside twenty-one times."

Annie giggled. "Shhh, Myra. My public

and my adoring fans await me. Get in character already, will you please. Remember, you are my wayward half sister, whom no one ever knew about because of your tacky lifestyle."

Myra sniffed, but good sport that she was, she slipped easily into her new persona. She pulled a flask from the purse that was dangling from her neck and took a long gulp . . . of iced tea.

Annie looked toward what she considered her people, waiting for the agreed-upon hand signals to let her know what her next move was. Suddenly, the area went quiet, with all the planes shutting down almost at the same time. Even the Little Bird sat quietly, sparkling in the sun, casting rainbows of color on the tarmac from its coat of shimmering gems.

Kathryn raised her arm and pointed to the lead Range Rover, which meant no meet and greet. But the second signal indicated Annie could pose for a picture with Myra at her side. Both women willingly obliged, with Myra taking an even longer belt from the gold flask that was studded with fake rubies. She made sure she lurched to the side so that Annie could grab her arm, which she did. At that point, Myra stumbled, and the ruby-studded cap to the flask rolled away. One of the Sisters/Brothers grabbed for it, then helped the two women into the backseat of the black Range Rover. The windows were darkly tinted, so it was impossible for anyone to see the two women collapsing in laughter. Annie kicked off the silly shoes she'd been wearing, lowered the window, and tossed them out onto the tarmac. No one rushed to pick them up.

"How'd we do, Myra?"

"I do believe we were Academy Award material. By any chance, did you happen to notice that gaggle of beefy men with bulges under their jackets? Since I was in character, I had only a moment, but I think I counted around twenty men, give or take one or two."

"Yes, indeedy, I did. I counted twenty-four. I do believe Mr. Spyder is now aware of our arrival. How cool is that? Are we having fun, Myra?"

Myra turned around to look out the back window. "We are having so much fun, I can barely stand it," she said through clenched teeth. "We're a regular caravan. I know what you're thinking, Annie. You are wondering which house Charles and Fergus are being held prisoner in. Tell me I'm right."

"You're right. I am. Every fiber in my body is telling me they're here. I just got here, and I hate this place. Look at those. . . . What are they, Myra? Castles, palaces, mansions? What?"

"Bricks and mortar, Annie. That's how you have to think of them. Yours probably looks the same. Relax."

Three minutes later, Myra screamed, "Quick, Annie! Roll down your window and wave till your arms fall off. Look up there on that stretch of boardwalk. Do you see the person in the wheelchair and the woman standing next to it?"

"Oh, dear God, I do." Annie waved frantically, hoping the girl in the wheelchair could see her. "But, Myra, she doesn't know who we are. Waving to her won't mean anything."

"I'm not so sure. I'd bet my last dollar she'd do anything to get off this island. She may already be plotting with her mother. We just think differently than most people,

Annie. Let's just hope that seeing our parade, she starts to think. I hope Stephen . . . Greg . . . sees her. Maybe he'll be quick enough to wave, too. That would clinch it for sure."

Little did either woman know that Greg Albright had spotted the wheelchair and the two women at the same time as Myra and Annie. He had the window down and was waving his arms as crazily as Annie had. Then he started to shout, until Sparrow yanked him back and smacked him hard alongside his head. "Screw this up, and you are dead meat, Albright."

"That's her. That was Gretchen!"

"We know. One more move, and we'll hogtie you, and you'll be no part of this. Tell me you understand what I just said."

"All right. I get it. I'm sorry. It won't happen again. I just had a knee-jerk reaction."

"You damn well better not have another one, or it's curtains for you, buddy," Sparrow said ominously.

Albright cowered in his seat. He closed his eyes and pretended he was running across the sand, up to the boardwalk, and into the arms of the love of his life. In your thoughts and dreams, anything was possible. He turned his head away so no one could see the lone tear trickling down his cheek.

But Sparrow saw it and winced.

Chapter 15

As Annie and the crew settled into what she referred to as "our new digs," Hank Jellicoe stood in the inner sanctum of his employer, who was exploding in rage at what he perceived to be happening.

I really do despise this man. I should just put a bullet through his black heart right now, Jellicoe thought. He waited patiently for the tirade to be over before he spoke. He cringed at the way the spittle was flying and took a step backward. When the ugly, frog-like man finally ran out of steam, Jellicoe wanted to clap his hands.

"Mr. Spyder, I told you that putting those

bugs in the countess's house was a mistake. She has security that's just as good, perhaps better, than mine. And now they all know that someone was intent on spying on the countess. I tried to tell you the countess was not someone to mess with. She is no innocent and is as wise to the ways of the world as anyone you can find. Plus, she has wealth beyond most people's imagination. It truly pains me to tell you, Mr. Spyder, but you, your security, me, my security are no match for hers. I warned you about this, but you made the decision not to listen to me. Now those same people are going to put you under their microscope, since you are the only one on the island who could have bugged the countess's house. What do you think they're going to find when they do that, sir?"

Angus Spyder's ugly face turned brick red as he blustered, cursed, then kicked out at the wall. Spittle flew in all directions.

Jellicoe decided to stick the knife in a little farther and give it a twist to boot. "If you recall, you were uptight when you found out she was richer than you were. You hated that it was a woman in the bargain. Royalty, no less. I did warn you, Mr. Jellicoe, business, and it will be all over the world in about sixty seconds, thanks to social media. The world press will be here in a heartbeat. Helicopters will hover, and ships will dock. Think **invasion.** Do you want to go down that road?"

"I want results!" Spyder bellowed as he kicked out at the wall a second time.

Jellicoe simply wanted to kill him on the spot. He took a deep breath before saying, "Then let me do my job."

"Offer a million. I don't care what it takes. If you don't find my grandchildren by the end of the week, I am cutting you loose." Spittle once again flew in all directions. It was all Jellicoe could do not to pull his gun and plug the bastard right between his eyes.

"Don't threaten me, **Angus.**" He had never called his employer by his first name. Ever. "Just so I understand, if no one takes your million-dollar offer, then you are cutting me loose. That is what you just said, right?"

"I guess you aren't deaf, after all. Get out of my sight now and do what I told you to do. Find my grandchildren or the man who fathered them."

Jellicoe itched to pull his gun. It was all

when you had all your number cruncher
fired and new ones flown in. She is riche
than you. You have to accept that and g
on from there.

"And, to address your other problem, you
grandchildren . . . My people have done ev
erything humanly possible to find them. W
have nowhere else to turn. We've hit a dea
end. I did find out something I didn't knov
before. It seems there may well be som(
kind of underground railroad that is rul
by . . . no one knows who and that spirit:
women and children to safety. It's only a ru
mor. I want to stress that. With all you
resources and mine, as well, we drew
blank, even with the hundred-thousand
dollar reward we offered."

"Then offer five hundred thousand dol
lars. No one turns down that kind of money,'
Spyder snarled. "Just as a reminder, I owr
this goddamn island."

"Even if you offered a million dollars, it
wouldn't change things. You don't understand that you are dealing with mothers and
children. Right there, that is an unbeatable
force. Accept it. And whatever you may
think, the countess **owns** her property. You
sold it to her husband. You try any funny

he could do to stare the ugly little man down. He didn't bother to wait to be dismissed but turned on his heel and walked out of the man's presence.

Outside, he jammed his security cap more firmly on his head and made his way to his own house, where he powered up his computer. He then called the operative he'd sent to New Jersey to look for leads on the Domingos.

"Sam, it's Hank. Listen, things are going off the rails here. I want to give you a heads-up." Quickly and concisely, he repeated what had transpired with Angus Spyder.

The silence on the other end of the phone bothered Jellicoe. He prodded his operative. "Say something, Sam."

"What's to say, Hank? You want me to go to Washington on a wild-goose chase and promise a million dollars for information. Only a fool would do something like that. Look, man, I've had it with that ugly little dictator. I want out. I saved my money these past years, and so have some of the other guys. The shit is going to hit the fan with that guy. I can already smell the stink. Then we're all going to go down. We're all fugitives. We got that rating the minute we aligned ourselves with you. I'm not complaining. I'm just letting you know it's time to move on. Consider this my notice. See ya around, Hank."

Jellicoe sucked in a mouthful of air-conditioned air. He didn't know why he was surprised at Sam Whitaker's response. He knew he could hit REDIAL into the next millennium, and Sam would never respond. The phone he'd used was already a pile of charred debris. Sam was the best of the best, almost as good as he was. He'd go to ground in sixty seconds flat, never to be seen or heard from again. That was how good Sam Whitaker was. He knew Sam and the others had millions stashed in off-shore banks and safe houses all over the globe. That was the first thing he'd taught his men. In the beginning, they couldn't comprehend that the day might come when they had to have a safe harbor to sail into. But, eventually, they got it and prepared for the day that would happen—this day.

The big question now facing Jellicoe was whether Sam would light out on his own or alert his team. If that happened, he would be left holding the bag. "Son of a bitch!"

His computer booted up, Jellicoe tapped

the keys until a map of Spyder Island appeared. He ran his finger down an invisible line that divided the island into two parts: the northern end of the island, where the resorts were located and the common people lived, the part that Spyder leased to the local government; and the southern end, which, except for the parcels he had sold to other billionaires, belonged to Angus Spyder and had NO TRESPASSING signs warning intruders that they would be shot if they stepped over the invisible line. So far, to Jellicoe's knowledge, no one had been shot. Yet.

Jellicoe closed his laptop. Time to get on the move and form a plan that would work for him and the rest of his men. For all he knew, he might be a security force of one. With that thought in mind, he walked into the room where he slept, opened his footlocker, rummaged until he found his old frayed and faded New York Yankees baseball cap. Then he sent the Spyder cap sailing across the room. He settled the slightly musty-smelling Yankees cap firmly on his head and headed out. To do what, he had no clue.

While Jellicoe was contemplating his future or lack thereof, Countess de Silva and her guests were traipsing through the mansion, oohing and aahing over everything as they removed their disguises. They chattered among themselves as they prepared to settle in.

"First things first, people. Is the freezer up and running?" Annie asked.

"It is," Dennis said happily.

"Why are you all standing here? Get our arsenal ready. We need to be prepared," Annie shouted. Feet stampeding down the marble hallway could be heard throughout the twenty-thousand-square-foot mansion.

"We need some downtime right now, even if it's just an hour or so. Let's all get a nice cold drink and go out to that pretty lanai with all those beautiful flowers," Myra said.

"Count me out. I'm going to the gym I saw on the first floor. I have to work my leg. I've been sitting too long today. I'll catch up with all of you later," Kathryn said.

"Where's Snowden?" someone asked.

A voice from the hallway responded. "He's with his people in the apartment over the pool house. From there, he has a view of almost the whole island. With binoculars, they can see for miles. The boardwalk, the road, even the Spyder mansion. From there he can see half of what we all thought was an empty house, which we think is where Jellicoe hangs out. And if we're right, Charles and Fergus, too." The voice belonged to Maggie Spritzer.

"Do I have to keep wearing this tiara?" Annie groused.

A wild chorus of yeses rang in the air. Resigned to wearing the sparkling headgear, Annie stomped her way through the house, mumbling and muttering about roller skates and skateboards or a moving treadmill.

A scribbled note from Avery Snowden lay on the kitchen table. It said that all bushes, shrubbery, and flowers around the property had been scoured for bugs. It went on to say that even with maximum-strength binoculars, the foliage around the mansion was too dense for any kind of real visibility. They could talk all they wanted. The note was signed with a large AS at the bottom.

Myra poured from two pitchers, iced tea and lemonade.

"We need to decompress and hit the ground running first thing tomorrow," Nikki said as she gulped the tart lemonade. "Ooh, this is good. I bet Snowden made it from that lemon tree in the yard."

"This is so beautiful. So peaceful. Kind of what I imagine paradise looks like," Isabelle said as she plucked a colorful bloom and stuck it in her hair. "It's hard to believe this peaceful place is a black hellhole of misery."

"Are you going to keep this place or sell it after we leave, Annie?" Yoko asked.

"I'm going to burn it to the ground, but first I'm going to take a match to Spyder's place. I'm not going to look real close to see if he's in there, either."

The others hooted with laughter, because they knew Annie meant every word she'd just uttered.

And then there was even more noise when Avery Snowden and his six operatives appeared, along with Dennis and the cache of firearms. They all gasped at what was being laid out on the colorful tiles at their feet. They watched in awe as Snowden and his people dried the weapons, cleaned them. Then they loaded them.

"We're good to go. I have a report," Snowden said briskly.

"Let's hear it, Mr. Snowden," Myra said.

"Earlier today I counted nine security. Meaning real security under Jellicoe. I can tell the difference between his security and the rent-a-cops Spyder uses. A little over an hour ago, the launch was boarded by all nine men. There are four more, whom I haven't been able to see. Those four might work shifts and be asleep right now. Jellicoe was not on board. Ten minutes ago, I received an alert on my mobile. The launch blew up. I would assume that's the gray cloud of smoke we all saw. You might have missed it since you were busy settling in."

"What does that mean?" Ted asked. "I did see that puff of gray and black smoke."

"It means someone blew up the launch. It's at the bottom of the ocean. My guess is that no one is going to investigate it. My alert said it didn't look like there were any survivors. That's how that guy Spyder operates. Here today, gone tomorrow. No questions asked."

Annie bristled. "Well, we'll just see about that. Mr. Snowden, alert someone. There must be an equivalent to the Coast Guard or a similar organization somewhere close by. That's inhuman. Those nine people were human beings. Bring the wrath of God down on these people."

Snowden eyeballed Annie. He knew an order when he heard one. Annie never made suggestions. He hated to be given orders. But in this case, he would have done on his own what Annie just told him to do. He nodded. "We'll be in the apartment over the pool house. I have to scramble my communications, and I can't do it from here. You guys, find a couple of trunks and load all the hardware in them, and then have the ladies decorate the foyer so they don't look like arms-storage cabinets."

Five seconds later, Snowden and his people were gone on the gentle breeze wafting through the lanai. The bustling noise that ensued was the hunt for trunks to hold the guns and ammunition. While the men squabbled among themselves about size and depth, the girls argued about what to put on top of the trunks to make them pass for royalty decor.

The girls stopped what they were doing to watch Kathryn limp down the hall toward them, her wet tank top plastered to her chest, her face glistening with sweat. As one, they wanted to rush to her, but they didn't. They waited till she pressed herself against the wall.

"No pain, no gain," Kathryn told them. "It was harder today because I sat so long. I'm okay. I would tell you if I weren't. I'm going to get in the hot tub now. Carry on, ladies. By the way, if you hang a picture on that wall, it will be perfect. Just my two cents."

The Sisters went back to arguing. Maggie made the final decision when she sprinted off, then returned with a painting of a twenty-eight-year-old Annie sitting on a throne, wearing her tiara. She looked to be nine months pregnant.

"It's so . . . so . . . tacky!" the Sisters exclaimed in unison.

"Exactly." Maggie grinned. "Tacky it is, just the way those trunks in the foyer look tacky. All eyes will be on the painting. Get my drift?"

Nikki burst out laughing. Yoko clapped her on the back, and then they were all rolling on the floor, giggling and laughing.

Annie and Myra came on the run. Annie took one look at the painting and shrieked in horror. "Where in the world did you find that . . . that . . . thing?"

"In a walk-in closet on the second floor," Maggie chirped.

"Well, take it down right this minute!"

"Just a minute, Annie. I think the girls have a reason for hanging that painting where they did. I think we should hear them out, don't you?" Myra said.

Annie sniffed. "Make it good, girls." She sniffed again.

Maggie explained, then pointed to the old trunks with the tarnished hardware. "We need eyes on the painting. We really need it, Annie."

"Well, in that case, all right. I just won't look at it. My husband insisted I sit for that painting. I was so miserable that day, I wanted to die. I gave birth the following day. I don't want to talk about this anymore." She trotted off, Myra in her wake. They whispered among themselves as only two old friends did.

Life would go on no matter if the painting hung in the foyer or not.

Up on the boardwalk, Hank Jellicoe stopped at the little snack shop for a bottle of water. He carried it to the bench in the shade, the same bench Gretchen and Felicia had sat on earlier in the day to eat their ice-cream cones.

He could hardly swallow the water because of the lump in his throat. Nine good men at the bottom of the ocean. Nine good, loyal men. Maybe not so loyal, after all, if they'd taken Spyder's launch out into deep water without an order to do so. Sam had to have called them. In the end, maybe there was no such thing as loyalty. So now it was down to him, his four remaining men, and Spyder's goon squad.

Jellicoe's cell buzzed in his pocket. He made a snorting sound when he pulled it out. "Yes, sir. What do you need now?"

"Would a report be too much to ask for?" the voice on the other end of the line snarled.

"I called my man in New Jersey, and he quit on the spot. I would have fired him, anyway, for the unflattering, unprofessional things he said about you," Jellicoe gibed. "Regardless, he's gone, and we have no operatives in the area who can do what you want. Of course, you could send a few of your own men, but they'd stand out like manure in a daisy field, so you might want to think twice about that. As I told you, no one is going to rat out mothers and children, no matter how much money you're offering.

"I did get an alert on my mobile saying the launch blew up. It appears all aboard drowned. I cannot confirm that one way or the other. Is that the report you were expecting me to deliver, Mr. Spyder? If so, consider it delivered. I'll have a written report to you by the end of the day."

"So, once again, Mr. Jellicoe, you failed me."

Jellicoe clenched his teeth. With as much cheerfulness as he could muster, he forced the words out of his mouth. "It would appear so, **Angus.** It would appear so."

Jellicoe jogged his way back down the boardwalk and on to his house, where he sent out a call to his four remaining employees to join him there.

Life was now going to take a turn for the better. At least he hoped so.

Chapter 16

The Sisters gathered in the lanai were munching on toasted Pop-Tarts and drinking orange juice. The new day had barely erased the black, star-filled night when they'd gathered with coffee cups in hand.

"Myra and Annie are usually the first ones up at this hour," Isabelle said, peering through the sliding doors that led to the great room.

"The boys are no slouches, either. Are we the only ones with any stamina?" Nikki queried. "I don't even see Cyrus. Wonder what that means."

"It means everyone was exhausted. I

guess it also means we have more adrenaline than they do," Isabelle said.

"Hey, Izzy, how's it going with Abner?
Are you guys back to being a married couple, or are you just winging it?" Kathryn
asked.

A frown built itself on Isabelle's face.
"We're winging it. I have high hopes, but I've
had high hopes before that have been
dashed, so I'm being extra careful, and so
is Abner. If it is meant to be, then it will be.
For now, it works."

"Good attitude," Yoko said. "What's our
plan for today? Does anyone know?"

"We get made up again and hit the island. We're guests, so we can explore. Or
if you prefer the word **spy,** that works, too,"
Alexis said. "I have to get to work, so whoever is going out first is who I have to work
on. Just out of curiosity, how many sets of
eyes do you think will be on us?"

"Fifty or so would be my guess. I also
imagine there are cameras everywhere, up
in the trees, along the beach road, the
boardwalk. Always be aware and be careful," Nikki said.

"Did anyone check online to see what the
media is saying about the explosion yes-

terday?" Kathryn asked. "By the way, Bert said to tell you all hello, and he's sorry he can't be here. He did say that if there was a way to get here, he'd make it happen. He hates to be left out."

Out of nowhere, Cyrus appeared like a black streak as he headed for the sand to find a place to do his business. Jack followed him as he waved to the others. He gave Nikki a quick peck on the cheek. "I can't get used to you being a guy and me a girl." He guffawed. Nikki gave him a playful swat before she handed him a Pop-Tart. Jack snatched one for Cyrus, who was partial to blueberry.

One by one, the others appeared, grabbing at the Pop-Tarts and pouring coffee and juice. Jack returned with Cyrus at his side to announce that he'd seen six different security guards patrolling the empty beach. He went on to say that Snowden was eyeballing the guards from the apartment over the pool house.

Alexis dusted her hands and announced that she was ready to go to work. Harry and Yoko went first.

"I like your sundress, Jack," Sparrow quipped.

Jack offered up his middle finger but grinned. Nikki just giggled.

Sparrow went on. "Ooh, your skin looks satin-smooth, but don't you itch from where they shaved your chest?"

"We have fragrant lotion for that," Jack snapped.

Ted Robinson did his best to blend into the shrubbery so Sparrow would ignore him. It didn't happen. "You would not be on my ten best list of datable women, Ted."

"Yeah, yeah, yeah. I'm supposed to be frumpy. So there. You want fast and loosey-goosey, go for Espinosa. He . . . she might be more your style."

It was all in good fun, and no one took offense.

"These high heels are a killer, I have to say. Nikki said we can wear sandals. No one wears heels in the sand," Jack snapped again. Cyrus barked shrilly to back up his master.

"So," Sparrow said as he zeroed in on Kathryn. "What's on the agenda for you girls? I mean guys. Oh, hell, you know what I mean."

"We're taking out the Harleys. We're go-ing to buzz the island, the north end and the south end. We want to make some noise. Not to worry. We all know how to ride a Harley. It'll just be me, Nikki, and Isabelle on the first one, unless Annie and Myra want to come along. They're just as good on Harleys as we are, so don't worry. Harry and Yoko are otherwise occupied. Dennis is going to take them out on the special cycle Alexis ordered. The one with the two sidecars. There's no traffic on the beach road since no one is allowed on this side of the island. We can make our statement without interference."

"Works for me," Abner said. "Gotta go now. Work calls. Buzz me if you need me for anything."

"What about lunch?" Dennis asked.

"Since you asked, you can do it, young man. You should be back from your excursion by then. Something simple. Maybe shrimp scampi and a salad and lots of iced tea. Make enough, in case people want seconds. How does that sound?" Annie asked. The look of panic on Dennis's face made Annie burst out laughing. "I'm teasing. Peanut butter and jelly sandwiches will do nicely, along with the iced tea and perhaps lemonade. Do your best."

Dennis dithered and fretted for a few minutes, thinking he was off the hook, but something told him Annie **wanted** shrimp scampi. Like Sparrow, he did not want to disappoint her. Maybe he'd surprise her. He knew how to make shrimp scampi for two. How hard could it be to make it for fifty? **Damn hard,** was the answer he came up with. He beelined for the pantry, where the freezer they'd brought with them was installed. He opened it and poked around. With all the firearms and ammunition gone, there wasn't as much food as he thought there would be. Still, the freezer in the kitchen held other kinds of food. He heaved a mighty sigh when he saw six bags of jumbo shrimp.

Dennis leaned against the freezer and ran the recipe over and over in his mind. **Garlic, butter, wine. Make small batches.** Problem solved. Another mighty sigh escaped his lips when he heard his name being called.

Yoko and Harry stood in the doorway in their Mama-san and Papa-san makeup. "C'mon, kid. Let's get this show on the road," Harry said. "Fire up that machine and take us on a tour. We've got our cameras attached, and they'll video everything as we tool along. You up for this, kid?"

"Oh yeah, you bet. I even have a map of this part of the island. Just so you know, I have to be back in time to make lunch, so don't get too carried away." Then Dennis remembered to whom he was talking. "Uh, sorry, Harry. What I meant was—"

"We know what you meant, Dennis. Let's just do it, okay?"

Dennis gulped and ran out of the house and around to the covered area that contained the Harleys and his special machine. He looked it over, frowned, and went back in his memory to a ride-on toy he'd had as a child. This looked to be the adult version of that particular vehicle. It was bumblebee black and yellow and almost as wide as a Mack truck. The banana seat made him laugh out loud. Harry was going to be so embarrassed to ride in it. Yoko, too, he surmised. He himself itched to sit on the banana seat and hear the roar of the engine.

Dennis looked around to see if anyone was watching him. He didn't see anything with his eyes, but he felt like he was being watched. Trembling, he climbed on the seat, turned over the engine, and almost fell off at the roar that ensued. "Holy shit!" was all he could say over and over as he made his way to the front of the mansion, where Harry and Yoko were waiting for him. Next to them were Nikki and Kathryn in their guy regalia, who were there to help the two oldsters into the sidecars.

Kathryn dug down deep to come up with a gruff belly guy voice. She patted Yoko on the top of her head and said, "Be careful, little mama. You, too, Papa-san."

Dennis took off on her order, going from zero to forty miles an hour in a nanosecond. Full of himself now, Dennis played the tour guide. "What we have here on our left is the ocean. On the right is sand. Up above the dune is a boardwalk, where there is a little shack, much like any thatched hut selling soft drinks and ice cream back in the States. The trees are palm trees and are in full leaf, limb, frond, whatever. Oh, and there is a bench beside the shack, under a palm tree. That's it for this stretch."

Harry spoke to Yoko, his lips barely moving. She didn't respond other than to nod.

"I'm not seeing anyone, but I feel eyes on me," Dennis said. "I'm going to be making a turn to the right in a bit. Pay careful attention to the second house. It's the empty one. Two turns later on the left is the Spyder estate. I can stop to attend to your . . . ah . . . needs if you want. Just wave your arm, and I'll know you want me to stop. Don't talk. I'm doing all the talking. This is fun, isn't it?"

When there was no response from the two sidecars, Dennis clamped his lips tight, knowing how Harry hated conversing. He let his thoughts go to the shrimp scampi he would be preparing later. He knew there was wine, but was there butter and fresh garlic? Now he had something else to worry about.

"Slow down," Yoko singsonged. "Okay, that's good. Papa-san gets upset when you drive too fast."

Ooh, if there was one thing Dennis didn't want, it was for Harry to get upset. He eased up on the throttle and barely crawled along. He waved his left arm a lot to indicate the fine housing, the flowers, and the exquisite landscaping. So far, he hadn't seen a car, a truck, a dune buggy, a cycle of any kind. Nor had he spotted a real, live person. Nor were there any animals to be seen. **How weird.** Maybe these rich people preferred goldfish in tanks. Or piranhas in a pool somewhere on the property. He shivered at the thought.

The piranhas were too scary to think about, so Dennis went back to worrying about whether there was butter and fresh garlic for his luncheon dish.

While Dennis was contemplating butter and garlic, Angus Spyder was glued to the seven different closed-circuit television screens in his suite of offices. He eyed the weird-looking cycle and the two old Asians, who looked bored out of their mind. The driver of the weird-looking cycle looked like a punk kid with his gelled, spiky hair. All he did was wave his arms and point to whatever he wanted the old geezers to look at. He couldn't help but wonder how these two ancient creatures fitted into Countess de Silva's life.

He stretched one of his deformed arms to grab the passenger list of all the people who had arrived with the countess. He looked for Oriental names and jabbed his finger at the paper. **Haya and Jiro Miyoko.** He snorted. Then he tried to Google the names and came up with nothing. He then spent five full minutes trying to decide if the couple, who looked as old as God, were a possible threat. He decided they weren't; nor was the spiked-hair driver. Probably hangers-on. Rich people always had hangers-on.

Spyder went back to the television screens. Now he had a visual of three black men doing calisthenics on the beach, with a massive dog doing the same thing. They looked to be in top physical shape, better than some of his own security guards. Amazing that an animal could follow a human like that. Maybe it was a wolf.

Another screen showed the countess and her lush of a half sister with her flask at her lips at this early hour. It irritated Spyder that the woman was wearing a tiara on the beach. That told him she was classless. She might have half the money in the world, but if you didn't have class, you were just someone with money. He refused to see the irony of his thoughts.

He moved his gaze to a different monitor to see a bunch of women comparing the colors of their nail polish. **How vain.** How ugly they were. Well, that made sense to Spyder's warped brain. The countess wouldn't want beautiful women around her. She'd want to be the center of attention. These were just hangers-on, also. How sad that a woman such as herself had no true friends, just people she bought and paid for to do her bidding. Again, he utterly failed to see the irony.

Spyder moved away from the monitors. He didn't see anything that posed a threat to him and his well-being. All he saw was a classless old broad with money to burn with a drunken half sister and a gaggle of people draining her bank account.

Where the hell was Hank Jellicoe? He went back and clicked the monitors every which way until he was satisfied Jellicoe was nowhere to be seen. **Bastard.**

Spyder knew he had to do something about Hank Jellicoe. Jellicoe had failed him; it was that simple. Jellicoe knew he could not, would not, tolerate failure of any kind.

Long known for his lack of empathy, sympathy, or anything closely resembling either one, Spyder had acted immediately when he'd tuned into Jellicoe and Sam Whitaker's phone conversation yesterday. He'd lost Whitaker, but he'd nabbed nine of his cohorts. **Four down. Five, if you counted**

Jellicoe, to go. But then, where would he get a new security force? His own guards had nothing between their ears but brain matter, a fact that Jellicoe had pointed out on more than one occasion. They might be bulky and brawny, but they were only fair to poor with firearms, whereas Jellicoe's men were military trained, sharp, and intelligent, and they were expert marksmen to boot. He recognized that if it came to a showdown, Jellicoe's men would take it hands down. Now, with only five left, the odds were a little more even.

The little, frog-like man paced his offices. He was going to have to make a decision sooner rather than later about Jellicoe's two **guests.** For now, though, that could wait.

Something was off. He could feel it. Something he was missing. Or maybe it was something Jellicoe knew and hadn't seen fit to confide in him. Spyder went back to the monitors, which now had no people in them. Obviously, the countess and her people had gone indoors to prepare for the day. He looked down at the passenger list. He ran one stubby finger down the list. **Stephen Wolansky, FBI agent.** His heart kicked up a beat. Why hadn't he noticed that before? Why hadn't Jellicoe mentioned it?

He heard a sound then and ran to the door. He looked up to see if a jet was over-head or possibly a helicopter. The sound was coming from his left, from the estate in back of his own, the sound carrying on the wind. He realized it was the sound of motorcycles revving their engines. He went back to the monitors. He gawked in disbe-lief when he saw the countess, complete with tiara and gem-studded leathers, mount one of the Harleys like a pro. The lush sis-ter, jewel-crusted flask in hand, mounted the one next to the countess just as ex-pertly, followed by three strapping black men all done up in leather and helmets. They laughed as they gunned the cycles, which were peeling out one after the other.

"C'mon, chickee baby, show me what you got!" Annie shouted to Myra at the top of her lungs so as to be heard over the roar of the cycles. Myra showed her as she took a gulp from her flask.

Up ahead, the Sisters giggled, their thumbs shooting high in the air.

"Are we having fun, old girl?" Annie bel-lowed.

"Damn straight, we are," Myra said, tossing the flask to Annie, who caught it expertly. She gulped at the iced tea and flipped the flask back to Myra, who caught it just as expertly as Annie had.

The Sisters up ahead convulsed in laughter.

Angus Spyder was so enraged, he tried to put his webbed fist through one of the monitors. All he got for his efforts was pain. He howled; then he thumbed his cell phone to summon all his minions in the compound. Within minutes, his entire security force was standing in his office. Jellicoe was the last one to saunter in, a smirk on his face.

"Stop them right now! Do you hear me?"

"How?" one of his men asked.

"Shoot them!" Spyder snarled. "I don't care. They're making a mockery of my island. They're thumbing their noses at me. I own this goddamn island, and I have rules. I don't give a damn how rich that bitch is, this is **my** island. You're still standing here. Move!"

Spyder fastened his gaze on Hank Jellicoe. "You're taking this rather well. When I give an order, I want it obeyed."

"You might want to rethink that order. Don't you hear what I hear?"

"What? What?" Spyder shouted as he ran to the door and looked upward. "Son of a bitch! Are you telling me that's the goddamn media with helicopters, spying on me and my island?"

"Actually, **Angus,** I think you're completely secondary. They're actually spying on the countess. She is news, you know. They don't give a good rat's fart about you. She's news. I'd rescind that order to shoot if I were you."

"You son of a bitch!"

"Among other things." Jellicoe grinned. "You never take my advice, but I'm going to offer it, anyway. Tell your goon squad to play nice and be a welcoming committee. You get more flies with honey than vinegar. Didn't your mother ever tell you that? Oops, that's right. You didn't have a mother, did you? You were hatched from some frog in some slimy pond."

"How dare you speak to me like that, you . . . you . . . criminal?"

Jellicoe laughed as he turned around and left the little man screaming like a banshee.

Outside in the brilliant sunshine, Jellicoe

sobered. He had to get out of here. Now more so than ever. Like Spyder, he knew that something was off, something was wrong. He could feel it in every bone in his body.

So much to do, so little time.

Well, he did have one ace in the hole. Maybe it was time to play it out.

Chapter 17

Jack, Ted, and Espinosa made their way to the lavish apartment over the pool house, knowing that many sets of eyes were on their backs. The possibility of hidden listening devices kept their chatter low and meaningless. Indoors, where they knew it was safe, they let loose.

"What's the game plan, Snowden? What do you have?" Jack demanded.

Always at odds with Jack, Snowden looked up from the computer he was watching. While he didn't like Jack, he was smart enough to respect his abilities. In the end, the only thing that mattered was the mission and the outcome.

"Well, unlike you three, who seem only to be concerned with the shade of your nail polish, we, as in I and my operatives, think, I say think, that Charles and Fergus are in Jellicoe's house. One of those helicopters you just heard dropped a heat-sensor gizmo on top of the roof. It's too complicated to explain. We immediately picked up on two heat sources, and we know for a fact that a man—can't tell for sure yet if it's Jellicoe or not—left the house earlier and hasn't returned. Uh-oh, he's returning now." Snowden waved his arm and pointed to the monitor while he raced to the window and pulled his binoculars up to his eyes.

"That guy is a pro for sure. Ball cap pulled low. Says NEW YORK YANKEES. It's old, worn. Same build, same strut. He's aware at all times of where he is and what's around him. That's the mark of a pro. He was one of the best back in the day. Can't get a full-face shot of him. It's like the bastard knows we're here. Even a side shot is not telling me anything. I ran our facial recognition software nine ways to Sunday, and we can't get a lock." Snowden looked at

Jack, a fierce look in his eyes. "I have an idea, but it could be dangerous. You want to hear it or not?"

Ted looked nervous; Espinosa, downright worried.

"Spit it out, Snowden," Jack said. "We aren't here to play games. The sooner we do what we have to do, the sooner we can get out of these outfits. I hate this cherry chiffon nail polish. If God wanted me to have cherry chiffon toenail polish, I would have been born that way."

"I hear you, Emery. Here's the thought. When the girls/guys, Myra, and Annie get back from their reconnaissance, I want you to agitate for a ride. Take the tour to what we think is Jellicoe's house, get off, march up to the door, and knock. I want you to invite him to a barbecue at Annie's. You'll just be three nutty, cuckoo women on vacation. At the same time, if Charles and Fergus are being held there, they might somehow be able to tip you off. You'll have to be on alert, because I want you to go when Jellicoe is not there. Be aware of security and wear those floppy straw hats. Be playful, kittenish. You know how to do that, right? Think your sophomore year in school and the way the girls acted back then. Coy. Yeah, yeah, **coy.** That's a better word."

Espinosa surprised everyone by saying, "I know how to do that."

"Well, damn," was all Jack could think of to say.

Ted just looked at his polished nails and didn't say a word.

"It might not be a bad idea to take that Albright guy and Sparrow with you. Happy, happy vacationers where there are no rules and your host is Countess de Silva. I'm thinking it will work. What do you think, Jack?"

Jack was stunned that Snowden was asking for his advice, but he didn't show it. "It's far enough out of the box that it just might work. Maybe we should also stop by Spyder's house to pay our respects and invite him to the barbecue. What's the worst thing that could happen? Nothing," Jack said, answering his own question. "As long as you get those helicopters up in the air and let them hover while we're doing our thing. If none of it works, we go to Plan B."

"And what is Plan B?" Snowden asked.

"I'll let you know when I figure it out. Call everyone back to home base now. We'll get

Sparrow and Albright clued in. Yeah, yeah, I'm liking this. What about you guys?" Jack asked, directing his question to Ted and Espinosa.

"Doable," the two **Post** employees chorused in unison.

"Just out of curiosity, Snowden, what are you and your people going to be doing?" Jack asked.

"I'm going to show some muscle. I'm going to patrol the beach with my people, but only on the side that affects Annie. Securing her perimeter is what we call it. We have AK-47s and a couple of Uzis. Spyder's guys have nothing like that kind of firepower. We're just flexing our muscles. We won't be doing it until the helicopters are overhead, and speaking of heavy-duty machinery, I think I hear a bunch of Harleys approaching."

"We're outta here," Jack said, leading the way out of the room and down the stairs to the lower level of the pool house. "Everyone, take a deep breath and start to giggle. Act like silly women."

"I wouldn't let those women out there hear you refer to them as silly," Espinosa said as he fiddled with a shoulder-length silver earring that was making his neck itch.

"I didn't mean **them.** I meant other women," Jack said defensively.

"Yeah, well, I don't think **them** as in **they** would believe you. I am in character. Gee whiz, I just love this turquoise bracelet. Don't you girls just love my turquoise bracelet? And my toe ring, it matches perfectly and sets off my new nail polish, which, by the way, is called Scarlet Blush," Espinosa trilled.

"Ooh, you are so funny, Joe. Watch me kick the shit out of you in another minute," Ted said.

Fortunately for Espinosa, Ted's words were drowned out by the sound of the Harleys. The **girls** tripped forward and fluttered their hands, making motions that they wanted to go for a ride. Already warned by Snowden, Annie motioned to her Harley, and Jack hopped on.

"We need to wait for Sparrow and that Albright guy," he said. "You know the drill, right?"

"I do. Isn't this exciting, Jack? Myra is having the time of her life, but she won't admit it."

Jack risked a glance at Myra. He thought she looked a little green around the gills, but he had enough self-control not to say anything. He watched as she gulped from the flask. The fake jewels sparkled on the flask, creating miniature rainbows. She looked over at him and grinned from ear to ear.

"We are having fun, believe it or not," Myra said. She lowered her voice and added, "When we were whizzing by . . . **that house,** I got the strangest feeling. It was all I could do to keep going. I wanted to drive right up to the door. Woman's intuition, something you probably don't understand."

"Oh, I understand. Nik makes sure of that. I would never discount what you just said. We're on it!" Jack replied.

Myra winked at Jack, who just laughed out loud.

Annie gave her tiara a quick tug. Satisfied that it would remain secure in the ocean breeze, she bellowed, "Saddle up, ladies and gentlemen. We're going for a ride on the wild side!"

Dennis just missed the cavalcade by a hair as he roared onto the drive on Annie's property. "Wow, did you see that! Something must have gone down. I know you don't want me to help you, but we have to stay in character, and that means **I have to help you.** Remember, you are the ancient ones. Play nice, Harry. Let me take your arm. Just play the game so I can go inside and start to cook."

Harry was as docile as a lamb as he allowed Dennis to help him first, then Yoko. They shuffled and teetered to the house, Dennis a hair away to help should they stumble and fall. They finally made it indoors, where Dennis fled to the kitchen, and Harry and Yoko made their way to the lanai, where they ripped off their disguises.

"They're here on the island, aren't they, Harry? Did you feel what I felt when we went by the house? I **felt** it, Harry, and it was not my imagination, either," Yoko whispered.

Harry held up his hand for silence. Then he went into the house and returned with two glasses of lemonade. He handed one to his wife and watched her drink. Then he sampled his own. He felt like sand was clogging his windpipe. "Yes, I felt the same thing you did, and five bucks will get you ten that Myra and Annie felt exactly what we did.

Because they are so tuned in to Charles and Fergus. We felt it because we practice Zen. End of story."

"You are so wise, my charming husband. Whatever would I do without you?" Yoko teased.

Harry trembled. This little bit of a woman could bring him to his knees with just a look. Not that he would ever admit it. But Jack knew, and it was their secret. He smiled because he wasn't seeing the look that told him Yoko was being insincere. Suddenly, the sun seemed brighter and warmer, the scent of the flowers more pungent, and the lemonade suddenly sweeter. And all because his wife was sincere. How happy he was.

"Do you think anything will go wrong?" Yoko asked. "I wish we were there. What if we're needed, and they get into trouble with the island security?"

"We can't go. We have to stick to the plan. Jack's on it, and so is Avery Snowden. Don't worry. Maybe we should offer to help Dennis. He looked a little frazzled."

"That is **not** a good idea. No cook or chef wants a second person in the kitchen. That boy is very resourceful, as we've come to find out. Let's just sit here and talk about our trip to see Lily in the fall. I wonder how Cooper is doing."

Harry slapped at his forehead. "I forgot to tell you in all the excitement of coming here. Julie Wyatt sent me a text. Her daughter gave birth to an eight-pound, six-ounce baby girl right on Cooper's schedule, and they are calling her Hope. She said Cooper woke her up at three thirty in the morning and urged her to get dressed, then ran to the door. She said they drove straight to the hospital because she got a call just as they were getting into the car. Cooper knew. That dog is . . . magical, ethereal, something. Anyway, Julie said he took all his gear and set up shop in baby Hope's room. Guards her night and day."

Yoko smiled. "Just the way he did with Lily. Let's talk about something else, Harry, so I don't start to cry."

Harry sucked in a deep breath. "Sure. Do you think the girl Gretchen and Albright have a chance at a life together?"

"I do. But first we have to take out that father of hers. Once he's out of the picture, I see no reason why they can't have a life together and raise a family."

"But what about the twins Gretchen gave up for adoption?" Harry asked fretfully.

"The twins belong to the Domingos now. If Gretchen and Greg are lucky, they might be allowed to be a part of their life, but only if the Domingos say so."

"So Greg will forgive her for not telling him and giving them up?"

"If he loves her, he will. I have to believe she was protecting him the only way she knew how. She was so young, Harry. They both were. Because they are young, they can have more children. If, and this is a big if, she gets the operation they were talking about. A lot of ifs, Harry. A lot to overcome. But you know what they say. If there's a will, there's a way."

"I wish we could take a walk on the beach," Harry said.

"We can, Harry, if you want to put on all that stuff again. Old people shuffle, as you know. I'm game if you are. But we need those big straw hats, and we go barefoot, okay?"

Harry raced into the house and returned with what he called the mess. They helped each other until they were satisfied that they looked the way they had earlier, with the addition of the floppy straw hats.

"Want to hold hands, Harry?"

Harry grabbed for his wife's hand. "If people see us, they'll think we're holding on to each other to stay erect."

Yoko laughed, the tinkling sound that turned one Harry Wong into pure jelly.

Charles Martin looked across the chess table at Fergus Duffy at the first sound of boots on the staircase. He said nothing. He didn't need to; his eyes said it all.

The two men were prisoners of Hank Jellicoe, although Hank Jellicoe referred to both Fergus and Charles as his personal guests. He was quick to point out the lavish rooms, the custom-made furniture, the wonderful, plentiful food and premium liquor he provided. The library was stocked with the latest books, magazines, and newspapers. The satellite television allowed for the latest shows, movies, and news. He allowed outside walks on the beach, plus pool and ocean swims. What he didn't allow were phones or any outside access to the world both men had once known. Even so, they were both prisoners, unable to leave the island. He paid both men a weekly visit, usually on a Sunday, when he chitchatted about what was or wasn't happening on Spyder Island, which was usually nothing, so the chitchat was minimal. Today was not Sunday.

Jellicoe opened the door. There was no point in locking it, because there was nowhere for either man to go. Cameras were everywhere, with sound. Both men turned at Jellicoe's entrance. They waited, neither man speaking.

"There are guests on the island. I'm afraid I'm going to have to ask you to stay indoors until they leave."

Charles smiled. "Dare I ask if it's the president, the queen, or the pope?"

Jellicoe forced a laugh he didn't feel. He eyed the two men, weighing how much to say, if anything. He admired both Duffy and Martin for their honesty and their integrity, the same two traits he himself had had a lifetime ago. Charles Martin had once been a dear, close friend, but that was another lifetime ago, also.

"Someone a lot more interesting. Countess de Silva. I believe you know her, don't you, Charles?"

Charles could feel his heart thunder in his chest. "I met her twice. She was a school friend of my wife when they were children. Quite rich, I believe."

Jellicoe fixed his gaze on Fergus. "And did you not have a rather long-standing affair with the countess, Mr. Duffy?"

"A gentleman never kisses and tells, Mr. Jellicoe. Believe what you want. And why do you care?"

"Because she's here with a retinue of people. My employer does not appreciate it. He does own this island, as you well know."

"And this means what to us?" Charles asked. "If your employer doesn't want her here, why doesn't he tell her to leave?"

"See, here's the thing," Jellicoe said, straddling one of the chairs at the chess table. "The countess owns the house. The count, her deceased husband, purchased the house many years ago, and at his passing the property passed to her. According to my employer, she has been here only twice in over twenty-five years. He wants to know why she's here all of a sudden with all those people."

Charles burst out laughing, as did Fergus. "And you think we know the answer! How ridiculous for you to have such thoughts. In case you've forgotten, we've been your prisoners for close to eighteen months. How could we possibly know anything about her and what she's doing?"

"Guests, Charles. I thought you might have some insight on the matter. Matters could become dangerous for them. Mr. Spyder is most unhappy."

"Tell that to someone who cares. I don't. And I don't think Fergus cares, either. Do you, Fergus?"

"Not a bit. But we are curious, I have to admit. Who are those men patrolling the beach with all that firepower? And what was that explosion we heard yesterday, or is that a secret?"

"The men on the beach belong to the countess. They're her security detail. It appears she never goes anywhere without them, which is understandable since she is the second richest woman in the world. Her wealth far exceeds that of my employer, much to his chagrin. The helicopters overhead are the media. The countess arrived yesterday with about twenty people. Give or take a few. Two Gulfstreams landed yesterday, followed by two C-130 cargo planes. That raised a red flag for my employer.

They brought a fleet of Range Rovers and six or seven Harley-Davidson motorcycles. All that for a simple visit to an out-of-the-way island no one ever heard of. Oh, and let's not forget that Little Bird. Back in the day, when all I needed to do to get something was make a phone call . . . I couldn't have gotten a Little Bird. The lady has some juice to pull that off, I can tell you that. A goddamn Little Bird!"

"And we should care about this . . . why?" Charles asked. His heart was beating so fast inside his chest, he thought he would black out. One quick look at Fergus told him he, too, was having a hard time holding it together.

"You still didn't tell us what the explosion was," Fergus said.

"My employer killed nine of my detail"— Jellicoe snapped his fingers—"just like that."

"So that means your . . . um . . . detail is down by nine men. Is that what you're saying?" Charles asked.

"Ten. One of my men in New York bailed on me because of the outrageous demands my employer was making on us. I have four left. Well, I have one other, but he's useless, so, yes, six in all. Mr. Spyder's elite goon squad numbers twenty. Do you see my dilemma here?"

Charles tossed his hands in the air. "Why are you telling us this? What do you want us to do? As you pointed out on many occasions over the past year and a half, we are over the hill."

Jellicoe got up and looked down at the two sitting men. "I'm sorry I interrupted your game, gentlemen. Remember, you are not to leave the house. My men have orders to shoot if you do."

"Point taken, Mr. Jellicoe," Charles said as he turned to stare down at the chessboard in front of him. When the door closed behind Jellicoe, Charles turned to Fergus. "Lord love a duck, mate. What the bloody hell was that all about?"

Fergus laughed.

Off in the distance, both men heard a thunderous roar. They looked at each other and laughed hard and long as they forgot about their game and raced to the French doors that led out onto a wide veranda. They watched as cycle after cycle roared into the compound. Their arms pumped high in the air when they spotted the spar- kling tiara on Annie's head.

"I love that woman," Fergus said between clenched teeth.

"Then you should have told her that in- stead of hightailing it back to Scotland," Charles said.

"I was afraid she'd say no if I asked her to marry me. I'm just a working sod. Got nothing to offer the likes of her. By the way, I gave away all my winnings. I did tell you that, didn't I?"

"You sold her short, Fergus."

"I know, and for that I will be sorry for the rest of my days."

Chapter 18

The driveway leading to Hank Jellicoe's house took on a life of its own as Myra and the gang roared up to the front entrance. Off in the distance, on the beach, Angus Spyder's security likened the cavalcade to the annual Myrtle Beach Bike Week back in the States. They took off on the run, slogging through the thick sand.

No one made a move to get off their respective Harley. They just sat, balancing the cycles as they revved their engines. Annie was the first to dismount. She patted down her star-studded leathers, settled her tiara more firmly on her head, and marched up to the front door. She leaned on the bell as she looked around. For one wild moment, she forgot everything but the thought that Fergus and Charles were inside and there was nothing she could do about it. She had to get back into character and fast. She risked a glance behind her before she gave the doorbell another jab. Her crew offered a thumbs-up, and then she saw Nikki point to the stampede from the beach.

Annie whirled around just in time to see a bald-headed, tatted-up thug in a muscle shirt approaching Myra. It was hard to ignore the rifle slung over his shoulder. "Do you live here?" Annie trilled as she watched Myra take a slug from her flask. The rubies on the cap sparkled in the bright sunshine.

"No, ma'am. The owner isn't home right now."

"That would be, 'No, Countess. The owner isn't home right now.' I am not a ma'am, as you can see." The girls revved their cycles to make Annie's point.

"Huh?"

Annie rolled her eyes. "Never mind. Who lives here?"

Baldy looked over at his colleagues, debating if he should give up the information.

After a nod from an equally tatted-up guard, he snapped, "Chuck Diamond. He heads up Mr. Spyder's security."

"Well, we just stopped by to invite him, and all of you," Annie said, waving her arms, "to a barbecue this evening at seven. Will you kindly extend the invitation?" Annie was thoroughly enjoying the role she was playing. "Normally," she said in a haughty tone, "I send out personal engraved invitations, but since this is a casual affair, it really isn't necessary. Plus, I extended myself by coming in person. I never do that. My press secretary does all that." Annie stifled a laugh. She'd lost him at asking him to extend the invitation.

"But it is casual attire," she repeated. "Tell everyone, please. Now, if you'll excuse me, we have to be on our way over to Mr. Spyder's home so I can personally invite him and his family to join us. I do promise a fun-filled evening. I so love jocularity when it comes to a party. I do hope you all like country and western. We're featuring Willie Nelson tonight."

"Huh?"

The girls/guys stomped down on the pedals and waited for Annie to peel out, which she did with a roar. Myra twirled her scarf in the air with one hand and bellowed, "Let's rumble, boys!"

Myra deftly maneuvered her Harley until she was abreast of Annie. "Oh, Annie, I am having so much fun. Thank you. They are in there. I could feel it. Did you?"

"I did. Stick with me, kid. The best is yet to come," Annie said out of the corner of her mouth. "Did ya get it, Myra? My best Humphrey Bogart impersonation."

Myra giggled. "I did, but I don't think anyone else would. That dates us, Annie."

Annie held her arm out to indicate she was going to slow down and make a turn. The others followed suit.

"The property is posted," Kathryn yelled. "No trespassing!"

"That certainly does not apply to me," Annie shot back. "I'm here to extend an invitation to a party. Just stay on my six and follow my lead."

Nikki took that moment to shout to the others, "Look up! Four media helicopters. Everyone, look pretty now!"

Kathryn and Isabelle waved wildly, while Alexis blew kisses in the air.

Kathryn screamed into the air, "Get our

good sides. We want to look chiseled. I'm
so glad I shaved this morning."

"I am just love, love, loving this," Myra
chortled as she took another swig from her
flask, which was almost empty by then.

Inside the Spyder mansion, Angus Spyder was apoplectic as he watched six of his
men spread out across the shale driveway.
Where in the hell was that goddamn Jellicoe? He looked to the doorway and saw his
wife and daughter. "Do something!" he
screamed.

"What would you have me do, Angus?"
Felicia said in a soft, gentle voice. "I'm sorry,
but I can't help you. You created this mess.
Now, clean it up yourself."

"Whatever you want done, do it yourself,"
Gretchen said, echoing her mother's advice
before she turned her chair around and
sped down the hall to an outside door that
would give her a full view of what was going on in the driveway. Her mother joined
her.

"I don't know what this means, but I know
it means something," Felicia whispered.
"This looks like a standoff to me. And it also
looks like those helicopters are here to stay

or will be here as long as the countess is out there. "She's lovely, isn't she?"

"I never saw a real, live countess before. Look at that tiara! It's gorgeous."

"Shhh, Gretchen. We need to listen. Oh, I so wish I could read lips. With the noise from the helicopters and the motorcycles, I can't hear a thing."

"Where's Hank?" Gretchen asked.

"I was wondering the same thing. I suspect there is something going on between Angus and Hank. I don't think I've ever seen Angus in such a rage before," Felicia said as calmly as if she were reporting on the weather. "I wouldn't be at all surprised if he has a stroke."

"Mother, we could not get that lucky. Besides, I don't think frogs have strokes, at least not fatal ones, the only kind that would do us any good."

In spite of herself, Felicia laughed out loud. She sobered almost immediately. "Do you know the first thing I'm going to do if we're ever set free?"

Gretchen looked up at her mother. "What?"

"I'm going to sell off all my jewelry and buy a ticket back to Russia, to see if I can

find my family. The family Angus promised to take care of. He has said all these
years that he kept his promise. I don't
know if I believe it or not. I don't even know
if they are alive or dead. What will you do,
dear?"

"Get my operation, then see if I can
find . . . someone very dear to me."

Felicia reached for her daughter's hand
and squeezed it.

Back in the driveway, the girls/guys were
still waving and blowing kisses to the occupants of the helicopters. Myra was gur-
gling from her flask, and Annie was being
haughty and arrogant as she once again
extended her invitation to her evening barbecue.

The line of security didn't budge, but they
did flex their muscles, until Annie whipped
out her gun from the small of her back. In
the blink of an eye she fired off six shots,
nipping the toe of each man's boot. Then
she brought the gun up and aimed for center mass of the man in the middle. "Well,
see if I ever invite any of you again," she
sniffed. "You can tell Mr. Spyder he isn't fit
to shine my boots." She looked up at the
helicopters, waved her gun for effect, and

laughed out loud, but not before she gave her tiara a good tug.

"I think we're ready to rumble again, Myra. Let's put some juice in our takeoff this time." In the blink of an eye, Annie straddled the Harley, revved the engine longer than necessary, and peeled away, the others right on her tail.

The six guards spread across the driveway looked at one another. "Man, we are so deep in shit, we might as well quit now. What in the damn hell was that all about?" the bald, tatted guard said.

"An invitation to a barbecue is what I got out of it," one of the guards said as he looked down at his boots. "The lady—excuse me, the countess—has a mighty fine eye, if you want my opinion. She looks like she was born on that beast she was driving, and she's one hell of a gunslinger."

Six cell phones pinged to life. The helicopters were still hovering, the **whump, whump** sound deafening.

The guards trotted off, the helicopters having left to follow the countess and her crew. The beach was now patrolled only by Avery Snowden and his operatives.

Off to the right, Felicia pushed her daughter's chair down the walkway and up to the boardwalk. "I think this calls for an ice-cream cone, don't you, dear?"

"Peach this time." Gretchen laughed.

"Oh, darling, this is the first time I've heard you laugh since you returned to the island."

Gretchen laughed again, a sound of pure joy, as she held up her hand for her mother to take in hers.

Back at the de Silva compound, as the women called it, they parked the Harleys and ran into the house to be met by the rest of the gang. They reported breathlessly on what had happened. Questions were asked and answered, and a lot of high fives, along with some backslapping, ensued.

"Now what?" Sparrow asked.

"Now we wait. The next move is Spyder's," Myra said as she fluffed out her wig, then decided that since she was indoors, she didn't need it. She tossed it onto a chair.

"What's that I smell?" shouted Kathryn, their food critic.

Annie made a face. "Peanut butter and jelly sandwiches."

"Nope! Shrimp scampi!" Dennis bellowed from the kitchen. "Come and get it!"

They did, and they ate till they couldn't eat any more. Dennis beamed his pleasure at all the accolades coming his way.

"We're having a barbecue this evening. We might or might not have a few guests," Annie said cheerfully. "If no one shows up, oh, well, more for us. Now, who is going to be doing the barbecuing?"

Ted, Espinosa, Sparrow, and Greg Albright volunteered.

"Then you better check the freezer and take out what you need now," Annie suggested.

"Let's hit the lanai," Jack said as he reached out to grab a pitcher of iced tea. Harry reached for a second one, and Yoko carried the plastic glasses. "We all need to talk now."

Angus Spyder, his face cherry red, stared down his men. Spittle and drool dripped from his lips and down his shirt because he didn't have a neck for it to roll onto. He cursed, using every vile, ugly word in his extensive vocabulary of vile and ugly words. Then he said it all over again in every language he knew. Jellicoe entered the room on the tail end of the tirade.

"All they were doing was inviting you and the guards to a barbecue. I have to admit, their approach was a little over the top, but you need to remember who you are dealing with. People like the countess thrive on publicity. You, Angus, can't afford any publicity. Be prepared to be looked at, scrutinized, and crucified. Your reputation is nowhere near what the countess's is. Now the media has it all on film. You couldn't leave it alone, could you, Angus? I warned you, and now what are you going to do?"

The little frog-like man hopped from one place to the other, still screaming the vile curses, which everyone was trying to tune out. "I don't know what I'm going to do. Yet. Is that what you want me to say? Well, I said it. This is not about some goddamn barbecue, and we both know it. Something is going on. I damn well want to know what it is."

"Then go to the goddamn barbecue and find out what it is," Jellicoe said quietly. "Just out of curiosity, what do **you** think this is all about?"

"I'll tell you what I think, you son of a bitch. It's about my daughter and the twins that she gave up for adoption. My heirs. My heirs, whom you swore you would find and bring to me. You failed. You bastard, you failed me! I do not tolerate failure. I told you that when I agreed to allow you to come to the island. And the other thing is those two men you have locked up at your house. Scotland Yard, MI6. Even if they're retired, they have more inside their heads than you will ever have. Somehow, someway, they got word out. If you think for one minute that gun-toting, tiara-sporting, motorcycle-riding countess came here by chance, you are a bigger fool than I thought. This is all a setup to take me down. I want them off my island. Right now. **Now!**" Spyder screamed, spraying everyone with his spittle.

Jellicoe sighed as he watched Spyder's men inch their way toward the door. "Well, Angus, short of shooting the countess and all her people, I don't see how that's going to happen. We do not have AK-47s and Uzis in our arsenal. Your men are piss-poor shots, and that countess can shoot better than I can. Thanks to you, I'm down ten men. As for your heirs, that's never going to happen. So you might as well give up on that pipe dream right now. That's another way of saying that you lost. If you want some advice, I'd be happy to offer some up. For free."

Spyder cast his evil, hooded eyes on his security head and waited. He gave a slight dip of his head to indicate that Jellicoe should continue.

"Leave," was the one-word piece of advice Jellicoe offered up, which was met with disdain. "And that's exactly what I'm going to do right now. When you're ready to talk sense, call me. Oh, one other thing, I quit!" Jellicoe stalked out of the room. Out of the corner of his eye he saw that Felicia and Gretchen Spyder were in the hallway, probably listening to everything that had been said. He decided that was a **good** thing and pretended not to see them.

Angus Spyder looked around and, for the first time, realized he was alone. But then, he was always alone, at least in his mind. Not that he would ever subject himself to a roomful of people. He would never do that, because of his appearance. Here in his hideaway, with only servants and guards, it didn't matter.

Drenched in sweat, Spyder could smell his own stink. He hated the smell. It reminded him of scummy pond water rife with green algae, where frogs were hatched and bred.

He made his way to his luxurious bathroom, which was bigger than some people's entire home in terms of square footage. The room was done in all-natural earth stones, with luxurious velvet green moss growing between the stones. A trickle of water sliding down the stones was a soothing sound to luxuriate in when bathing. The only problem was that no one ever bathed in the deep tub with the gold faucets. Angus preferred the massive shower, which was almost as good as walking through a rain forest, with its 127 jets pummeling his shrunken body.

Angus never looked at his body, so there were no mirrors in the huge bathroom, only art hanging on the walls. He didn't need to look into a mirror to shave, since he was basically hairless. And he used an electric razor when he did shave.

A wide shelf above the sink held every exfoliating cream on the market, creams that he used three times a day because he felt the need to shower that much in case scales of some sort started to form on his swarthy skin. Sometimes he rubbed himself raw, but he didn't care.

Before he stepped into the shower, he pressed a button that flooded the room with soft, mellow music. He was partial to Frank Sinatra and Dean Martin. As he listened to his favorite tunes, Angus wondered what it would be like to dance with a woman to the music on a moonlit night. Dreams and fantasies.

When Angus got tired of dreaming about dancing and the soft, mellow music, he recalled his life and how he'd gotten to this point in time. He thought about all the people he'd ruined, stepped on, killed, plowed under to garner the wealth that sat in many banks around the world. The one thing he was most proud of was the slick deal he'd pulled off in England, right under the queen's nose, with her new age city. He actually laughed out loud, choking and sputtering when the spray of water went into his nose and mouth. When it was finally finished by the end of the year, he would make billions and billions of dollars. So much for the queen and her MI6 and MI5, Sir Charles Martin and his buddy from Scotland Yard, Fergus Duffy. Over-the-hill action players. He laughed again, but this time he closed his mouth.

Angus no longer knew what his potential worth would be at the end of the year, when the new age city took off. And what was he going to do with all that money? How much was enough? There was nothing left to buy or acquire that he didn't already have. That was when he'd set his sights on acquiring his illegitimate grandchildren. He'd make them kings. Or at least that was the plan. He realized for now that he was going to have to shelve that plan and wait. Sooner or later, they would surface. Or he'd force it out of his slutty daughter. She'd give it all up if he threatened to kill her mother. Or would she? He should have done that months ago. If he had, he wouldn't be in this predicament right now. But, no, he'd listened to Hank Jellicoe, and look where it had gotten him. Nowhere. And now he had a crazy countess on his island, and he was willing to bet that she and her entourage were here for Gretchen.

His thoughts stayed in the past. He had done **one good** thing: he'd kept a promise he'd made to his wife. He'd made sure Felicia's family was taken care of, not lavishly, but taken care of. He continued to do it to this day, and he would never welsh on that promise. Never. Try as he would, he could not come up with any idea for why he did it. One good thing. That had to count for something.

Fall back and regroup. First things first. A trip to Jellicoe's house to pay a visit to the two guests.

Chapter 19

Hank Jellicoe walked along aimlessly, trying to get rid of his anger. He was surprised to see where he was when he looked up. Angus Spyder's personal security hut, the building out of which his men worked. He was stunned to see the gaggle of men lugging backpacks and gear out of the building. He frowned. He turned when he heard his name being called. Don Finley, a man his age who was the head of Angus Spyder's personal security, the only man on the team worth a good spit. To his eye, Don Finley looked happier than a pig in a mud slide.

"Hank! How's it going? You here to wish me bon voyage? No offense, man, but I can't get used to calling you Chuck Diamond."

Jellicoe ignored the reference to his bogus ID. "What are you talking about?" he asked. "Where is he sending you now?"

"Rotation. We're leaving. New guys coming on board. You know how it works. I have a few minutes. C'mon, let's take a walk, just two guys. What do you say?"

"Sure. Why not? When was this decided, Don?"

"Last week. Two weeks ahead of schedule, too. I was surprised, but, hey, it works for me. It's fine with us. I can't wait to get off this damn island. Ten years is way too long to stay in one place, rotation or not. I don't know how you stand it. And just between us professionals, I'm not planning on coming back, but keep that to yourself. I made my money. So have the others. Look, man, I had nothing to do with blowing up that launch with your guys on it. I swear to good Christ none of us know who did it. Hell, that crazy bastard might even have done it himself. Regardless, that was our wakeup call."

Jellicoe listened to the words. He had no beef with Finley. If he said he didn't do it, then he didn't do it. It was that simple. Hell, he actually liked the guy. "You plan on swimming? Or are you taking the same boat the rotating crew comes in on? Take some advice. Swim."

"I'm not that crazy. That's what Spyder thinks we're going to do, but we're leaving from the northern end of the island. Got a flight chartered, and we're wheels up in two hours. I'm 99 percent sure we'll get off. Aw, you worried about me, Hank?" The big man grinned.

"Yeah, actually I am. Where is this new crew from?"

Finley shook his head. "Not sure. Miami, I think. Bunch of badasses. No integrity there. Thugs. Five steps down from some of these guys," he said, nodding in the direction of his own crew. "Give some people a gun, and they think they're king of the hill. All I know is they've never put in time here. You need to get out, Hank. **Now!**"

"I know. I know. I've been biding my time. Want to give me the name of the pilot who's going to ferry you out of here?"

"I'll do better than that. I'll clue him in, but

who the hell knows if he'll even come back here once he gets us out of here? I had to pay some really big bucks to make this happen. Spyder's reach is long. As you well know."

"Tell me something I don't already know. I've stayed six months too long."

"Then come with us. Your call, **Mr. Diamond.** I know you have a safe haven somewhere, but it's the getting there that's the clunker. Right now, no one is watching except Spyder himself. If I tell my guys to stand down, they'll stand down. You might not get another chance, Hank. Your call."

Jellicoe thought about it. For a whole minute. Thought about his gut instincts, thought about Charles Martin and Fergus Duffy, and then he thought about Countess de Silva and the way his stomach crunched up because he knew he was being set up. **To go or not to go?**

A sharp whistle caused both men to turn around.

"We're locked and loaded. Time to shove off. What's it going to be, Hank?"

"I can't leave with you, but I can drive myself. He might pick up on it, and he might not. Do I have time to pack any gear, or do I go cold?"

"You have about sixty minutes. I'll hold the plane as long as I can, but you need to roll, buddy."

Jellicoe nodded. He held out his hand to Finley. The grip was hard and firm, one mercenary to another. Honor among thieves, that kind of code. Right or wrong, he'd take it. Like he had any other choice.

Jellicoe sprinted off. Inside his house, he raced up the stairs, unlocked the suite of rooms where Fergus and Charles had lived for so long under his watchful eye. "Listen up. I only have a minute here. I'm leaving the island. If you agree to remain in this suite for one full hour, you are then free to leave. Make your way to Countess de Silva. She's here to rescue you with her crew of vigilantes. Don't look at me like that, Charlie. Do you take me for a fool? Now, here's the thing. If you leave or try to leave before the hour is up, this place will blow up. You know how I like to wire things. You following me here?" To make his point, Jellicoe held up a small black square that glowed with two red dots. "This will tell me if you open a door or a window. I will press this

button immediately. Tell me you understand."

Fergus and Charles nodded, their eyes
wide, in shock at what they were being told.

"Let's hope we never see each other
again," Jellicoe said.

Five heartbeats later, Jellicoe was in his
truck, racing up the coast road that would
take him to the northern part of the island,
where his escape waited. He kept one eye
on the road and one eye on the oversize
watch on his wrist. Out of the corner of his
eye, he saw Felicia and Gretchen Spyder
at the snack shop at the end of the boardwalk. He leaned on the horn and waved.

Good-byes were sweet, and some were
bitter. One small corner of his heart wished
the two women well. And then he forgot
about them and concentrated on his own
survival. He floored the gas pedal.

Back in Spyder's lair, the little man
hopped about like a frog on steroids as he
glared at the monitors in front of him. He
knew that this was going to happen. Knew
it in every fiber of his body. His new people
should have been here two hours ago. In
time to thwart Finley's betrayal. He'd delib-

erately pushed back the time so Finley would get caught in the act and mowed down. What he hadn't counted on was Hank Jellicoe joining forces with Finley or Finley beating him to the punch. How could he have been so stupid? His small webbed hands smacked down on the desktop. Pain shot up both his arms. Then he kicked out at the desk with his stubby legs and was rewarded with even more pain. He howled and cursed.

The e-mail alert glaring at him on the screen told him that his new security force was being delayed because of engine problems. Revised ETA was twelve hours away.

Aside from the pain shooting up his arms and legs, the only thing Angus Spyder could fathom was that he was unguarded. He couldn't even shoot a gun for the simple fact that he couldn't hold one in his webbed hands. A knife was also out of the question.

Spyder started to rant and scream again about how he'd made all those people rich beyond their wildest dreams. And this was the thanks he got for his generosity. **Bastards.** Unguarded. Anyone could get to him. He wasn't safe. He was vulnerable. For one wild, crazy moment, he thought about summoning his wife and daughter and holding them hostage. And how exactly would he do that? Another stupid thought. Felicia, if she knew what was going on, would not think twice about sticking a knife in his chest or slitting his throat while his daughter egged her on.

Felicia was in excellent shape. She worked out for hours in the gym. She swam five miles a day in the pool on top of all the exercise, then she used a tanning bed, preferring it to the real sun, and she ate healthily. He hated how perfect she was. Hated the disgust he saw on her face each time she was in his presence. And still he'd provided for her family. Where was her gratitude? She should be kissing his feet.

He needed to lock up, to fortify himself somehow. His eyes bulging in fear, the little man scurried as fast as he could to secure the bolts on all the doors that led to his suite. He kept one eye on the monitors as he hopped about, sweat dripping from every pore in his stunted body.

Angus Spyder had never experienced such fear in his life.

Breathless, he hopped up on his special chair and fixed his gaze on the monitors.

He watched as the countess's men ran up the beachfront to gather in a knot. He could hear the sound of the ocean, but the voices were muted, the words all running together. A scrambler of some sort must be in play. Why weren't they chasing after Finley and his crew? Another stupid question on his part. Why would they do that? With Finley and his people gone, the countess's people could invade his compound with no resistance. Talk about a sitting duck. Rage once again took over, but this time the little toad just screamed and yelled because his hands, arms, and legs still hurt. Sweat continued to roll down Spyder's swarthy face.

Another monitor showed him his wife and daughter licking ice-cream cones like they hadn't a care in the world. His rage was so overwhelming, he spit on the computer monitor.

Spyder blinked. Two men were walking up the road toward the countess's house. Two men! Jellicoe's prisoners! The bastard had set them free. His rage continued unabated. He spit again at the computer monitor. His bug eyes moved at the speed of light. The two old-time spooks would spill their guts to the countess, who in turn would call in her security, and they, in turn, would call the authorities. Which authorities? His brain felt so scrambled. He tapped at the computer keyboard with his little fingers, demanding that his new security force charter a plane and do it immediately. His frazzled brain tried to calculate the time it would take for them to arrive. At best, six hours, possibly five. They could kill him in five hours.

The computer e-mail pinged. He leaned forward, sweat dripping onto the keyboard.

His new security force would land in four hours. Four hours was an eternity. Could he survive for four hours on his own?

Consumed with fear for his well-being, Spyder leaned back in his special chair to think. He needed a way out. He had enough money to last a hundred lifetimes, and it wasn't doing him one damn bit of good. He thought then about all the people he'd had killed so he could make money, take over their businesses, or steal them for pennies on a dollar, and it wasn't doing him one damn bit of good. He laughed when he thought about how he'd skinned Hank Jellicoe and made millions off his cyberspy crap. Right now, this very minute, this very

second, he'd give it all up for safe passage
out to his yacht.

Spyder wished then for a friend, a confi-
dant. Someone to trust, someone to call on
when he was in trouble. He'd read somewhere that to have a friend, you needed to
be a friend. Felicia. She was the one who'd
said that. He had laughed in her face and
had been so cruel when he said he didn't
need friends. Money was the only thing he
needed.

Money wasn't going to help him now.
Right now, what he needed was safe passage. And it wasn't going to happen, no
matter how much money he had. He let his
thoughts go back to months ago, to when
he issued the order to kill the Domingos and
snatch his grandchildren. Just like that, kill
them and take the children. No one had
questioned him. They'd simply nodded. A
done deal. Only, it wasn't a done deal.

The toad-like little man leaned back
again and closed his eyes. He wondered
if there really was a God and what He held
in store for him. Felicia was forever pray-
ing with a string of beads, for all the good
it did her. He turned his thoughts to the
devil and wondered if he was real. Such

jibber-jabber. The only person he believed in was himself.

Spyder looked again at the monitor and saw his wife and daughter preparing to leave the snack shop. Gretchen was propelling the wheelchair, while his wife was twirling her straw hat in the air. He looked past them out to the ocean, where his yacht lay at anchor. He sighed so loudly, he scared himself. If only . . .

Avery Snowden ran faster than he'd ever run in his life, his men right behind him. He shouted orders, which were carried on the breeze, as he headed for the dune buggies that would carry him and his men out to the coast road. Snowden hopped onto one of the dune buggies and said, "The bastard is going to make a run for it. C'mon, c'mon! Move it, guys!

"He's got at least a fifteen-minute head start. Son of a bitch! He cut a deal with that guy Finley. We can't let him get away again. The first time was a fluke. Twice, and our ass is grass where those women are concerned. C'mon, c'mon! Can't you make this thing go any faster?"

Snowden hung on to the overhead strap

as the buggy raced down the road, his men right behind him. **This isn't happening. This is not happening,** he kept saying over and over to himself. But it was happening. Hank Jellicoe, aka Chuck Diamond, was getting away. Snowden knew he was going to lose him, knew it in every fiber of his body.

"We're here. Which way, boss?" the driver shouted.

"Take a right. See that plane over there! Head that way."

"Can't, boss. The barrier is up. We need to get out and run the rest of the way. Oh, shit! There goes someone up the steps with a backpack. Look! Look! He's turning around. Ah, the famous middle-finger salute, boss. Talk about stupid, dumb luck. The door is closing. Double shit! The plane is taxiing down the runway. No way we can make it unless you want a shoot-out right here."

"Son of a bitch! The bastard pulled it off," Avery Snowden said hoarsely.

"Bad timing, boss. Hey, we tried. There was no way to know how this was going to go down. Until those guys started packing up their gear, it was business as usual.

Not your fault, boss," barked Jim Ryan, Snowden's right-hand man.

"Try telling that to Countess de Silva and the other women. The first time he got away, **we** let it happen. Those women captured him fair and square, and we let him get away. They are never going to forgive this one. We're going to be damn lucky if we aren't exiled here on this damn island for the next hundred years. Those women are not the forgiving kind. Nor should they be. This falls on my doorstep. I'll take full responsibility."

Snowden's men hiked back to the dune buggies, their weapons out in the open. No one questioned them or opposed them.

"Now what, boss?" asked Jim Ryan.

"Now we head back to the countess's villa and get our asses handed to us on a silver platter. Don't even think that guy is better than we are. He's not. He caught a break out of the blue and was smart enough to grab it. We came here to take out Angus Spyder or, I should say, exfil him, when the women are done with him. He was and is our primary objective. Hank Jellicoe was a bonus. A twofer, if you will. That part of our assignment has not changed."

Snowden looked upward and off into the distance. He undid the red scarf around his neck and twirled it in the air, the signal for the helicopters to stop burning fuel and head back to their home base.

Avery Snowden felt lower than a snake's belly as he watched the landscape whiz by. He wasn't used to failure. It just wasn't in his makeup.

"Where to, boss? You still want to go to the villa? You sure you don't want to talk this out before . . . those women hand us our asses on that silver platter you mentioned?" asked Jim Ryan.

"The villa. We need to get this over and done with."

The remainder of the ride to Annie's villa was made in total silence.

Failure was failure, no matter how you looked at it.

Chapter 20

Charles Martin and Fergus Duffy stood eye-ball to eyeball in the foyer of Hank Jellicoe's house. Charles reached out for the door-knob, then drew his hand back. He looked down at his watch. One hour and ten minutes had passed since Jellicoe had said they could leave.

Fergus chewed on his lower lip as he stared at the door that could lead him and Charles out of captivity. He was light-headed with the thought. He sucked in a deep breath and said, "Do it, Charles!"

Without a moment's hesitation, Charles reached once again for the ornately carved doorknob and thrust the door open. Wide. "Run, Fergus, like you've never run before!" he bellowed.

Fergus needed no more urging. He ran like the hounds of hell were behind him. Five minutes later, breathing hard and gasping for breath, the two men came to a halt along the side of the road and clung to each other.

"I think we made it, mate," Charles said, his face beet red from the hard run.

"Jesus, Mary, and Joseph, we're free, Charles! We're free!"

His breathing returning to normal, Charles leaned back against a luscious palmetto and said, "There's free, and then there's free, Fergus. We still have to face . . . ah . . . the ladies, not to mention our island host, Angus Spyder. I don't know about you, but while I'm looking forward to it, I am also dreading it. The meeting with the women, not with Angus Spyder."

Fergus dropped to his haunches as he tried to get his breathing under control. "I think what you're trying to say is that if the women turn on us, we could be here for the rest of our lives, as guests of Angus Spyder."

Charles chuckled. "One thing is for certain. We'll be paying for our absence for the rest of our lives. Especially me. I left Myra high and dry. And then it all went to hell in a hand-basket. The first thing we have to do . . . I have to do," Charles said, correcting himself, "is call . . . and report in. God alone knows what Lizzie is thinking, and I'm not talking about Lizzie Fox here."

"I'm no authority on women, Charles, and I am the last man who should be giving you advice, but I'd say that is the **second** thing you should do, not the first. Calling your childhood friend is not of the essence right now, and calling her isn't going to change anything at the moment, whereas—"

"I get it! I get it! And you are right. Have you given any thought to what you are going to say to Annie?" Charles asked, hoping to send the conversation in a different direction.

Fergus looked so uncomfortable, Charles took pity on him. "Just let the cards fall where they fall. Those women are human, you know. Well, at least at times they are," Charles said, correcting his statement. "Other times they—"

"Don't say it, Charles. Listen, I love that

woman. Think about it. What's not to love? Annie is everything a man could want. She's witty, she's charming, she can shoot like a Wild West gunslinger, and she can **pole dance.** Her cooking leaves a lot to be desired, but I can live with that because my mum taught me how to cook at an early age. She can be kind, gentle, and she is caring. She's also an experienced safecracker. A woman of many talents.

"You don't know the half of what she gives away. She is probably the most generous person walking the face of the earth. Do you know that she has a pair of rhinestone cowgirl boots that she polishes regularly and that she has had resoled **three** times? She could buy new ones, but those boots mean something to her. Who does that these days? She used to drive me crazy when she'd wear that tiara. I just wish she weren't so rich. I have a hard time with that, like I told you. She's used to the fine things in life. I don't have anything to offer her but my pension, and it is so measly, it's not worth mentioning."

"And yet when you had a ton of money from your sweepstakes winnings, you gave it all away. Here's the thing, Fergus. Annie was devastated when you didn't ask her to go back to Scotland with you. Devastated. She doesn't care about your lack of money."

Fergus hung his head. "I thought about asking her to go with me, but my pride wouldn't let me. I had myself convinced she'd say no. I have a hard time with rejection, as do most men. She wouldn't have liked living there. She couldn't handle being dirt poor."

"Ah, but you see, my friend, that was her decision to make, now wasn't it? You made it for her instead, and now look at what and where you are. Women do not like it when men make decisions for them. I did learn that the hard way. Come along now. We've dillydallied long enough. We need to face the lionesses and take whatever is coming our way."

Charles clapped his friend on the back and urged him forward. "It feels great, doesn't it, Fergus?"

"You mean that we're walking on our own to either our salvation or our doom?"

"I suppose you could put it like that. If it is any consolation to you, my insides are in double knots. I'm hoping for the best and expecting the worst."

Fergus stopped in midstride. He looked around. "There's no one following us, Charles. Where is that insane man who owns this island? Why isn't someone chasing us?"

Charles looked around. All he could see were palm trees swaying in the breeze. The scent of the island flowers was heady. He looked out at the ocean as the small waves washed to shore. A paradise of sorts, if you didn't peel back the layers of evil that lived here. "To answer your questions, Fergus, I do not know. I think we should pick up our pace, in case this is some kind of fluke and we get ambushed."

By the time the two former prisoners reached Annie's villa, they were sweaty and disheveled. They looked at one another and groaned out loud.

"So, what do we do? Do we just march up to the door and ring the bell? Is there some kind of protocol that we should be observing in a situation like this? I feel like I'm out in left field, with no ball in the air. Oh, I hear people. Sounds like it's coming from the back of the property. Maybe we should go around. There might be a lanai, like at

Jellicoe's house. What do you say, Charles? You're top gun here."

Charles pondered the questions. If he was top gun, as Fergus implied, it **was** a position he didn't want or need. His stomach felt like an army of angry wasps were chewing away at his insides. Plus, his mouth was dry, and he knew he looked awful, probably as awful as Fergus looked.

The two men walked single file along a colored flagstone walkway to the rear of the property, where a loud conversation mixed with laughter could be heard. When one especially loud voice permeated the air around them, Charles reached out to pull Fergus to a stop. "I think that's Avery Snowden talking. That means the girls and Avery and his men are here on a mission."

"To free us?" Fergus hissed in Charles's ear.

"No. I think we came with the deal. They came here because of our host, Angus Spyder. I don't know that for sure, but what I do know for sure is there is no way Myra and the girls could possibly have known we were here. We need to think of ourselves as a bonus, Fergus." Fergus looked so crushed, Charles patted him on the back. "Regardless, they're here, we're here, and as far as I'm concerned, we're rescued. Shhh. What's Avery saying? My hearing isn't as sharp as it once was. Can you hear?"

"He's being a bleeding heart. He just told them that Hank Jellicoe got away. He's apologizing all over the place and taking full responsibility. Avery is saying that Jellicoe has a new identity or used it here on the island. Said he goes by the name Charles Bennett Diamond. The workers called him Charlie or Chuck. Not that any of it helps us right now."

"How are the women taking his confession?" Charles asked as he cupped his hand around his right ear in an attempt to hear better.

Fergus grimaced. "I'm hearing some spicy, dicey words. Most from Annie and Kathryn. The others are muttering, but I can't make out what they're saying. We're going to be Snowden's encore, Charles."

Charles pulled a face and backed up a few steps, pulling Fergus with him. "Maybe we need to fall back and regroup," he said nervously. "All their venom is going to spill over onto us when we make our presence known. What do you think, Fergus?"

Fergus didn't know what to think. He closed his eyes, hoping something would come to him. Nothing did. He didn't object when Charles dragged him farther back into the flower-scented foliage.

"We should go back till we decide what to do," Charles whispered.

"To that house! Never!" There was such outrage in Fergus's voice, Charles flinched. "Listen, Charles, how bad can it be? They scream and yell at us, they chastise us, and then they end up throwing their arms around us, knowing we are safe and sound and didn't really abandon them. Think about it."

"I'm thinking you are insane that you think as you do. That simply is not going to happen. I need to think. I wish I had a cigar."

"I wish I was on an airliner at thirty thousand feet and headed for the States. A cigar is not going to cut it, my friend. How much longer do you think Avery and his people are going to take that dressing-down? They should be headed our way any minute. Make a decision, Charles, and make it quick."

"They'll stay until those women say they

can leave. You know how they work. But you're right. They should be cutting them loose shortly. The big question is, do they stay or do they go, **go** meaning 'to leave the island'?"

"Look, Charles, Snowden is your compadre. Why don't we just lie in wait, and when he leaves, we follow him and his men? He's not going to blow the whistle on us. Or will he? You know him. What is your opinion?"

"We're so close, Fergus. We can hear our beloveds' voices."

"Yeah, well, I'm not hearing any kind, endearing words, that's for sure. Going in there now would be the same as sending a hen into the fox den, or whatever that saying is."

"So, then, your vote is to go with Snowden when he leaves?"

"Damn straight that's my vote."

"Then I guess it's mine, too. Can you hear anything this far back?"

"No. It's quiet. Oops, they're leaving and heading our way. Do we just fall in line or what?"

"Yes, and don't speak above a whisper. Let me do the talking."

Super-spook that he was, Avery Snowden

almost peeled out of his skin when Charles stepped out of the bushes and onto the path.

"Just keep walking and act like we're part of the group," Charles said.

"What the bloody hell—"

"Never mind that. What happened back there?" Charles asked, drifting closer to Snowden, Fergus right behind him. It was a flawless fill-in, and he was certain that if anyone was watching, they would not immediately notice the two extra men on the team.

"What happened was I got my arse handed to me is what happened. I let Jellicoe go free. For the second time. I expected to be handed my walking papers, but it didn't happen. While vitriolic, the women didn't fire me. Because . . . Jellicoe was not the primary objective when we arrived here. In fact, we weren't even sure he was here. Nor were we certain you were here. Like the Yanks say, Jellicoe was the cherry on top. You and Fergus are two more diamonds in the countess's tiara. They don't even know for sure that you're here. They're bitter—make no mistake about that—but they're also intelligent women.

There are just some things that no amount of planning can foresee."

Snowden looked around at his posse and said, "Close in and shield these two as we go up the stairs."

Inside the cool, lavish apartment suite, Snowden whipped around and said, "Talk!"

Ninety minutes later everyone was caught up. The huge pile of ham sandwiches was gone, only crumbs remaining. The beer bottles stood sentinel on the kitchen countertop.

Charles threw his hands in the air. "Now what?"

"Now this," Snowden said as he whipped his computer into place and booted it up. "Abner Tookus is logged on to Spyder's computer. His new crew is due at the north end of the island in four hours. Three now. Spyder rotates his security crews every three to four months. According to Tookus, once in a while he makes them stay six months. What that means is this crew is new. They've never been here before. Twenty men out of Miami. He pays top dollar, so every hired gun who can shoot straight applies for the job, and Spyder isn't particular. The only real professional on a par with Jellicoe was Don Finley. I explained all this to the women. With a three-hour window to do whatever they have to do, it is going to be dicey. We also have to think about the wife and daughter."

"What about that yacht moored out there?" Fergus asked.

"We have to get them there. Spyder had the launch with nine of Jellicoe's men blown up. Just like that!" Snowden said, swallowing hard. "The man, and I use that term loosely, is one wild-assed son of a bitch."

"So he's unguarded and vulnerable right now?" Fergus asked.

"Yes, except for the two women, and don't forget, the girl is in a wheelchair. That's an additional problem right there."

"How did you leave it with Myra, Annie, and the girls?" Charles asked.

"They were switching gears and reformulating their plans. Jack Emery said there are two cigarette boats and one regulation speedboat in the boathouse. I didn't ask him how he knew that, either, so stop glaring at me, Charles."

Charles ignored Snowden's remarks as he tried to figure out the timeline and what Myra, Annie, and the girls might have in mind. "How long does it take to get to the north end of the island, where that little airport is?"

"Thirty, thirty-five minutes tops. Annie's plane is on the runway, gassed and ready to take off when she gives the okay. The airport has only two short runways. We're going to need a diversion at the airport when that new security crew arrives. I'm thinking a welcoming committee of sorts to slow things down. Jack Sparrow is here. He's the current director of the FBI. Not that he has any jurisdiction here, but he sure as hell can play the part. He can say Angus Spyder sent him to bring them to his end of the island. Their firearms, I assume, will be in their bags. The only glitch to that is Spyder getting in touch with them. He can't do it while they're in the air. But the minute they land, he can. Unless that genius Tookus can scramble his signal. Dicey at best."

"Did you explain all that to Myra, Annie, and the girls?" Charles asked.

"I did. Then I repeated it all. At that point I left. You do realize that Spyder can see every inch of this end of the island, right?"

Charles and Fergus both nodded.

"Our best bet would be to get to the women, but he'll still see us coming. I'm sure a man like him would have a safe room, a bunker of sorts, and he's holed up in there at the moment. The wife might be of some help. She does live there. She might know how to entice him out or how we can blow our way in. We can't count on it, though."

"Three hours!" Charles said.

"And counting," Snowden replied.

"We need to go back to Annie's villa," Charles said.

Snowden agreed.

Fergus looked green around the gills, but he got to his feet, ready to follow his leaders.

"Avery, call ahead and have Sparrow head to the airport now. See who he wants to take with him. Maybe Ted or Jack. He can't go alone. Unseen firepower, to let those men know he's in charge. By the way, is Harry Wong here?"

"You bet. Everyone is here."

"Harry is his own army, and with Yoko at his side, we've won the war," Charles said, feeling better immediately.

"You're sure there are two cigarette boats and one speedboat?" Fergus asked.

"If Jack said there are two cigarette boats and one speedboat, then yes is the answer," Snowden shot over his shoulder. "C'mon. Move it, men. The clock is ticking."

Fergus looked at his watch. So did Charles.

Chapter 21

Jack Emery likened what was going on at Annie's villa to a Chinese fire drill gone wrong. The women were shedding their disguises and doing their best to scrub off the brown dye on their skin.

"I didn't like pretending to be a guy," Isabelle groused as she scrubbed harder.

"I hate wearing baseball caps and messing up my hair," Nikki grated as she did her best to fluff out her blond locks. "And your head sweats!"

"No flip-flops, girls. Lace-up sneakers. We need to be steady on our feet. Fashion doesn't count," Kathryn said as she bent over to tie her Nikes into a snug knot. She stretched out her bad leg and winced. The others pretended not to notice.

"I think Harry and I had the worst costumes," Yoko said as she piled up the pounds of clothing Alexis had assigned to both her and Harry to make them appear ancient. "I feel like I can breathe again." To prove her point, she danced around the lanai, doing a few pirouettes for everyone's benefit. Harry beamed his pleasure as he flexed his fingers.

Jack felt as jumpy as a cat in the middle of a rainstorm. Something was niggling at him. Something he was sure he had missed. He said so aloud. Everyone just looked at him, but no one offered any advice. "Anyone want my push-up bra?" he said, twirling it in the air for all to see.

He had no takers, so he tossed it into the bushes. "Your loss. It had modesty pads."

In spite of himself, Harry burst out laughing. Harry never laughed.

Annie and Myra looked at each other, and both nodded. "Change of plans, people," Annie said.

Nikki looked at Jack and mumbled, "How

do they do that? They didn't say a word out loud, yet they both agree on whatever is coming. And ninety-nine times out of a hundred, it is the right decision. I hate that, Jack. I really do."

"That's because you're a lawyer, and you think things through. They just do it. Let's see what the new plan is."

"Myra and I do not think it's a good move to send Mr. Sparrow, Maggie, Ted, and Joseph to the airport. While Maggie and the boys are legitimate, and the exposure they would be touting to the rotating crew might make sense to us, it won't to the crew. And neither one of us is comfortable that the crew won't recognize Mr. Sparrow even in his disguise. Plus, there is no viable means of transportation back here. They number twenty. I think hiring a taxi would raise a red flag. This is our fault—we did not think it through—so someone call Mr. Snowden and tell him to get to the airport ASAP."

Jack squeezed Nikki's hand. "See? It makes sense now, doesn't it?"

Nikki mumbled something under her breath, which Jack couldn't quite hear, and he was thankful he couldn't.

Ted held up his iPhone and was texting furiously. He beamed and nodded at the return confirmation. "They're on their way."

"I feel like Jack. I think we're missing something," Annie said, a deep frown building on her face. "We need to hustle here, people. Our window of time is shrinking rapidly. And we still don't know how we're going to penetrate Mr. Spyder's home."

"I know how," Dennis said, raising his hand like he was in the fifth grade again.

All eyes turned to the young reporter.

"How?" they chorused as one.

Dennis pointed to Greg Albright. "All he has to do is show up, knock on the door, and Gretchen will let him in. I think. I say I think, based on the fact that I think Mr. Spyder will be in his bunker. He can bang on the door, call her name, whatever. I don't think either she or her mother will be able to resist. Bear in mind here that we are assuming neither woman wants to be there but has had no viable means of escape. If we all go as a group, and Greg takes the lead, I think it will work."

Harry tilted his head to the side and fixed his gaze on Dennis, who immediately started to shake.

"I said, 'I think,' Harry. I'm not 100 percent sure it will work."

Harry smiled.

Harry never smiled.

Greg Albright bounced up off his chair like he was spring mounted. "I'll do it! I'll do it! When? I'm ready right now!"

"You need to cool your jets, young man," Myra said sternly. "You do not do anything until we tell you to do it. Tell me you understand what I just said." Her tone softened a little. "I understand how you are feeling right now, but you need to understand that if you do something that goes awry, all our planning will go down the drain."

Albright took one look at Myra's fierce expression and sat down. He started to nibble on his thumb, his gaze sweeping the room, wishing for something that would give him hope. He saw nothing in anyone's expression. His shoulders slumped. So close yet so far.

Harry gave his slim shoulders a shrug as he got to his feet. "Take a walk with me, Jack. I need some exercise."

"You need exercise like I need a watermelon taped to my head. What's up?" Jack asked.

"You're right. Something is off," Harry replied as he and Jack walked outside.

"What did we miss, Harry? It's not like us to miss something. Yeah, maybe for a minute or two, but this . . . whatever we're missing is crucial. I'd bet my life on it. We're losing minutes here. I hate it when the girls cut it so close."

Harry looked at his watch. "The way Snowden drives, he should be halfway to the airport by now," he said, looking up at the bright sun. "I don't like this place, Jack. I can smell and sense the evil here."

"Yeah, I know what you mean." Jack looked out across the deep blue of the ocean, the sun shimmering down creating little rainbows on the dancing waves. And then it hit him. Hard!

"Son of a bitch! Harry! Listen to me. Those new gunslingers from Miami—they aren't flying in. Well, they are, but they're coming on a seaplane, not a regular 747. **They're coming here.** We need to call Snowden to warn him and his people to get back here on the double. C'mon, Harry. Our current timeline just took a big hit."

Jack raced up from the water's edge, across the small dunes, and literally belly flopped onto the lanai. "We gotta go **now!** Those new rotated security people aren't arriving at the airport on the northern end of the island. They're coming here by seaplane. They're coming **here!**" he gasped like a fish out of water.

"Hold on, Jack. How do you know this?" Annie asked.

"My gut, that's how. It's the only thing that makes sense. Someone call Snowden. Isabelle, find Abner and ask him to break in, hack in, whatever the hell he does, to see what kinds of flights left out of Miami, if any. Nikki, round everyone up and get your gear together. We need to leave ASAP. We need to be **inside** that house before those creeps land. Otherwise, we abort the mission now, and once those guys arrive, Spyder will be as safe as he was in his mother's womb. Shake it everybody. Move! Move!"

The Sisters moved. The way they always moved when they were on a mission. Like a well-oiled machine. Within minutes, the women were on the Harleys and the boys were in the Rovers, with Greg Albright bellowing that it was about time. Dennis gave him a chop alongside his head, to Harry's approval.

"You need to pipe down right now, or I'm going to jam my foot down your throat," Dennis roared into Albright's ear.

"Okay, okay."

Still in a daze at Snowden's abrupt departure without a word, Charles and Fergus paced the spacious apartment over the boathouse. Both men walked over to the huge bay window that overlooked the whole island in time to see the Sisters mount up. Charles's hungry gaze immediately found Myra, who looked to him like she'd been born to ride the Hog she was sitting on. He blinked when she steered the Harley to the front of the line. She held up her hand as an earth-splitting sound filled the air. Fergus almost jumped out of his shoes when he saw Annie sidle up next to Myra.

Both men watched in delighted horror as Myra twirled her red neckerchief in the air and bellowed something neither man could hear. She peeled out. Evel Knievel couldn't have done it better. Charles almost had an orgasm at what he was seeing.

Charles turned to Fergus. "What do you think she said?"

"I think she said, 'Let's rumble!' I think all

bikers say that when they take off. I read that somewhere a long time ago," Fergus said, dithering. "Would you look at those ladies go! I don't know about you, Charles, but I'm getting a hard-on just standing here. **Those are our women!**"

"Why are we still standing here?" Charles demanded.

"Because Snowden told us not to move or leave, that's why," Fergus shot back.

"Let me get this straight, Ferg. You want to stay here because he said so. Well, you can stay, but I'm leaving. Join me or not," Charles huffed as he hustled to the door.

Fergus raced after him. "Where are we going, and how are we going to get there? I counted the vehicles. They're all gone."

"Then we walk, jog, run, whatever it takes. Think of this as our daily exercise routine. We need to get in shape, anyway. As to where we're going, this is just a guess on my part, but I rather think the gang is headed to Spyder's mansion. For all I know, they might be planning on blasting their way in. We need to be there if that happens. We need to be there, period."

"Don't you think we might be a distraction,

Charles? I, for one, certainly don't want to throw off their timing, and you know that will happen if we show up."

"You have a better idea, Fergus?"

"Actually, I don't. You were always the planner. You always said, 'When in doubt, do nothing.' So, what are we doing?"

"We keep going. When you stop, you drop. You know that, Ferg. I think we can handle whatever comes our way."

Fergus nodded, but he wasn't so sure about handling things on their own. When they'd tried that back in England, they'd been blind-sided, and they'd ended up here, under Hank Jellicoe's watchful eye. But, loyal to the core, he followed Charles, his heart beating faster than that of a racehorse crossing the finish line.

The airport was small, like all island airports. But unlike most island airports, which were busy, this one was not. Snowden hopped out of his all-terrain vehicle and ran up to the check-in counter. He talked bullet fast as his eyes raked the board overhead. No incoming flights were due until tomorrow. When the pretty blonde behind the check-in counter confirmed what he was reading on the board, he turned and raced back to the all-terrain vehicle.

"The guys were right. There are no flights due in today. Not till tomorrow. Emery was right. They're coming on a seaplane. You don't need an airport or a runway for that. Goddamn it! This has been one damn snafu after another. Burn rubber, Pete," he told his driver.

"Time?" Pete, the driver, bellowed to be heard over the ocean's roar.

"Don't know much about seaplanes. My guess would be anytime soon," Snowden bellowed in return.

"You planning on a shoot-out O.K. Corral style, boss? Or are we the welcoming committee?"

"For now, let's go with the welcome wagon. I managed to jam all the signals coming into the island, so if nothing went wrong, Spyder has not been able to contact his crew. They're coming in blind, and I'm hoping what they will be seeing, which is us, won't set off any alarms. I think we can pull it off. If not, oh, well, then it's O.K. Corral time."

"Six of us and twenty of them. Not good odds, boss."

"Mom! Mom! Come quick," Gretchen Spyder shouted at the top of her lungs. "God, Mom, hurry up! We need to get to the front door. Look outside! They're all here! Mom, what does this mean?"

Felicia Spyder kicked off her spike-heeled shoes and ran as fast as she could to the front door, where Gretchen was waiting for her. She opened the door wide just as a batch of Harley-Davidsons ground to a halt. Four Range Rovers stopped one after the other in a straight line. People appeared out of nowhere.

Greg Albright broke ranks and ran forward. "Gretchen!"

If Felicia hadn't been holding on to her daughter's shoulders, she would have toppled out of the wheelchair. They all watched as Greg scooped Gretchen out of her chair and danced away, their lips locked together.

"Well, that went rather well," Annie said, a smile on her face. "Mrs. Spyder?"

"Please don't call me that. My name is Irina Dasha. Angus named me Felicia when he took me away. Just for the record, his birth name is Feodor Kostya Spyovich. Please tell me you are here to take me and my daughter to safety. Please tell me that."

"That's why we're here," Myra said gently. "But first we have some business to take care of. Where is your . . . that man?"

"He's got himself locked in his suite in the back of the house. It's like a bunker. He literally seals himself in there when he's alone. He's waiting for his new security team to arrive. Today, sometime, though I don't know when. What can I do? How can I help you?"

"Can you reach him by cell phone?"

"Yes, normally, but nothing in the house is working. Everything is full of static. I saw a TV program once where that happened because someone was jamming the frequency or something like that," Irina said. "Can you really take me and my daughter away from here?"

"Yes, my dear. Gather up what you each want to take with you, but first show us where . . . Mr. Spyder is hiding out."

"With pleasure." Irina risked a glance at where Greg Albright was still holding her daughter. They were smiling at one another, their eyes and their expressions saying it all. Their grip on each other was fierce. "Follow me."

"I can't believe this. I simply cannot believe this," Irina said over and over as she raced along the path and pointed to a section set off from the main part of the house by a covered breezeway. "There are no windows. The door is specially made. A while back, Angus boasted that not even a rocket launcher could penetrate the door. I believed him."

"Okay, Felicia . . . Irina, we can take it from here. Go back to the house and gather your and Gretchen's things. Where will you go?"

"First to Miami, so my daughter can have her operation. I have to pack up my jewelry so I can sell it to pay for the operation. I have no cash money. Then, when Gretchen is safe and she has recovered and can walk again, and is with the one who I hope will be my new son-in-law, I will go back to Russia to see my family, and perhaps if I can find a way, I'll bring them here so we can all be a family. Thank you so much for coming. Gretchen and I had all but given up hope of ever being able to leave here. You are a godsend to us both."

Irina raced off, while Albright and Gretchen continued to bill and coo at each other, oblivious to everything else on the planet.

The group huddled. What to do? How to do it?

"No windows to shoot out," Jack said.

"A door a rocket launcher can't take out," Sparrow said.

"His lair is a stand-alone structure," Ted said.

"But," Harry said, holding up his hand and pointing to the breezeway, "that's just a plain old stucco wall at the end of the breezeway. Take one of those massive Range Rovers and back it right up and into and through the wall. It might take you a couple of tries, but I think those trucks have the horsepower to do the job."

"Brilliant, Harry, just brilliant," Jack said, clapping Harry on the back. "I'll do the honors."

In the blink of an eye, Jack was behind the wheel of a champagne-colored Range Rover. He slipped it into gear, backed up, then shifted again to go forward so that he could drive into the breezeway. He plowed down a row of sweet-smelling bushes full of crimson flowers. He straightened the truck out, moved forward again, then shoved the gear into reverse and floored the pedal. The air bag exploded on impact. When he finally extracted himself, Jack looked into the rearview mirror to see how much damage he'd done. Not too much, by what he could see. He called out to Sparrow, who was assessing the damage.

"Maybe two more good hits, Jack. You need to use one of the other trucks since the air bag went off. You okay?" he asked as an afterthought.

"Good to go," Jack said as he hopped out of the Rover. "Ted, move it, okay?"

Ted slid behind the wheel and mowed down the other side of the sweet-smelling bushes in his haste to get out of Jack's way.

The Sisters cheered Jack as he slid into a money-green Range Rover and fired it up.

"Be careful, honey," Nikki called out.

Jack grinned. He loved it when Nikki called him honey. She called him other sweet names, but he liked honey the best. He waved to indicate he had heard her and would be careful.

The moment Ted had the champagne-colored Rover a safe distance away, Jack maneuvered the money-green one forward and floored the pedal in reverse. An air bag hit him for the second time, but he knew he'd knocked through the wall, because a cheer went up behind him. He jumped out and down and looked to see what damage he'd done. Enough, he saw, that they could gain entry to Spyder's lair if they went single file, one person at a time, but first they had to move some of the chunks of masonry out of the way.

They all fell to it while Espinosa moved the money-green Rover to a safer spot.

Inside Spyder's lair, all manner of bells and whistles were going off. The sound was deafening. Spyder's alarm system was going crazy, the sound bouncing off the walls.

Angus Spyder stood rooted to the floor. He felt fear and rage consume him as he tried to think of what he could do to save himself. He looked at the white noise coming from all his computer monitors, listened to the shrieking whistles. He looked at his Bloomberg terminal and cursed. As far as he was concerned, he had all the money in the world, and it wasn't doing him a damn bit of good right now.

With nothing else to do, he cowered in the corner.

And waited.

Chapter 22

Nikki led the way, her gaze sweeping her surroundings. She marveled at the space, thinking it hadn't appeared from the outside to be as big as it was. She estimated the bunker to be about two thousand square feet. And not a window in sight. But the bright light more than made up for the lack of windows. **Solid** was a word that came to mind. **Safe** and **secure** were two more words that invaded her mind. Then she wondered how any human being could live like this.

"Look, there's a full gym. And there's a hot tub and a tanning bed. I thought someone said the guy was a pissant. Why does he need all this equipment?" When no answer was forthcoming, Kathryn continued to follow Nikki, who was in the lead.

The door at the end of a short corridor was closed and locked. Annie peered at the door, at the lock, and decided it was an ordinary interior door with a standard lock. She pulled her gun from the small of her back. She waved the others to the side in case of a ricochet and fired. The sound was earsplitting. Sparrow moved forward and hit the door with his shoulder, causing it to fall inward. Sparrow bent down, picked the door up like it was a toy, and tossed it across the room. A painting full of red and orange slashes fell to the floor. The others peered at it, shrugged, and moved into the room to see Angus Spyder curled up in a corner.

"Abner, unjam everything," Annie ordered.

A wicked gleam in his eye and an even more wicked grin on his face, Abner sat down to do as ordered.

Angus Spyder straightened his back, then hunched forward. "You are trespassing on private property. I demand that you leave, but before you do that, you will please pay for the damage you've done to my home."

Annie laughed. "That's not going to happen. Take a look around, Mr. Spyder. Do you see how many we number? Of course you do. Just so we're clear on things, we are in charge. End of story."

"Well, there are a few other things you should know before the end of the story," Myra said. "For starters, your wife and daughter will be taking the speedboat out to your yacht. They'll weigh anchor and be off to Miami within"—she looked at her watch—"fifteen minutes. Gretchen's friend, Mr. Albright, did join us, and he's with her as we speak. He is the father of the twins. The man you moved heaven and earth to find but couldn't. We found him. Your daughter will live happily ever after with no interference from you from this day forward. Her children, who you so desperately tried to find, will live wonderful lives, and one day, when they are old enough, they will come to know their biological parents."

"We're good to go," Abner bellowed. "What do you want me to do now?"

"Find all his passwords and give away his money," Isabelle bellowed in return.

"By the way, Mr. Spyder, we don't want you getting your hopes up that aid is coming. That new crew you hired from Miami . . . you know, the ones who encountered engine trouble and were forced to travel via **seaplane,** they aren't going to be able to help you. When they land, they will be taken into custody," Jack said, hoping what he was saying was true.

"What are your passwords, Spyder? I'm waiting," Abner singsonged as he flexed his fingers to get the show on the road.

Everyone turned when Irina blew into the room like a wild wind. Her gaze swiveled around the room till she spotted her husband. Her eyes narrowed as she advanced farther into the room.

Maggie Spritzer, the closest to Irina, thought of her as a stalking cat. They all watched, their eyes wide, as Irina moved closer to where her husband cowered in the corner. Her eyes were narrowed to feline slits. Before anyone knew what she was doing, one foot struck out, then the other as she brought her closed, clenched fists down on Spyder's neck. "How's that feel, you bastard? Huh?" Then she rattled off a string of what they all thought were Russian obscenities.

"Uh . . . ma'am, I think you knocked him out cold. He's not going to be able to answer you. At least not right now," Jack said.

"Oh. Well, at least I finally did something right. I just came here to tell you something. Better yet, let me show you where it is." She babbled as she ran into the grotto-like bathroom and rummaged in the cabinet under the whirlpool tub. She groped and cursed, but finally she withdrew a large, old-fashioned hardbound ledger. "This is a record of all his business dealings. He liked the computer but wanted to be able to see things in black and white whenever he wanted to. He made all the entries himself. In some ways, it was a sensual thing for him. If it helps, fine. If not, at least you can compare what's in the computer to what's in the book. We're ready to leave now."

"I imagine you are," Myra said. "Ted, you and Joseph help Irina and her daughter. Dennis, you go, too." She threw her hands in the air. "Good Lord, we never thought to ask. Do you know how to drive the speedboat?"

"I do," Dennis chirped. "I grew up on the Maryland shore."

"I can drive it," Irina said. "Angus had one of the men teach me in case of an emergency."

A flurry of movement ensued as the group prepared to depart, and Angus Spyder started to come around.

"Hurry," Annie urged. "You need to get out to the yacht before the new crew arrives. We'll be in touch."

Tears rolling down her cheeks, Irina turned and blew a kiss to them all.

"Go!" Annie roared.

The minute Irina was out of sight, Kathryn, her leg burning, advanced on Spyder. She bent down and hauled him to his feet. "The man asked you a question. Answer him."

Spyder's big head wobbled on his neck. Kathryn shook him like a rag doll until he started to curse, telling her what she could do and how to do it. Kathryn's eyes narrowed. She did not understand a word of what he was saying or calling her, but she had a pretty good idea he was not inviting her to a picnic or a dance. She slammed him back against the wall. He clamped his lips tight, a sure sign he wasn't giving up a thing.

"How about this, you little monster?" Abner said, waving the old-fashioned ledger in the air so Spyder could see it. "I'll get it all with this to help me. It's just going to take me longer. The longer it takes me, the longer you're going to suffer at their hands."

Spyder sneered. "A bunch of women!" he spat. "What? They're going to beat me to a pulp while batting their eyelashes? Ooh, I am so scared."

"Oh, shit. Wrong answer," Jack mumbled under his breath.

Jack inched closer to Harry in time to hear Yoko whisper, "You need to sit this one out, sweetie. I think we have it covered." That was all Harry and Jack had to hear as she slithered toward the doorway.

The room went still, as though all the air had been sucked out of it. In two short minutes, the air returned in a rush of sound and motion. Jack didn't realize what a death grip he had on Harry's shoulders until Harry yelped in pain. Both men watched as Angus Spyder flew through the air, only to be caught and tossed from one woman to the next as they peeled off his clothing in midair. Jack closed his eyes. When he opened them, he saw that Yoko had a hammerlock on the little man. The others crowded around, forming a barrier to his eyes.

"What are they doing?" Harry hissed.

"I can't bear to look, but I heard your wife say they are going to flay the bottoms of his webbed feet, and then they're going to fry him in the tanning bed," Jack hissed.

"Yeah, yeah, I heard that, too," Sparrow said, his dark eyes as wide as saucers. "They won't really do that, will they? I mean . . . that's just a threat, right?" His voice was so shaky, Jack felt sorry for him.

"Easy to tell this is your first rodeo, Sparrow. If my wife said it, you can take it to the bank. It's probably going to get a little gory in here in another few minutes," Harry said, his eyes on Alexis and what she was pulling out of her red bag.

"This might be a good time for you to check the women, to see if they got off okay," Jack said.

Sparrow hastily withdrew. He felt like a wuss when Maggie Spritzer laughed right in his face. She shook her head at what she perceived as his squeamishness.

Abner held up his hand. His eyes were on Alexis, who had two straight razors in her hand. "Last chance, Mr. Frogman!"

A string of curses filled the air. "Crazy people. My men are going to slaughter you!" Spyder snarled.

"Crazy?" Abner boomed. "Only a crazy person would write down the passwords in a ledger and hide it in a bathroom." He continued watching Alexis to see what she would do with the straight razors. "I'm in," he chortled as he tapped away on the keyboard. Blizzards of numbers whipped across the screens. "Lookie here, Mr. Spyder! Let him see, girls!"

Nikki grabbed one of Spyder's ears, Isabelle took the other, and they hoisted the little man up so he had a full view of what was flashing on all the monitors. A fresh wave of curses and spittle filled the air.

"Move it all out, Abner. The Netherlands Antilles. But keep fifty million dollars and move it to Goldman Sachs. I gave you the routing numbers earlier. Move another fifty million dollars to Wells Fargo."

"What do you want me to do about that Spy Trap or crap business? The one that spies on everyone."

"Make it crash and burn," Annie shot back.

"There are billions of dollars sitting in that account. No code, no password. Why is that?" Abner asked.

"The man asked you a question," Yoko said quietly. "Hold him steady, girls. Who is doing the carving?"

"Me." Alexis giggled. "I'm doing the right foot, and Nikki," she said, handing her the second straight razor, "is doing the left foot. On the count of three!"

Spyder struggled in vain to free himself. Abner kept shouting for the code and password, while Yoko pinned the little man to the chair he was sitting on. Myra grabbed one webbed foot to hold it steady, while Annie grabbed the other.

Maggie Spritzer leaned forward and stared at the man's webbed feet. "I didn't expect him to have toenails, for some reason."

"One!"

"Two!"

"Three!"

The scream was so primal that Jack and Harry scooted out the door. Jack sucked deep breaths of air into his lungs. Harry did the same thing.

"I don't think they need us in there," Jack said.

"I think you're right," Harry agreed. "Let's check to see if the women got off all right."

Both men loped along and down to the boathouse. Off in the distance, they could see the two speedboats returning to the island. The yacht was moving. Both men looked at the motorized wheelchair sitting in the boathouse. The wheelchair made it all real.

"No sign of the seaplane," Jack said.

"Where's Avery?" Harry asked.

"Good question. Where is he? We should have heard the plane by now." Jack looked over his shoulder just as Dennis maneuvered one of the speedboats into the boathouse. Ted, Espinosa, and Sparrow were right behind them. They secured both boats and hopped up to the deck.

"That was a very rewarding experience," Dennis said. "But in a way, it was sad, too. At least we know the women are safe, and Gretchen and Greg will live happily ever after. I heard Greg whisper to Gretchen that if the operation wasn't a success, it wouldn't matter to him. He told her it wasn't her legs he fell in love with. Gretchen cried, and so did her mother."

Harry clapped Dennis on his back. "You did good, kid. I'm glad to see you have heart."

"So, what's going on here?" Dennis asked.

"Well, ah . . . we weren't needed, so we came out here to see what was going on," Harry replied.

"In other words, you couldn't take what they were doing, so you bailed out," Ted said.

Jack grimaced. "They were filleting his feet. He wouldn't give up the password and code for that spy company. If he didn't give it up, they were going to toast him in the tanning bed. Abner crashed the site."

"Holy shit!" Espinosa said.

"So now what do we do?" Dennis asked.

The boys all looked at one another and shrugged.

Jack Sparrow sat down on the deck and looked at his bare feet. "Tell me your boy really crashed the site, Jack. That goddamn company is a thorn in everyone's side. Tell me I can go back and say, 'It's gone. No more spying on anyone.'"

"You can tell them that, Sparrow, and it will be the truth. There are billions in that account. That's billions with a **b**. And we're going to return a good portion to his victims and give the rest away. And we will take a hefty chunk for the BOLO boys."

"Well, that's going to make my life a lot easier. I imagine the White House will be relieved. I didn't tell you this, because I was sworn to secrecy, but the bureau was tasked with taking the site out. As much as I hate to admit it, we didn't have a clue how to do it, and you just handed it to me. Man, you guys . . . um . . . and the girls are something else."

"Someone should call the Domingos and tell them they're free agents again and they can get on with their lives," Dennis said.

"It's not that simple, Dennis. I'll call Pearl Barnes in a bit, and she'll put the wheels in motion. We can't upset the railroad," Sparrow said.

"Okay. That's good. Right. I understand. I just thought they should at least be told they're in the clear so they can sleep easy tonight."

"They will, trust me," Sparrow said.

"Do you think maybe we should be . . .

you know . . . be getting back, in case the girls need some help?" Ted said.

The others hooted with laughter.

"That's a joke, right?" Jack said.

"What? We're just going to sit here until . . ."

"I guess until they fry his ass in that tanning bed," Jack said.

The boys sat down on the deck in the boathouse, their feet dangling in the water.

"Where the hell is Snowden? Where is the seaplane? Where is the rotating crew?" Harry asked.

"I can't see the yacht anymore," Dennis said, shielding his eyes to peer out at the ocean.

"That's a good thing, kid," Ted said.

The BOLO boys stared out at the calm ocean, their thoughts and feelings reflected on all their faces.

"So this is where you've been hiding," Snowden said as he came around the side of the boathouse.

The boys jumped to their feet, each of them shouting questions, the main one being, "What's going on?"

"Well, I and my crew are happy to report that the rotating crew arrived and was quite happy to take us up on our hospitality, and they are now sleeping off a king-size Russian vodka drunk. By my best calculations, we have about two hours to split this place and return to safety. Where is our . . . ? I want to say 'patient,' but I think 'victim' would be more appropriate."

"I think he's sizzling in that tanning bed back in his gym. Maybe it's time to check on things. Strength in numbers, that kind of thing," Jack mumbled under his breath.

"Let's do it," Snowden said, striding off, the boys trailing behind.

Once they were back in Spyder's bunker, the boys lined up like soldiers, waiting to see what they should do.

"What took you so long?" Kathryn snapped. "He's ready to go."

"Did he give it up?" Jack asked.

"He did," Abner said cheerfully as he tapped away. "I've got all I need right now, but I want to finish up back in the States. Got it all on flash drives. We are good to go, ladies and gentlemen. I have to say, he put up a good fight. He didn't cave till his skin started to bubble up. He's all yours. My job here is done."

"And you did it so well, dear," Isabelle said as she took his arm.

"Clear out!" Snowden said. "I need to get my men here to clean up this mess. Do you have any special instructions?"

Annie fixed a steely eye on Snowden. "Three times is the charm, Mr. Snowden."

Snowden bit down on his lip. "Point taken, Countess."

Annie poked Myra in the arm. "What do you say we hit Vegas for a bit? We can drop everyone off at Reagan National and take off again for Vegas. I'm feeling lucky all of a sudden. Race you back to the villa."

It didn't quite happen like that. Outside, there was such a clamor of laughter, squeals, and shouting that Myra and Annie ran through the crowd in time to see Charles and Fergus pumping hands and being hugged. Both women watched as they started to shake from head to toe.

Annie pinched Myra. "Are they real or figments of our imagination?"

"They look pretty real to me, Annie. Charles looks thinner."

"So does Fergus," Annie whispered. "What should we do?"

"You're asking me? You always have all the answers. What do you **want** to do?"

"Good Lord, Myra, do not ask me that. What I want to do and what I should do are two different things."

"I hear you."

The group parted to allow Charles and Fergus to walk forward.

"Myra."

"Charles."

"Annie."

"Fergus."

The two couples stared at one another.

As one, Charles and Fergus spoke. "What took you so long to find us? We've been waiting forever for you to spring us."

Myra made an instant decision at the same time Annie did. "You weren't exactly easy to find, Sir Charles. But we found you. That's all that is important. Is it really you, Charles, or am I dreaming?"

"You're not dreaming, love."

"You didn't ask me to go with you," Annie whispered.

"I thought you'd say no. Look at me, Annie. I have nothing to offer you but my person and my very small pension. I wanted to ask, but I was afraid."

"Are you offering now? Because if you are, I'll take it."

"You will?"

"Damn straight I will. How'd you like to join me and Myra and probably Charles now? We're going to Vegas. You know what they say, Fergus. 'What happens in Vegas stays in Vegas.'"

"I'm your man, then."

Myra looked back over her shoulder and winked at Annie.

Annie grinned as she settled her tiara a little more firmly on her head.

The Sisters clapped loudly, while the boys whistled and hooted their approval.

"Doncha love it, Harry, when things end so well?" Dennis asked.

"I do, kid. I do."

Epilogue

Seven months later . . .

While the world watched Mother Nature help spring transition into summer with barely a drop in the temperature, then nudge what most meteorologists called a perfect summer into autumn, the residents of Pinewood and their guests barely noticed the change in seasons.

It was the day before Thanksgiving, seven long months since the Sisters' return from Spyder Island. The lights at the command center at Pinewood burned brightly

24/7 as the gang worked nonstop to right all of Angus Spyder's wrongdoing.

Thanksgiving was their target date to wrap things up, and as Annie de Silva said, they were right on target.

To say the women were tired would be an understatement. The guys were just as tired but were refusing to admit to it. And then there were the squabbles, the small turf wars that ensued with Charles's and Fergus's return to the fold. In the end, though, it all came together, and they worked as the well-oiled team that they were.

Charles, to his chagrin, relinquished his position on the dais in the war room to Abner Tookus. Myra appointed him chief cook and bottle washer, with Fergus as his top aide. With so many mouths to feed and the long hours of work, it was necessary to keep everyone nourished. Since the order came down from Myra, Charles thought it best if he pulled in his fighting horns and did her bidding. To say the menus were flawless would be an understatement. One day, the meals would be exotic; and the next day, comforting; followed up by downright perfect. Charles and Fergus allowed themselves to bask in the compliments, while Dennis watched and took notes, sometimes feeling brave enough to offer a suggestion.

On the first day after their return from Spyder Island, assignments were handed down. It was up to Ted, Maggie, Espinosa, and Dennis to let the world know about Angus Spyder, and they did with a once-a-month in-depth article, a series that had the four of them on the way to a Pulitzer. The **Post**'s readership tripled during the seven months the articles ran. The last article, which would run on the weekend after Thanksgiving, was being tweaked one last time.

After much debate, Annie gave the final okay for a warlike banner on the front page of the **Post** that read, VIGILANTES END REIGN OF EVIL. The rest of the front page carried photos of Angus Spyder, thanks to Joseph Espinosa. It was Maggie's suggestion, one that Ted had seconded, to wait till the last article to show the world the little, ugly man who had created such evil around the globe. She said it would be a fitting end to the whole ugly story.

It was midafternoon on the day before Thanksgiving. A light, blustery wind was blowing outside, but it was cozy and warm indoors, where all the gang was gathered, packing up the files and stacking them neatly in the war room. What they would do with them later on was anyone's guess. Myra thought they should be dropped off at either the FBI's front door or on the CIA's doorstep. A decision had yet to be made, but the most likely vote would be for the files to be transported to the **Post** warehouse, then sent to the FBI, to the attention of Jack Sparrow. He could then make the decision about what to share and what not to share with the CIA. Sparrow said he liked that idea best of all and knew the president would laud him forever if he made it happen.

There were many good things that had happened during the seven months at Pinewood. Abner and Isabelle had made peace and were cohabiting once again, to everyone's delight. Espinosa and Alexis had formally announced their engagement over the Fourth of July. The wedding, to be held at Pinewood, was scheduled for Valentine's Day the following year.

Annie and Fergus were once again best buds. They billed and cooed and never once mentioned money. Charles had stood his ground on his famous leave-taking at Thanksgiving two years before, and Myra had finally forgiven him, because, as she put it, she loved him and didn't want to spend the rest of her life without him in it.

Kathryn's leg had finally healed, with the promise from her doctors and surgeons that she could take to the open road after the first of the year. She had said the only good thing to come out of her accident, aside from the monetary gain, was that she could now accurately predict the weather better than any meteorologist.

There were two surprises left for the group as Thanksgiving approached. To Nikki and Jack's delight, Cyrus became a father to five rambunctious pups, three girls and two boys, over the Labor Day weekend. The new pups were to be delivered to their daddy on Thanksgiving Day.

And then there was Dennis, who had fallen in love with one Mitzi Overton, a red-haired, freckle-faced UPS driver who picked up and delivered to Pinewood. He was a goner the day she let him ride with her on her deliveries. The day he confessed to be-ing a spook for the CIA, as a joke, then told her how rich he was, Mitzi blacked out and

Dennis had to make the rest of her deliveries himself. As he told the others, it was a relationship made in heaven. He did take back the story about being a CIA spook, to everyone's relief.

Harry and Yoko had simply done what they normally did and had waited as they counted down the hours till they could head to China to see their daughter, Lily.

At three o'clock, Myra got up stiffly and hobbled around, craning her neck to the right and the left to ease the tension. "I am so glad we are done with all this. I have to be honest, I thought we'd never finish." She tapped the old-fashioned ledger and said, "If it weren't for this, we'd be here till this time next year. I so hope we covered everything. Abner's idea for that eight hundred number for people to call will tell us if we got all of it right this time around. If not, we can always come back here and finish up. For now, I think we're all golden. I say we hit the showers, then join Charles for some much-needed refreshment and a magnificent dinner, which I am sure he is preparing as we speak."

The others clapped and did stretches and knee bends to limber up after their long hours of sitting and poring over reports and files.

And another mission was filed away with the word SUCCESSFUL stamped across the final box.

"Hold on, hold on, people!" Annie shouted. "These boxes aren't going to walk their way upstairs. We need some strong arms to do that. You boys are elected. While you're all doing that, we ladies will be headed for the showers. Dennis, you need to call your friend Mitzi to have these boxes delivered to Mr. Sparrow. If you have any clout with her, ask her to come in an empty truck. We don't want any of these boxes getting mixed up with residential deliveries."

It wasn't a suggestion, it was an order, and Dennis recognized it as such.

Upstairs in the kitchen, the women swooned at the heavenly aromas that greeted them.

"Cocktails in ninety minutes, Charles," Myra said as she swept by him to make her way to the back staircase that would take her to the second floor, the girls right behind her. She giggled, as did the others, when Charles swatted her tush with a dish towel.

Life was looking good.

Ninety minutes later, everyone was in the huge family room, with a fire roaring in the fireplace. While they were bone tired, there was still excitement in the air as drinks and canapés were handed around. The dogs all curled by the fire and snoozed in utter contentment.

Annie took to the floor. "I think we should make a toast to a job well done." She held her wineglass aloft. The others joined her. Cyrus barked twice to get his vote in; then Lady echoed him. "That makes it official, people!"

And then they talked, giving Charles and Fergus, who were out of the loop, a detailed summary of what had gone on below for the past seven months. Myra took the floor. The others listened, spellbound. She ended forty minutes later with a parched throat, which she corrected by downing her glass of wine and holding it out for a refill.

"We gave away billions. I truly don't think we missed anyone Angus Spyder, or Feodor Spyovich, trampled on. It's possible, so we set aside monies, should that come to pass. Believe it or not, it is not easy deciding what someone's life is worth. You simply cannot put a price tag on it. We did our best. We tried the best we could to make those people and their families whole again. Anonymously, of course. We have one billion dollars left offshore, which we can tap anytime we need to, thanks to Abner.

"We donated to Doctors Without Borders, the Wounded Warrior Project, every medical charity out there, no-kill animal shelters across the country, Seeing Eye dog farms all across the country, women's shelters, children's causes, different hospices that need help, scholarships, the Salvation Army, breast-cancer centers. We donated hundreds of thousands of computers for schools. We even set up free screening clinics for walk-in patients. We set up a fund nationwide where people can get free medicine if they can't afford it. We donated to clinics so people can get free care if they can't afford it. We donated heavily. Even so, we barely made a dent in Spyder's fortune.

"Realizing that, we set up an organization to which every one of the places I just mentioned can apply for more funds. The paperwork took forever, but we did it. Nikki and Jack are going to hire an outside group to monitor it all. For now, it's the best we can do. We can do more. There's a never-ending need for help, and we'll see to it that every cent of Spyder's money goes where it will be needed the most. It goes without saying that we helped ourselves to a good portion of the money, to be used by us to continue to right the wrongs of others. We did take a vote on that, too. We were all in agreement."

"What is the latest on the Domingos and Irina and Gretchen?" Yoko asked.

Charles spoke up. "Pearl called me yesterday to tell me the Domingos are safely housed in Miami. They were given new identities, and no, she did not tell me what they are. She said they accepted twenty-five million dollars, and she had to twist their arms to agree to it. They now live in a nice tree-shaded community with, as she put it, real sidewalks, where the twins can walk to the park. They agreed to send pictures of the twins monthly to Pearl, along with little progress reports for school, their activities, and such, so she can forward them to Gretchen and Greg. Gretchen and Greg both agreed not to interfere in their lives, with the understanding that when the twins reach eighteen, they be given the right to see or not see each other."

"Where are they now? What about Irina?" Isabelle asked.

"Gretchen's surgery was a success, to a point," Charles explained. "She can walk, is in intense therapy, and will always have a noticeable limp. But she's okay with that. She says she can dance again, albeit a little lopsided. She and Greg plan to marry over the Christmas holidays, when Irina's family is due to arrive here in the States, thanks to Jack Sparrow and Immigration. We set aside monies for Gretchen and Greg. She was adamant about not wanting it, but we put it in a trust for them.

"Felicia, or Irina, as she prefers to be called, didn't want any money, either. We pointed out that she cashed in her jewelry and that came from Angus, so she agreed to a fund for her family. She wasn't greedy at all. All she wanted was for her family to have nice little houses with picket fences so they could have gardens full of flowers and vegetables. Her only real request was to be near a Russian Orthodox church, which we made happen. They are all going to take up residence in Reston, Virginia."

"Guess that means all is well that ends well," Nikki said happily. "I think this was our worst case so far, but the most rewarding in the end."

"Except for Hank Jellicoe," Annie said sourly.

"There's always tomorrow, Annie. One of these days, we'll nail that son of a bitch," Jack said cheerfully. "Listen, I'm starved. When are we eating, Charles?"

"How about right now?" Charles said, getting up and heading for the kitchen.

Dinner was all everyone wanted it to be. Delicious, pleasant, good friends surrounded by other good friends.

When dinner was over, the girls took charge, and within minutes, the kitchen and dining room were sparkling clean and everyone was once more in the family room, with coffee and brandy.

Ten minutes into the last toast of the day, eyes drooped wearily as heads tilted to the side.

"Guess it's just you and me, Fergus. Dress up. Time to take these pooches out for a stroll. I've got the cigars and the treats for the dogs. Then, my friend, we come back in to get ready for our Thanksgiving feast tomorrow."

"Why didn't you tell them, Charles?" Fergus asked.

"Tomorrow is soon enough. To be honest," Charles said, shrugging into his anorak, "I'm not sure how Myra is going to take it."

"Now, **that** I understand."

Thanksgiving dinner was the same for Pinewood as it was across the country. A giant thirty-pound turkey cooked to perfection, every side dish known to man, along with Charles's plum pudding and, of course, pumpkin pie made from the fruits of Myra's own garden.

The moment grace was said and Charles picked up the carving knife, every person in the room froze in place as he or she remembered another Thanksgiving, when dinner was interrupted and Charles was whisked away by the spooks of MI5.

Charles looked up from the turkey and said, "I'm here to stay."

The conversation picked up as plate after plate was passed around the table.

Everyone was there, even Elias Cummings, Nellie's husband, whom no one had expected to make it so far into the year. Elias was having a good day and for brief moments recognized one or another of the group. Pearl was antsy and said she was going to have to leave the minute dinner was over because she had a family she needed to send on its way, and today was the perfect day to do it since everyone was with family. The group offered up a toast in the middle of dinner for the wonderful, secretive work she did safeguarding families from those who wished them harm.

Charles was just about to serve dessert when the outside warning monitor came to life. Myra turned white at the sound. Charles reached for her arm. She shook his hand off as memories assailed her.

"Relax, everyone. I think Cyrus's kids are being delivered," Nikki said as she ran through the dining room to the kitchen.

She was right. Two women stood at the door with blanket-wrapped bundles. A third woman held bags of something or other. Nikki opened the door wide, and suddenly the kitchen was flooded with people and animals.

"Hey, buddy, your kids are here," Jack said, bending down so he was eye level with Cyrus, who was eyeballing the blanket-wrapped bundles. And then he whooped and pounced as he saw his offspring for the first time. He moved then at the speed of light as he picked up one pup. Lady picked up another, and then Lady's pups picked up the rest and ran to the family room, with the people beings tripping behind them. They all watched as the dogs settled the new pups into their own beds, then sat down to watch over them.

Jack swiped at his eyes, as did every-one else. Cyrus threw back his head and howled. Translation . . . "Where are the cigars?"

Jack ran to the kitchen and brought out a box of cigars he'd bought earlier to cel-ebrate the occasion.

"One puff in celebration, and then you have to put them out. Cigar smoke is not good for new puppies," Myra said. No one knew for sure if that was true or not, but they did what she said.

Cyrus yipped his approval as he checked on his sleeping kids.

"Time for dessert," Charles said, breaking

the spell. "And I have a surprise for you all. Can we please get to it?"

Dessert served, coffee poured, Charles walked around the massive table, handing out heavy cream-colored invitations with a huge gold seal. He then took his place at the head of the table and waited for the re-action of his little family, which wasn't all that little today.

"Oh my goodness. It's an invitation to din-ner at Buckingham Palace on Sunday," An-nie said. Her expression was so neutral, Fergus flinched and Charles swallowed hard.

His gaze was on his wife as he waited.

Nikki nudged Jack. She whispered, "See, see? She's looking at Annie, and she's mak-ing a decision with no words. How do they **do** that?"

Jack shrugged.

"How nice, Charles. But since we are all scheduled to depart for China on Sunday morning, how is that going to work?" Nikki asked.

"We'll leave a day later out of Heathrow. That's if it's all right with all of you. I told Lizzie I would call her after dinner. She's ex-cited, doubly so, now that the new age city is back in her hands. Are we all in agreement? I was hoping for a little more enthusiasm for some reason."

"Why is that, dear?" Myra said sweetly.

"Quit while you're ahead," Fergus whispered into Charles's ear.

"I guess because the queen never invites people to dinner. And she is making a special exception because she wants to meet all of you and to thank you in person."

"How sweet," Myra said, tongue in cheek. "I do not curtsy to any woman, Charles."

"Me either," Annie shot out.

The other girls voiced their agreement.

Charles knew he was in hot water that was going to boil any second. "I just had a thought. Why don't I give her a call and say, 'Thank you, but we can't make it at this time, as we are going to China to see Lily'?"

"That, dear, is a very sweet idea. Isn't it, girls?"

"We just love, love, love it, Myra," Kathryn said.

"Good thinking, fearless leader," Fergus hissed into Charles's ear.

Charles's sigh was so mighty, it could have blown out the fire in the family-room fireplace.

"Cleanup time!" Annie announced.

The gang fell to it.

The hustle and bustle at Pinewood as the group prepared to depart for the airport would have made a sane person insane. Bags were being loaded into the **Post** van and extra cars. Presents for Lily were stacked high by the door. The dogs were yipping and yapping, adding to the confusion. Cyrus was at the door with his beloved duck.

Jack whistled, and Cyrus ran to him. "Listen, buddy, you can't go. They have this thing in foreign countries about animals. They keep you in a cage for days. You don't have the right shots. You'll get sick from the different food. I want you to go—we all do—but it's impossible."

Cyrus looked at his master, and Jack swore he saw tears in the big dog's eyes.

"You aren't buying this crap, are you?"

Cyrus barked loudly.

"Okay, here's the skinny on things, Cyrus. You're a dad now. You need to stay and watch your kids. You don't want someone else messing with them, do you? Of course you don't. They need you, Cyrus. Yeah,

Lady is good with her own pups, but these are **yours.** Yours, Cyrus. So, what's it gonna be?"

Cyrus waited all of one minute, then put his paws on Jack's shoulders and licked his face. Then he barked in his ear. Translation . . . "Okay, I'm giving you this one, because you're right." He flew out of the room, his beloved duck clenched in his teeth.

Jack offered up a sloppy salute to his dog, his eyes wet.

"Okay, let's get this show on the road," Annie bellowed.

"China, here we come!" Yoko and Harry cried out happily in unison.